DANGEROUS SCORE

Michael Bearcroft

Dynasty
Press

Dynasty Press Ltd.
36 Ravensdon Street
London SE11 4AR
www.dynastypress.co.uk

First published in this version by Dynasty Press Ltd.

ISBN: 978 0 9568038 3 2

Cover Artwork from an initial design by Sue Bearcroft and Typeset by Shore Books and Design, Blackborough End, Norfolk.

Printed and bound in the United Kingdom.

In one week the footballer George Clooney goes from hero to zero. After scoring the goal that takes his club into the League for the first time.

After claiming to have dated a girl who has been missing for a year he is pilloried by media and fans alike.

Fighting to prove his innocence he helps bring down a major crime ring, falls in love, achieves a new career in football and learns more about himself and life in just 100 days than he could have ever believed possible.

It's a roller coaster ride of football, mystery, love, crime and even more football providing a story with a real difference.

This book is dedicated to:

The Hillsborough Family Support Group

and

the 96 in 89

'They will never walk alone.'

Chapter One

There were six thousand people packed in the ground with hundreds more locked out. This was the biggest night in Kettering United's history. A win against Leominster Athletic would put United in the Football League for the first time. If they were to lose, it would be the lottery of the play-offs.

Sky television was covering the game live, local papers, BBC and commercial stations were all in attendance.

Reportedly fans would travel from as far afield as the USA, Australia and just about everywhere to see the game that would define a season, if not a club's history!

The tension in the crowd matched that on the pitch. With an hour gone there was no score. A draw would take Leominster up, but Kettering had to win. The home team were giving all they had to get a goal, the opposition's game plan was simple; everyone back, chop every opponent who came near, then boot the ball up-field for giant centre forward Jonas Maglowski to chase. The Serb stood six foot six, and was known in football circles as 'the gorilla'.

Play was certainly not pretty, but for the away team it was effective.

Four of their players had been booked so far, while a fifth, midfielder Jo Jo Watson was lucky not to have been red carded for one particularly cynical challenge, unseen by the referee.

The home crowd was getting restless, the players nervous, on the bench Tony Bradshaw, Kettering's under pressure manager signalled for substitute Jason Clooney to get stripped. When Clooney, known to everyone as George, began to get ready the supporters reacted with shouts of "George, George, we want George!" and "Come on the Aussie!" - the latest catcall not being strictly true as George was born in Sheffield though he had just returned from playing in Perth, Western Australia. He waved an acknowledgement to the crowd as he prepared, ignoring the boos of the visitors' fans and the abuse from the Leominster dugout. As he loosened tense muscles with a warm-up run and stretches, he knew his moment had come. Two years ago he had moved to join Perth Glory, where he had sold cars part time for the main Holden dealer. He had a club bungalow on the beach and with his partner Lara Mindage, a former Miss Australia, at his side he thought he had it made.

Then she left him for a surfing champion, the goals dried up and it was back to Blighty! He had missed the last five games through injury thanks to that animal, the Stafford centre back. But there was only the faintest hurt now and as the club's leading scorer he was needed, and he was ready.

The assistant referee checked George's boots, the gaffer had given him final instructions: "Stay up top, put yourself about, try and get a penalty and so on." The females in the crowd lusted after him at 6 foot 2 inches tall and two hundred pounds of muscle, with his dark hair and tanned skin he had the looks of his actor namesake, and the appeal as well. Male fans urged him to get out there and get stuck in; away supporters hoped he would break his leg. Nothing like football to bring out the best in people!

There was a momentary hush to hear the

announcement, and then polite applause as Dave 'Tick Tock' Clockmine, the young Kettering forward, left the pitch. Then a huge roar as George, the new gladiator, entered the field of play.

He ran past skipper and midfielder Tommy Ferguson, passing on the basic instructions: "Scotty, Jim up front, every ball high to me, get Aggas to go wide." Scotty duly passed on the new game plan. Dele Aggbolalure, the reserve striker who had been playing in George's absence, was to go wide on the right in place of 'Tick Tock', allowing George to resume his rightful place leading the charge. It was a throw-in which had provided the break in play enabling the substitution to take place. Once it was taken the field became a battleground again.

Immediately after the restart Cherill, the Leominster defender, punched George in the back. "That's just a start, wanker!" was his not so quick witted verbal insult. That just wound Clooney up even more. He chased every ball, appealed every decision. But eventually he too struggled, as his team mates had, to get that elusive goal. He had a header strike the bar, a shot round the post and he brought a couple of smart saves out of the keeper 'Desperate Dan', so named because of his permanent face stubble; plus his real name, Marcel Desperon, reminded everyone of the cartoon character.

With less than a minute remaining George won a corner on the left. 'Pernod', Kettering's two footed wide man, real name Vincent Perolido, born in Peterborough of Italian father, sprinted across to take it; he signalled 'high outswinger'. George rushed in, taking two defenders with him before stepping back smartly to meet the ball, unchallenged. With his markers nowhere he had time to pick his spot, and do so with accuracy and some power.

He guided his well taken header into the top right corner. 'Desperate Dan' was pinned in by team mates and opponents so couldn't get near it. The fullback on the line was slow to react and didn't jump high enough. It was a goal, *the* goal, and when the whistle sounded a minute later it proved to be the goal that took Kettering into League football for the very first time.

Chapter Two

The crowd went wild. Home stewards and police battled to keep them off the pitch. All of Clooney's team mates jumped on him in celebration. Then, game over, as they left the pitch the victorious players were mobbed by jubilant fans. The defeated left the field in tears. They had nearly done it, but nearly wasn't enough. Soon they would have to pick themselves up for the play-offs, but for Kettering this was their moment.

Cameras and microphones were thrust in the players' faces, everyone wanted an interview and a picture of the 'new legend' Jason 'George' Clooney, scorer of that goal. He lost count of the times he was asked "How did it feel?" He just wanted to relax, to celebrate in the dressing room as the champagne flowed. The skipper made a speech, followed by the gaffer, then the Chairman and even the Mayor.

Finally, after a brief warm down, it was showers, change and ready to party. All the players could talk about was what they would do with their bonus? What kind of contract would they get as a League player? Should they buy a new car? Go on holiday, or what? For this one night they were Gods, could do no wrong, and the world belonged to them alone.

A celebratory meal had been planned by the club for Friday at Wickstead Park. Attendance expected by everyone. But for tonight the instructions were, visit the Supporters Club bar for one drink and thank them for their backing. Go careful with the boozing as the cops would be watching, so no one spoiling the day please with a drink driving charge. Sunday would be an open top bus ride around the area to meet and greet the fans, details to be confirmed. The players groaned. 'Wethers', legally christened Norton Weatherall, followed skipper Tommy Ferguson into the clubhouse. The cheering was ear splitting, there were more handshakes, hugs and kisses, not only from the ladies, then more and more champagne. George mingled with the fans, graciously accepting congratulations whilst pledging his future to the club.

Finding himself trapped between the out of order fruit machine and the very busy ladies toilet he contented himself with yet another orange juice while waiting for an opportunity to leave.

A very beautiful dark haired girl came out of the loo. She was tall, slim, dressed in a black suit and white sweater, and as she passed she gave him a killer smile and whispered "Well done," in a husky voice. The smell of her perfume said expensive, and she certainly oozed real class.

She stood a few feet from him, taking a wine glass from the adjacent table. Hesitantly he tried to converse with her above the din. He fought his way to the bar and back to bring her another glass of wine when hers was spilt in the crush. She was surprised that he was teetotal. He was amazed she was on her own. Making conversation over the noise was near impossible and he suggested they adjourn to a quieter bar he knew. She agreed and he was delighted when she followed him to his car. He had discovered her name to be Jess short for Jessica and that she lived nearby. She was surprised that the 'legend' was only driving an old Volvo. He explained how he now worked part time for MotorGiant in Northampton and this was a car he had taken in part exchange.

They drove to the Hunting Lodge, a country hotel in Corby, home of one of Kettering's rivals, so less chance of there being fans celebrating there. "Unless they'd have lost," he thought. George had stayed here when he first signed for Kettering so was confident they would serve them, despite the hour.

The venue was set back in the trees, easily missed as you drove through the village of Cottingham.

They relaxed into the sumptuous green leather chairs of the residents' lounge. The night porter Scott was delighted to serve them tea and chicken sandwiches with all the trimmings. That meant crisps, lettuce and a tomato. They ate, each deep in thought. Clooney's dad raved about Catherine Zeta Jones. "He'd love Jess," he mused, as she looked just like Pop Larkin's little girl.

He found himself telling her his life story, with her prompting. Growing up in Sheffield, his family, Australia, everything. Jess was a good listener, but he did learn that she was a nurse and lived in Loddington, a village less than two miles from his apartment, and that she had a sister who was a journalist. For a few years she had lived and worked in Peterborough until she came home from a shift one day to find her partner in bed with her then best friend. Returning to the family home hadn't been easy, but at least she got to see more United games. She had been a fan all her life and knew more about the club and its history than he ever would.

It had been the perfect end to the perfect day, but now he was flagging. That's the problem with relaxing. His adrenaline gone, limbs tired, he didn't need to look at his watch to know it was late, neither did he want it to end; but Jess, seeing that he was knackered, suggested he take her home.

He thanked Scott, tipping him generously, then with great reluctance climbed once more into the car. They drove back the scenic way through the picturesque village of Middleton, its Northamptonshire stone buildings without any lights because of the time. They listened to Michael Bublé on the CD, each seemingly content with their thoughts about the night, each other and what happens next.

Through Rothwell, across the A14, and into sleepy Loddington they drove. Jess told him to pull into the village pub car park. The Red Lion was quiet and dark, nothing seemed to stir. George asked her out for dinner on Saturday and she agreed. They discussed eating places and Jess opted for the Thai Garden at Rothwell. Though he was concerned they would be plagued by fans, because basically he was a gentleman he agreed.

They exchanged phone numbers and email addresses, and then, because it seemed the most natural thing to do, they kissed, deeply, passionately. Despite tiredness he was soon aroused. She told him she wouldn't sleep with him on this first date, but then uplifted his spirits by coyly raising her sweater. "I don't want dirty marks on my clothes," she said, as she unclasped her lacy bra, unleashing her generous breasts. As his lips swept over the heaving mounds of silky soft skin she whispered in his ear whilst reaching for his zip: "But I won't leave you frustrated either."

Later, after they had both cat-napped for a while, Jess asked him to take her home. She lived a short distance away in a gated house set back from the road. Very modern and very expensive it looked. In their own words, each told the other how much they had enjoyed the night, and how much they looked forward to Saturday. Jess blew him a kiss as she passed through the gates. He drove home in a dream, so much had happened in such a short time.

A defunct private hospital alongside the main east-west highway of the A14 had been turned into luxury flats, complete with gym, pool and gardens. The club had helped him acquire a penthouse apartment with secure underground parking and a receptionist during the day-time. With its high-tech security and fire alarm system it was probably the best address in town for a man who was on his way up. He crawled into bed, couldn't be bothered to read emails or listen to voice messages as it was 5 a.m., and in three hours time he no doubt would be woken again by someone. Oh the price of fame!

Chapter Three

He awoke surprising himself, no calls, but upon checking his messages and emails, of which there were over two hundred, it suddenly hit him just how much life had changed.

This was the first property he had ever owned. Even though he had a mortgage it felt good looking out across the fields towards Loddington, to think about Jess, about that goal. He really did believe that from now on things could only get better. A fortune teller he was not!

He showered, shaved, dressed, had breakfast, turned on the box and saw himself scoring, being interviewed, being talked about. Then back to reality. It was Thursday, a working day, so cologne and blue suit on and it was off through the rush hour traffic to MotorGiant in Northampton. In the queues and at traffic lights people recognised him and shouted greetings and waved. When he arrived the staff stood and applauded him. The whole day was unreal as more and more people called to congratulate him. Several bought cars just so they could be photographed with him. Life didn't get much better than this.

It might be a small pond, but he really was a big fish. In truth he would have been a liar if he didn't admit he was loving it.

His boss, sales manager Andy Curtis, even took him to a meeting of the directors, where over a celebratory drink the company photographer captured the unique occasion.

With all that had happened, or was happening, it was mid-afternoon before he realised he still hadn't spoken to his parents. They had left countless emails and voice messages for him. His dad Graham had been a good amateur footballer in Sheffield, before a career in accountancy beckoned. He was deeply proud of his son's achievements, though he rarely showed it. Mum Ann loved him as only a mother could. She cared more that he wasn't hurt on or off the pitch, and just wished he could meet and settle down with a nice girl. This year they would be celebrating thirty-five years of marriage, and constantly told him they were as happy now as when they first met, and it showed. He couldn't help it, he told Mum about Jess. All dad wanted to know about was that goal, and what would he do next?

The day finished with drinks at the Tudor Gate, Finedon, a small country hotel owned by the Rothwell F.C. Chairman Stuart Andrews, courtesy of the Kettering sports writer Trevor Wolfe, in return for an exclusive story.

By the time he got to bed he was all in, but fell asleep thinking about Jessica.

He had needed that earlier night, for Friday was the club's annual dinner where he was presented with the 'Player of the Year' award. The drinks were endless, the speeches more so, but he had fun with the lads, and he was now just one night away from seeing Jess again.

He tried texting her and left voice messages, but he supposed that nurses were busier than footballers. So he booked a table at the restaurant and concentrated on what might happen on Saturday night.

With a lot of luck she might come back and view the digs, the bedroom at least!

He had to work Saturday to compensate for all those he'd missed because of football. Business was fantastic, everyone it seemed wanted to buy a car and be photographed with the man who scored that goal.

The Thai restaurant was full, and though his booking was for 8, he arrived early and bumped into head groundsman Bill Lawrence and his wife Sue, and a group of friends. At 8.30 he had drunk two orange juices and a coffee, but still no sign of Jess. Nor could he get an answer to his texts or voice messages. Had he, the legend, been stood up?

Bill persuaded him to have a drink with his party who were about to leave. Then disaster struck. Sue asked him the name of the lucky lady he was waiting for, and when he told her it was Jessica Thresham an uncomfortable silence fell on the group. Before he could sidestep out of the way, he was attacked by a visibly shaken woman, who slapped him smartly across his face.

Bill grabbed him and dragged him outside, the cold hit his smarting face, but it was nothing compared to the atmosphere he had just experienced. He was confused, stunned, literally gobsmacked.

"That wasn't funny," Bill told him, "in fact it was sick." George hadn't a clue what he was on about. Bill realised the boy was lost, so calmed himself down and explained how Jessica Thresham of Loddington had vanished about a year ago, and despite extensive police enquiries had never been heard of since. Clooney couldn't believe it, surely Bill was having him on, but his look said not. "Well that's the name she gave me," was all he could think to say, before making a hasty excuse to leave, feeling weighed down with sadness, confusion and acute embarrassment.

Tonight he was driving a black Saab Cabriolet he'd taken in that day. As black as his current mood. He drove far too fast. He thought to go to Loddington and find out what was going on, then he changed his mind, veering off left, back to his home.

When he arrived he grabbed a brandy. He always kept drinks in for guests and the rare occasion he partook. Online he soon got up the story of Jessica's disappearance, how she was a nurse, had moved back to live with her parents and hadn't been heard of since April last year. There were photos of her with different hair styles taken at different ages. But there was no doubt in his mind this was the same girl he had met on Wednesday night.

Chapter Four

Knowing something is one thing, understanding is another. The more he read the more baffled he was. He feverishly searched the archives for more and more background and information.

Jess was thirty-two, her parents had gone to wake her for work and found she was gone. When she didn't return that night they phoned the hospital and, upon being told she had not been in that day, they called the police. The family had been on TV appealing for information and a nationwide search for her had begun. Living in Australia he knew none of this at the time, he had never heard of Kettering, never mind Jessica Thresham.

He must eventually have fallen asleep because Tony Bradshaw phoned to remind him to meet up at the Kettering Park Hotel for the celebration drive. Just about the last thing he felt like doing at the moment. What a way to spend a Sunday. He printed off some of the articles and photos, then dressed in regulation club blazer and trousers before setting off to meet the lads and to do his duty. A bus trip round Kettering and afternoon tea with the Mayor. The perfect way to spend a day!

The hotel was located alongside an industrial estate and a retail park. But it was the best around. It also took him less than ten minutes to drive there, so he would get home quickly as well. The lads were wandering around the foyer like naughty schoolboys on a field trip. Because they felt embarrassed by their blazers they were even noisier and more stupid than usual, or so it seemed to an unhappy Clooney.

Shepherded on to the open top bus surrounded by adoring crowds, photographers and the rest, they departed for the grand tour of the district. A slow predictable journey of heavy traffic, loads of stops and noisy people. Tea at the Town Hall wasn't bad, and the Mayor was a true fan, not a hanger on. George made his apologies and left, as he was doing an interview for local radio that night. A taxi returned him to the Kettering Park, then there was a short drive to Radio Kettering's studio. The manager himself, Patrick O'Leary, had him in and talked him through the plan. It would go out as a thirty second teaser after each of the next day's news bulletins. Then the full interview would air on the Monday night sports programme.

George couldn't have cared less. All he wanted to know was, was he the victim of a sick joke, or was something more sinister going on? Should he contact the police?

Pernod called him at 10, they were going to a club in Bedford. George certainly didn't want to go, and was quite off hand with his friend and team mate. He just wanted to sit and stew in his misery.

Trevor Wolfe buzzed on the intercom, could he see him urgently? Clooney let him in. Unlike other journalists Trev had played a bit himself and was always fair in reporting, so he was trusted by the lads.

The bad news was the story of what happened at the restaurant, which was now going the rounds, and he urged George to give him his version of events. Clooney wondered what to do. He could be branded a nutter or worse. Should he lie or perhaps say nothing? But of course Clooney being Clooney, he told the truth. Trev recorded it, no shorthand for him. He only interrupted to ask a couple of questions and for permission to use the landline, mobile reception being notoriously poor in the area. George could hear bits of the conversation. Legal view was being sought, orders issued that would give the paper a scoop but at the same time prove it had acted in a responsible manner. Clooney wondered again if he had done the right thing. Trev told him the story would be on the front page of tomorrow's paper and the police would be informed an hour before it appeared.

That way the cops couldn't pull it, or sell it, and the paper could demonstrate how law abiding it was.

Too late George realised. Things would only get worse. Hero to zero in just a week.

Chapter Five

Monday started okay. Wethers phoned to see if he was alright. Clooney felt bad for not bringing him up to date on events. Reception buzzed him, there was a recorded delivery letter for him. Blister had signed for it to save him coming down. The old soldier who manned the desk was a great guy. He dealt with tradesmen, fans, salesmen and con merchants, so George was never bothered by unwelcome visitors.

On his way to work he stopped and chatted with Blister, or Steve, to give him his proper name. At fifty-six and with a lifetime in the army behind him Steve Blister, or Blister as everyone called him, was the ideal man to have front of house. Tall, fit, smart with short cropped hair, he was the model of discretion and had been a good friend to Clooney since day one.

In the car he opened the envelope, her perfume drifted up from the paper and he savoured the moment before reading the short note. "I'm sorry," it said, "and I hope we meet again. All my love J." He scanned the envelope, it was a London postmark. What did it mean, and what the hell was going on?

At work everyone was rushing around getting ready for Tuesday night's grand opening of the new van showroom. For the first time they were going to be selling cars and small commercial vehicles. The sales force was on an incentive scheme to get potential car and van customers to the grand party. George was to be a top table guest, given his new-found fame making him a minor television celebrity, and was also going to host the event. He worked the phones drumming up prospective guests, and forgot about last night's interview in all the hustle and bustle going on around him.

Then at 11.30 a.m. precisely, a detective from the Kettering C.I.D. phoned him to invite him in for a chat, only this time no one was talking football. Wethers and Pernod sent texts. Radio, paper and even TV from all over the country jammed the switchboard wanting to talk with him. He looked online, and there he was the front page, not the back of the Kettering Daily News. His picture, and one of Jess, under the lurid banner **"Soccer Ace Claims to have Scored with Missing Girl"** - a headline so outrageously untrue he could have screamed. Now the proverbial really had hit the fan.

Mum phoned, she had seen it on TV. Dad was at work. George calmed her down, he hoped!

Later, Andy Curtis called him into his office for a chat and an explanation. Andy said little, but did suggest that George might want an early night, and perhaps he should visit the police sooner rather than later. Clooney agreed, though what choice did he have?

He borrowed a fairly anonymous Passat from the show room and drove to Kettering. He turned his phone off, but put Radio Kettering on. He was getting stick from all the callers, branding him a liar, a disgrace, and worse still, some unnamed team mates were quoted as being ashamed of him. That really hurt.

He parked in the municipal car park beside police headquarters. The officer at the desk took his name and left him waiting. He read the posters on the walls out of boredom, well the English ones anyway. There was stuff in Polish, Hindustani and who knows what! A tall young guy stood over him, he looked familiar though he couldn't place him. He was invited to follow him to an interview room and it was then the penny dropped. Detective Sergeant Burns was the son-in-law of Steve Blister. He had met him at the flats several times. It really was a small world.

Burns offered him refreshments, George declined. He asked if Clooney minded the chat being recorded. George said fine. He asked Clooney to take him slowly through the events of Wednesday night, excluding the game. George obliged. "Has anything happened since, that might be relevant?" the detective asked. Clooney showed him the letter and the envelope. He asked if he might borrow it; George having little choice said yes. They chatted about Saturday night at the Thai Garden, then it was over, he was free to go, so he left.

He texted Pernod and Wethers. They came round to the flat, and he brought them up to date.

They were sure 'Death Wish Bronson', the club's reserve keeper, was the player who had spoken out against him. Bronson was jealous of everyone and everything. Still, they supposed that was only because he couldn't face the fact that he was crap! Pernod had seen Jess leave with Clooney after the game, and when he saw the pictures on the internet he also believed she was the 'real McCoy'.

Feeling better for his mates' support, George called it a day on the brain storming, and they all settled down to watch some mindless violence on the box! By the end of the night Clooney's mood had lifted, and he was able to sleep instantly, as if he didn't have a care in the world.

For the big day at work George took an extra shirt

and toiletries. "Got to appear like a true star for the punters," he thought. His dad phoned to check he was coping, and without a word of a lie he was able to tell him things were getting better again. Andy Curtis asked him how the meeting with the police had gone, but as ever, offered no comment. Over two hundred people had said they would be attending that evening. A rehearsal was scheduled for 3 p.m. Until then, 'get selling' was the order of the day. However, nobody came in the showroom wanting to buy a car from Clooney that day.

James Boardaman, the television presenter, was far too smarmy when they met, and Clooney took an instant dislike to him. Fake tan, built-up shoes and a wig. Was anything about him real? Most of those invited did turn up and everything was looking good until George was accosted by a hefty, florid faced tosser of about sixty years of age, with flashy suit and manner to match. This was Martin Thresham and he really didn't like Clooney very much at all. He told him so, and a whole lot more, then he made the big mistake of aiming a punch at George. That was very stupid.

Clooney had taken the insults out of respect for the man's concerns about Jess, but he was not going to be a punch bag for anyone. He blocked Thresham's fist then landed one of his own on his assailant's nose. It bled immediately and profusely, and Mr Thresham had to be taken away for treatment. Andy Curtis, struggling to contain his anger, told George to go home straight away. With the eyes of the startled onlookers bearing into him he duly obliged.

But as he was about to drive away in his favourite Saab Cabriolet, a face appeared at the window. It was Detective Sergeant Burns, who invited him for a quick drink. This time at the nearby Holiday Inn rather than the nick. George led the way wondering what now, at this unexpected turn up? They sat facing each other at a table in the empty bar. Both drinking orange juice. Clooney unsure what he was doing there. The detective told him they had checked with immigration and the Australian police. They knew he wasn't even in England when Jess disappeared, and they believed also that he wasn't lying about the events of last Wednesday.

George was relieved but still puzzled as to why then, were they enjoying this chummy drink?

Burns admitted Blister was his father-in-law. He asked Clooney what he thought of the old man. George, truthful as ever, told him of his respect for him and the many kindnesses he had received from the tough old soldier. Then Burns let it slip that Blister could probably tell him a whole lot more about what was going on than he could, off the record so to speak. Then they talked about that match and the goal. Seems Burns was a regular at the games, and he was keen to know what George thought about their chances of survival in the League.

When they parted Clooney suspected he might have made an ally in the copper, and he certainly would be talking to Blister, first chance he got.

It was after 9, and hunger was creeping in, so he ate a burger in the hotel bar before heading back to Kettering. One thing he was going to do was have words about that scandalous headline. That was bang out of order.

Trev was expecting his call and was brave and honest enough to admit it was wrong, and he would like to meet him to apologise in person. He also intriguingly said he had news for George, best not said over the phone. Very mysterious. They met at Clooney's apartment an hour later. Seems Trev was appalled with his editor's headline, but couldn't stop it. All he could do was offer his regrets.

The real news though, was that the editor had been to a secret meeting with the regional crime squad, local bobbies and some strangers who were never introduced. There had been all sorts of rumours over the years about Martin Thresham and his business activities, and Trev's boss thought the police were just as interested in the father as they were in the daughter. Not that he was the real dad anyway, Jess's real father was called Colin Granger and he had been the victim of a hit and run when she was only a year old. Thresham was her dad's boss and he had taken care of the family, then three years afterwards, married Jess's mum and they had all become one happy family. Or not, as the case might be. George was even more determined now to quiz Blister in the morning. He thanked Wolfe for coming round, and both agreed to let bygones be bygones. They would pool information, and who knew where it would lead next.

Clooney was online and listening to voice messages. There was mail from Robert Hardy, head of human resources at MotorGiant. It informed him he was suspended from work on full pay, pending investigations. He was not to visit the company premises unless invited to do so, and he could continue to use the car which they would insure, but he was to be responsible for fuel and repair etc. etc. Just when he thought he was getting somewhere, it was one pace forward, three steps back.

Chapter Six

Wednesday he woke early, was it only a week since the game? With no job to go to he watched television, scanned the post, read emails and planned his day. Hc buzzed Blister on the house phone, they arranged to meet at lunchtime in the flat. Having done no training for a week, George decided to go to the ground. It would be a tonic to see the lads, and a bit of hard physical work would improve his wellbeing.

The pitch was being re-laid for next season, so the few lads there were training on the car park. Pernod and George enjoyed some banter but the others were definitely cool. Bloody newspapers. There was a directors' meeting going on, so the gaffer was on standby for any summons to attend. Of the eighteen full time pro's, only eight were at training. Must be a lot on holiday, George thought. The workout hurt but improved his mood and after a massage from veteran club physio, Charlie Adams, he felt a new man.

As he dressed, Pernod came in to tell him Bradshaw wanted him in his office, pronto. George knocked on the gaffer's door and was invited in. You could tell when the boss was embarrassed and lying because he stayed seated, was unable to look you in the eye, and constantly fiddled with his wedding ring. In short, George was told the club would not be renewing his contract.

From June 1st he would be a free agent. They were

grateful for all he had done and would not, therefore, be seeking a transfer fee for him if he found a club before then. He could continue to train at the ground and use its facilities until he was fixed up, and his contract was being paid up with immediate effect, so his bonuses and wages until May 31st would be in the bank by the end of next week.

Shocked, speechless, Clooney could only just manage to keep tears from his eyes as he turned around and walked away. Now they had taken this away... his life as well as his job. He bumped into Francis Collins, the club's solicitor and a man he had met many times, and had great respect for. But today Mr Collins did not speak or smile as he moved swiftly by. Quick as he could get away, George headed for home. Now the tears did flow. Tough guy or not, he was a sensitive man, and the hurts were really getting to him.

He phoned his union, the PFA. Their advice stank. The club were being very fair and generous, but they would circulate his details to other clubs as being available. It suddenly hit him. No football, no job, no mortgage being paid. What a mess.

Blister rang the doorbell at 1 p.m. on the dot. They shared a sandwich, tea and the silence. George then told him all that had happened. Blister sympathised, confirmed what Wolfe had told him; that Thresham was a dodgy character and more. Apparently he and his web of companies were being investigated for tax evasion, fraud, people smuggling, drugs, protection rackets, illegal gambling, theft, prostitution and just about every other crime you could think of it seemed.

Blister had to go back to work, but asked George to meet him later. It was agreed they would meet at 7 p.m. in the Charter pub in Rothwell. Clooney phoned his dad and gave him all his news. His folks wanted to come down, but he thanked them and said no, promising to visit them as soon as he could. Wolfe phoned. The paper had received a media release from the club confirming his departure. They would be running the story that day.

Wethers phoned. The lads couldn't believe it, they all wanted to help, even 'Death Wish'. That cheered George up, but he couldn't talk, as more calls were coming in. The media wanted quotes, fans wishing him dead, fans thanking him. How did they manage to get his ex-directory number? Some saying he would be missed. Players, friends, acquaintances, workmates, or should that be former workmates? Everyone wanted to talk to him.

One person he needed to speak to though was Burns, but the cop had no news for him, still no sightings of Jess, yes forensic confirmed it was her fingerprints on the letter and envelope. As grainy CCTV pictures from St. Pancras post office showed, there was a woman who might have been Jess at the counter Saturday morning. But no other sightings at rail and bus stations, though tons of stuff was still being studied.

When he asked the detective about Mr Thresham, Burns was less communicative, but he did suggest George might find out more later, if he grasped his meaning?

Clooney wasn't stupid, naïve perhaps, but he knew now Blister would have lots to tell him.

On line he checked his finances, he was a saver not a spender, didn't smoke, drink or gamble, not that it was helping him at the moment, his current account balance was healthy and he had over £15,000 of savings, so he wasn't exactly skint yet. The next call he took was from Dave Evans, club director, successful national builder and former professional footballer; he hadn't been at the board meeting.

Business pressure prohibited him. Now he had heard the outcome he was outraged. As an old pro he respected George's achievements on the field, and as a businessman he knew something was not right.

Clooney didn't realise that Kettering's ground was owned by Abbeydale Estates, a Martin Thresham company, or that Thresham had loaned the club £200,000 the season before last when they were struggling. So put two and two together and you could see what had happened. Dave offered to help in any way he could, job, loan, free flights. As a qualified pilot Dave kept his own helicopter at Sywell Airfield so he could fly around the country keeping tabs on his business empire when he liked.

George thanked him profusely, promised to get in touch, and then, in frustration, sent an email to Jess venting his anger at her for the mess she'd got him in. As for her step-father he was tempted to drive round to his house and break his nose again. Fortunately discretion got the better of him, instead he read the evening paper which had been passed under his door - presumably by Blister?

He had been stabbed in the back again. To cover themselves the club were hinting that they couldn't meet his wage demands and so had reluctantly let him go. Talk about covering their arse! He got straight on the phone to Wolfe demanding the chance to set the record straight. An interview was booked for the next day at their offices at 10 a.m. He took calls from both the local BBC and commercial radio, again agreeing to be interviewed the next day. He was determined to pay Mr Thresham back, big time.

Gary Wicks, his solicitor and a mate, was next on the phone. Couldn't he help? Professionally, or as a friend. George arranged to meet him tomorrow as well. It seemed Thursday was going to be a busy day. Then, just when it seemed it couldn't get any worse, he received a text from Pernod. Seemed the rumour at the club was they were going to sign Ashcroft, the defender from Stafford who had done him in January. Now that was adding insult to injury.

In the hours before his meeting with Blister he was fully occupied reading the mail coming in from all over the world. It seemed clubs from Australia, America, Europe and home wanted to talk to him about next season. Either the internet, the PFA or Interpol were getting him lots of publicity and his notoriety was making him in demand. There was even a message from his ex, Lara. She sent her love and best wishes. The surfer had dumped her, so if he needed a place to stay or to get away for a while, he was welcome over there. "No chance," he thought.

It was amazing how time could fly when you weren't working. A quick frozen meal, wash and brush-up then it was off to meet Blister. There was no reply from Miss Thresham to his message. He still had the black Saab Cabriolet from work. "Nice motor," he thought, as he drove the four minute journey to his meeting.

The pub was quiet. After work drinkers had gone home for dinner. Those over for the night hadn't yet arrived. Blister and two other old guys were sat at the back of the lounge. Each had a pint of beer in front of them. George bought a J20 apple and cranberry, the group declined his offer of a drink. They looked serious, but friendly, unlike some of the patrons whose glares told Clooney he wouldn't be winning any personality contest in the place that night.

Blister made the introductions. John (call me 'Doors') Dawson aged fifty-seven, a former paratrooper, and Paul Scowcroft aged fifty-eight, an ex-Royal Marine. The three of them had seen various kinds of active service together and now in retirement were settled in the area for one reason or another. Blister was the spokesman for the group. They all wanted to help, felt he had been wronged and all had their own reasons for wishing Thresham harm. Clooney felt moved by the support of these tough old soldiers. Thanking them from the bottom of his heart he brought them bang up to date with the sad story of this last week.

'Doors' Dawson broke the silence when George paused, emotion getting the better of him. When he, with the consent of the others, told Clooney of the group's dealings with Thresham, George realised that what he was going through didn't compare with their problems. 'Doors'' wife had fallen behind with HP payments on a carpet she'd brought from a Thresham company. A thug had visited the house, threatened her, then groped her as he left. When confronted by 'Doors', Thresham denied all knowledge of the incident. A week later his wife was grabbed walking home from her keep fit class and had been mugged and beaten. Now she never left the house and their lives were shattered. Though he could never prove it, he just knew Thresham was behind it.

'Doors' lapsed into silence with tears in his eyes. Scowcroft took up the litany of sorrow. He had worked for a transport company in Wellingborough, owned by a local farmer Tom Rawlins. One night working late he found Tom sat in his office drunk as a lord and blubbing his eyes out. It seems he owed money to Thresham's casino in Northampton; if he didn't pay up they were going to take the business and the farm. His home had been in the family for over two centuries and now he had lost it. Scowcroft offered to get a loan to help, he was sure the other staff would help as well, rather than see the business go under. But it was too late. Thresham called in the debt and sold both the business and the farm. Faced with the shame and homelessness, old Tom killed himself with his own shotgun. But as far as Scowcroft was concerned, it was Thresham who had pulled the trigger.

Blister didn't want to go into his reasons for hating Thresham. He just hinted it surrounded his late wife. So they sat, four men united in sorrow, with hate in their hearts for the same man.

They all had words of warning for George. He had made a dangerous enemy and needed to take care. Thresham was evil and vindictive. Clooney had hurt his pride and his nose, the man would want revenge. It seemed to George like he was getting plenty of it already. No job, sacked by the club, pilloried in the press. But he accepted this might only be the beginning.

The pub was filling and Clooney was attracting black looks from the customers. He suggested they adjourn to his place. He bought some bottles of beer to take with him, and sensed the hostility of those around him. They had probably got out just in time.

'Doors' drove back with Scowcroft, and Blister went back with George. On the way he listened to his sad story. Blister's wife forgot to pay for some items in one of Thresham's shops, was apprehended by a female store detective, and, no doubt in a state of panic, she allowed herself to be strip searched, not realising it was being filmed. Later, after being shown the clips, she agreed to carry drugs rather than be seen on the internet. She was caught. To her daughter's shame and son-in-law's embarrassment, made all the worse as he was in the police force. So she over-dosed to avoid the scandal. As they drove into the underground car park Blister was crying, his body shook, and not knowing what to do George picked up the beer, deciding to leave Blister in peace while he let the others in.

Chapter Seven

They sat and drank and talked about football until Blister joined them. His eyes were red but he had obviously pulled himself together. They were unanimous, they were going after Thresham - enough was enough.

From the little things they said Clooney guessed they had met during the first Gulf War, all of them attached to their own special operations unit, but they had worked together and become life-long friends. Despite the fact they were as old as his dad he felt in safe hands. But with a lot to learn.

Keep yourself fit, stay alert, was their advice. They would arrange some equipment and special training for him. There was a world of difference between being a fit footballer and a fighting solder he was about to learn. When they left he checked again for messages, none that were particularly interesting had been received. His mother wanted him to call urgently whatever the time. Fearing the worst he did so. But for once it was good news. They were going to Canada to celebrate their thirty-fifth wedding anniversary, staying with mum's sister Aunty Cynth, and they wondered if he minded. Daft sods.

Mum had wondered if they should be here for him with all that was going on. He told her he was pleased they were going, and said he might get over to visit. Then his father came on, really pressurising him to make the trip, so this time when he promised, he meant it.

Remembering what he had planned for the next day he hit the sack and was soon dreaming of old battles, and even older soldiers.

The newspaper's meeting room was bland, the gathered group sullen. Expecting only to meet Trevor Wolfe, George was surprised to be introduced to a po-faced editor, Martin Powell, and an even more po-faced solicitor Mr Daniel Mathews. He gave his version of events but wondered if they would ever see the light of day. Then, after a few questions from Trevor, he was dismissed like an undesirable. Never mind, he had told his story, the true story, and he felt better for it.

Kettering Radio was angry with him. They had listeners phoning in condemning him and were not sure now if they wanted to speak to him. What would the advertisers think? He told them to get stuffed and drove over to Northampton for lunch, window shopping, and to meet with the BBC.

That was the best interview of the day. Because they weren't on the doorstep they seemed to take a more relaxed approach and he got the chance to tell it as it was.

Blister phoned, he had listened to the interview which had been broadcast, and he was most impressed. He hoped to catch up later.

Several of the lads phoned to wind him up, but they did say they thought the boy had done good.

Feeling pleased with himself, he drove over to Wellingborough Golf Club where he had arranged to meet Gary. Stopping for petrol he picked up the evening paper. Reading it over a coffee in the Little Chef, he was even more pleased with the tone and support it offered. Good old Trev, he must have won this one. He felt he came out of it almost smelling of roses.

The golf club was busy, warm May evenings made for better play than some of those winter mornings he'd slogged round with Gary. They had met when he needed a solicitor for his flat purchase, hit it off straightaway, and in the six months he had been in the area they had golfed a few times, dined and wined. Well Gary had certainly done the wine bit. George was expected it seemed, and the head waiter showed him to a table in one of the private rooms off the bar.

Gary rose to meet him, a huge smile on his face. He was almost as tall as George but ten years older and sixty pounds heavier. Always smartly dressed with a mop of silver hair, he exuded a charm and a confidence you wanted in your legal representative.

For once Clooney joined him in a glass of wine. They made small talk while ordering a meal, then food in front of them they got down to the serious stuff. From the newspaper articles and radio interviews Gary was up to speed on events, but he had 'off the record' words of wisdom regarding George's suspension from work and his football contract position. The key to the former was, did George really want his job back? If not, he, on Clooney's behalf would argue employment law with MotorGiant and would, if necessary, find witnesses to prove Clooney was a victim of an attack, not the perpetrator. He was sure he could get a great deal out of them for constructive dismissal. Reminding George that if he was going to pursue a football career elsewhere the money could come in handy, and he probably wouldn't be able to commit to work in Northampton, even if he really wanted to. While Clooney thought that over, Gary addressed the other matter.

Legally the club had done nothing wrong. Indeed by

paying him all his monies due, a month early, and allowing him to leave without a fee, it could be said they were more than generous, though stupid. Offloading a player in demand for free didn't make for good business, which Gary was sure would come back to bite them. Really, he felt where Clooney ended up was his choice. Did he fancy playing abroad again? With the interest he was getting it seemed George was in the driving seat.

Until now Clooney hadn't thought of leaving Kettering as he had only had the flat for six months. In that case, Gary suggested, why not look for a club in commuting distance, get at least a two year contract on the best terms he could and take it from there. It made sense to George. But how did he do it? In the past, clubs had come to him with a package and he had said yes or no. When he was in Perth and had told his boss that Lara had gone and that he wanted to return to England, the club had circulated his details, and Kettering had made him an offer. He had never seen the place before he drove up from Heathrow, had a medical and signed terms.

Danny Brown, the partner in Gary's firm who ran the Northampton office, had handled several players' contracts, and Gary knew he would be delighted to handle George's negotiations if he wanted, for a fee of course! Clooney said yes at once, he needed to sort his life out speedily and then perhaps he could take a break in Canada. Business done they relaxed and made small talk before they headed for their respective homes.

George drove there feeling better about life in general and his in particular. Listening to a local radio phone in programme it seemed fans were now much more supportive of him, and were turning on the club.

There were even comments about Thresham's role

in all this, accusing him of meddling behind the scenes. A car followed him as he turned into the grounds of home, possibly Blister? As he drove up to the automatic doors that provided access to the apartment's underground garage a dark coloured saloon car shot out from a visitor's parking spot, deliberately blocking him. With the car behind effectively sandwiching him he was trapped. Before he had grasped what was happening rough hands grabbed him. He was dragged from the car and three burly figures began to kick the shit out of him. You don't play professional football for fourteen years as a centre forward without learning how to handle yourself and Clooney landed a few kicks and punches of his own, despite the odds against him. But he would no doubt have taken a savage beating or worse if Blister and Scowcroft had not joined in. Within moments his assailants lay on the ground moaning, the old soldiers had not even broken sweat. Blister told him to get in the flat and wait for them, they would be with him shortly.

When George looked in the full length mirror on his bedroom wall he saw both eyes had been cut, his knuckles were skinned and his clothes would have been rejected by any self-respecting tramp looking for a new outfit. He realised he was shaking, shock he guessed. Blister came in, realised the problem, and told him to take the hottest shower he could stand, get some pants on and report back to him in the bedroom. Clooney duly obliged. Despite the heat of the shower he was still shaking. Blister had a field medical kit open for action. First he used antiseptic on all the cuts and bruises. Then a sort of strip on the eyebrow. "As good as stitching," he told George. Dressings and plasters as appropriate were applied and then he handed Clooney two large tablets and a small glass of water. They were military issue pain killers that would also knock him out. Blister told him he would stay in the apartment that night as guard, but he needed George to just take the tablets and then let Mother Nature take over. George obeyed his orders.

Chapter Eight

When he awoke he was stiff, sore and disorientated. As he got out of bed there was a knock at the door. Blister had heard him wake and had brought him tea, toast and more pills. Though these, he promised him, would dull the pain then pick him up, not put him out. As he sipped his tea the old man explained that when he saw last night's paper and heard the radio interviews he'd guessed Thresham would be out for revenge. Unknown to Clooney, 'Doors' had kept an eye on him at the golf club, then followed him back home. Blister and Scowcroft, waiting in the lobby, had seen the opposition vehicles arrive and got ready for action. They had interrogated George's attackers with little success; they were just three Corby boys who had been hired by a villain unknown to do a job, so after taking their pictures for future reference they had let them go. But they had confiscated the loot they were going to share for doing the job on Clooney.

Blister thought it advisable to fill Burns his son-in-law in on what had happened, if George agreed. He did so, and they phoned him. Then Gary called them. His partner Danny was available at 9 a.m., the office closed at noon on Saturday if Clooney wanted to meet. George confirmed he would be there.

Gary also wanted to talk about Jess. Thinking it over he was sure someone with money and contacts must be helping her. To have stayed off the radar for a year suggested to him someone, like perhaps a London based journalist sister, might be worth a call? It made sense, and Clooney said he would follow up and let Gary know what happened. He decided not to burden his friend with the details of last night's punch-up, instead he thanked him and promised again to let him know how he got on.

The next day he arrived early for the 9 a.m. meeting with Danny Brown. Relaxing in the waiting area of Watson Green's office George caught up on the football headlines in the papers. Apparently he was about to sign for Exeter, Watford, Rochdale or Luton, depending which paper you read. Laughable really, but maybe if he kept reading he might finish up at Manchester United! Danny appeared and they made their way into his plush air conditioned office. Danny introduced him to Fraser Wiltshire from the Allstars Allsports Agency. Fraser was about Clooney's age, smartly dressed with natural blonde hair. No one commented on Clooney's battered appearance.

Dan explained that Fraser was a FIFA registered agent, recognised by the FA Football League and the PFA. Watson Green would draw up all the legal contracts required but Fraser would handle negotiations if that was acceptable to Clooney. George knew Gary well enough to know that he wouldn't be a party to this if it wasn't kosher, so he agreed and signed on the dotted line. He didn't understand all the talk about image rights and the like, but if the guys could get him more money he was all for it. They all shook hands on it, and now Fraser had the real good news. Three clubs wanted to meet with Clooney and all were offering a two year contract with a generous signing fee. They were division one Watford, division two Bury and non-League Stafford, who had no chance after what the centre back had done to him.

Watford appealed the most as it was a high standard of football, and only an hour and a half from Kettering the way he drove. Fraser fixed up for him to meet their manager Steve Goddard at 1 on Monday. Allstars Allsports needed photographs and a full CV they could show prospective clients, so George promised to email the CV through later and Fraser told him his photographer at Demon Photographic would contact Clooney direct. With that, the meeting closed.

He asked Gary if he could borrow an office for ten minutes and was allowed the great man's own room. Online he abstracted details of Amanda Thresham. He emailed to ask if she would meet him for a drink in a London venue of her choice. Monday night. Might as well go on from the Watford meeting as he was half way there. He had more messages and mail. His parents wanted to know if they would see him before they flew to Canada next Thursday. Wolfe, Blister, Pernod, Wethers, and another thirty people were all trying to get hold of him, but for now it was 'me time' to head home for lunch.

When he entered the apartment he saw immediately the devastation. Everything he owned had been hurled about or smashed. It looked like a bomb had gone off. But why, and who were the thugs that did this?

He couldn't believe Blister hadn't heard or done something and he phoned him to give him a piece of his mind.

It had been the old boy's day off, he had taken his daughter with him to visit his wife's grave. He was mortified when he heard the news and came straight over. Just behind was the law. Blister had called Burns on his way to Clooney's; soon fingerprint men and others swarmed over the wreckage.

When just the three of them were left and the rooms had been returned to some semblance of order it was time for a council of war. Was this attack a warning? Or were Thresham's men looking for something? Assuming it was him behind it.

On a positive note Burns believed Thresham was running scared. First the attack on George and now this, he just wished they had the means to push him further and really nail him. Blister had an idea, but he wasn't telling his son-in-law yet. Though he did explain to George his anger and frustration that Thresham could do what he liked and then be protected by the laws of the land that he was abusing. If he was the dictator of a foreign country the army would go in, take over the infrastructure and then him, and hey presto answer questions later. This was giving the old soldier ideas. His pride was hurt that villains could have struck at his place of work and now he wanted revenge. He suggested George stay away for a night while he got the place back to how it was; and he needed time to think about his master plan. George phoned his parents. He didn't mention the fight or the attack on his home, he just told them he would like to see them before they left for Canada. In football parlance they were 'over the moon' when he announced his intended visit. Though they wished he'd given them more than two hours notice.

Chapter Nine

He arrived at his parents' home in Dronfield about 8 p.m. On the way he had stopped at Tesco's in Chesterfield and bought flowers and chocolates for mum and a bottle of brandy for his dad. As he pulled into the close he thought back to playing football in the street, the nosey Mrs Holden next door and the tantalising Janet Morton at number 62. As thirteen year olds they had sat in her dad's car in a pitch black garage and she had allowed him to see her bare breasts, in return he had let her see his cock. It might have gone further but her mother had hammered on the door to fetch her in. He was smiling with the memory when he drew up in the drive.

They both ran over to greet him but his mother shrieked when she saw he had been in a fight. He laughed it off with the old joke, you should have seen the other guy. Although the bungalow was sixty years old and they had lived in it all their married lives they kept it immaculate. Constantly decorating, replacing and improving, it was a home to be proud of. As ever they congregated in the conservatory, which offered a stunning view of the well -kept garden. He and mum had tea while his father cooled down with a local beer.

They were excited about the trip to Canada. The first time she would have seen her sister's house. But they were more concerned about him and what was happening in his life. He fobbed them off as if everything was fine, he talked about the clubs that were in for him and listened to all the ideas they had about what they would do in Canada. George's Aunt Cynthia lived in Burlington, a small town set halfway between Toronto and Niagara Falls. They intended to do all the tourist things, as well as catch up on events. Dad had never taken a month's holiday in his life before and that in itself was something to get excited about.

When the prodigal returns home he gets the equivalent of the fatted calf. In George's case this meant they sat down to his favourite meal, melon followed by mum's special turkey and vegetable pie with mashed potatoes and sweet corn, followed by bananas, raspberries and homemade ice cream. You certainly wouldn't want to try and play football after that!

They all cleared up and stacked the dishwasher - then, mugs of coffee in hand, it was back to the conservatory.

Clooney tried to keep them happy talking about their Canadian adventure. But his mother kept bringing the conversation back to him, trying to fathom what was going on. His father had printed off reams of articles and photos about the Threshams, George and football. His mother thought Jessica looked a real stunner and was worried for this young girl she had never met. Eventually she was persuaded to call it a day and the two men relocated to the lounge for a last word and drink before bed.

Clooney joined his father, thinking he might be becoming an alcoholic. This was about the eighth drink he had consumed in the last ten days. Once Graham was sure his wife was not in earshot he proceeded to tell George all he had managed to discover about Thresham senior. He had called in favours from friends in the police force, revenue and customs and accountancy firms he knew. When he told his son what he had discovered George understood why he also should be very, very concerned.

Martin Thresham was the youngest of seven children brought up - or should that be dragged up? - in a council house in Raunds, a small old shoe making town in Northamptonshire. Martin was almost expelled from school at the age of eight when he hit a fellow pupil with a house brick. The authorities suspected bullying so Thresham escaped with a warning. Age twelve he was convicted of shop lifting and demanding money with menace from two eight year old girls. He was taken into care and put on probation. Three years later he was banged up in a young offenders' institution. He had taken part, indeed the police believed he was a ring leader, in a vicious attack on a courting couple. The man had been beaten so badly he was hospitalised for three weeks and the woman had been subjected to an appalling sexual attack. Upon his release he obtained his first job as a labourer on a building site in Peterborough. Six months later he was caught stealing materials from the site. Back inside he certainly didn't learn the error of his ways and within a short time of his release he was involved in a fight in a brothel in Bedford. He had punched the prostitute he was with, the owner and two policemen before being overpowered. His next sojourn at Her Majesty's pleasure was the last to date.

After his release he had worked abroad, doing what no one knew, and then had returned with enough cash to buy a small caravan manufacturing firm, Nene Valley Caravans, that was close to going under. He must have had some talent for business because from that he opened holiday sites in France and Spain. Over the years a hotel in Florida, various companies and a casino in Northampton followed. By the age of forty he was a multi-millionaire.

Although it could not yet be proved, the authorities also believed he was involved in tax evasion, people trafficking, drugs and prostitution. This surely was a man to be wary of.

Collin Granger was the name of Jess and Amanda's real father. He had been the manager of Shipsmore Removals, a small transport company acquired by Thresham. Collin and his family had lived in the village of Woodford and after work each day he popped into his local, had two half pints of beer - never more - before walking the hundred yards or so back to work, collecting his car, then driving home. At his inquest it came out that he had followed his usual routine, though he had only had one drink. He was said to have appeared aggressive and not his usual self. On the way back for his motor he had been knocked down and his body flung into the roadside ditch, either by the force of the accident or by the hit and run driver.

Paula Granger, his wife - and now Thresham's - had phoned the police at midnight when he didn't return home and she could get no reply from his cell phone or the office. His body was found at 2.30 a.m. The Coroner's verdict was manslaughter by a person unknown. The case had never been solved.

Thresham supported the family through the bereavement process. He paid off the mortgage on the Grangers' home and provided a substantial pension for Mrs Granger, ensuring financial stability for life. He paid for holidays and bought Paula her own car. It seemed almost ordained that they would marry and the children's names were officially changed to his. The house at Loddington was built and the family continued to live there still, as George already knew.

George had always perceived his father as a man of

few words but what he had told him was a surprise on many levels. That his dad should so painstakingly have carried out this research for him, that the old man was so obviously worried and yet the quiet confident way he had told the story made him reflect yet again, does anyone really know their parents?

There was little to say when his dad had finished, except to reiterate that he would be careful and to thank the old man for his interest. But there was still one more surprise in store that night. His father told him how Blister had contacted them. As a father himself he knew George's parents would be worrying. He had promised them that he and his mates would look after their son and he would keep them in the picture with what was going on. He could see that had meant a lot to his folks and he mentally thanked Blister for his forethought.

They said their goodnights and he retired to his old bedroom. A quick check on the Blackberry showed nothing of interest so he climbed into the bed in the room he had called his own all of his life and, putting thoughts of Thresham to one side, enjoyed a good night's sleep.

After breakfast they all visited Meadowhall for last minute holiday shopping. It was lunch out, George's treat, then back to Dronfield. Clooney promised he would visit them in Canada, then they phoned Aunty Cynthia and Uncle George and he was made to repeat his promise to them. So now he was cornered, full stop. He left them an anniversary card and details of the hotel accommodation he had paid for them at Manchester airport prior to their trip. Dinner, champagne, the works. It was a privilege and it made him happy to have done so.

Blister had been as good as his word. The apartment was back to normal. He phoned him to thank him and for contacting his folks. The old boy muttered it was nothing. Amongst the hundreds of emails and messages waiting for him was one from Amanda Thresham. She would meet him at 7.30 p.m. in the bar of the Ivanhoe Hotel just off Euston Road. Now he might find out some more.

He joined Pernod for a drink at the George Hotel in Kettering. Pernod knew a couple of the Watford lads, he'd played with them at Peterborough. The news around the club was that they were getting some flack for releasing Clooney. Dave Evans was being suggested as a new Chairman for the club and Bradshaw's position as manager was deemed to be under threat. It saddened George to hear of the turmoil surrounding his old club but he wouldn't be shedding any tears for them. He cheered up though when he was told that half a dozen of the lads had signed up with Blister on his revenge mission if it ever happened. Though they didn't know what was in store.

Chapter Ten

After a leisurely breakfast he set off for a punishing run across the fields. His training regime had gone to pot with all that had happened and he wasn't sure he would pass a medical if Watford wanted him to have one. At least appearance wise he looked better than Friday night. Blister would have been a great asset at any football club with what he'd achieved with George. He decided to take an overnight bag in case he stayed in London. Then, after a brief natter with Blister, he set off for Watford.

He stopped near the ground for a quick bit of lunch and arrived five minutes early to meet Steve Goddard. He remembered Steve from his playing days with Liverpool and England and though they had never met he expected to get on with him. The Watford manager appeared on time. He was 20 pounds heavier than his playing days but otherwise looked no different. Same short fair hair, Liverpool accent, always a smile and a powerful handshake. The jacket and trousers he wore looked made to measure and he had a distinct confidence about him.

They did a quick tour of the stadium before settling down in the manager's office. Steve made him a coffee whilst explaining his future plans.

New investors from abroad had taken over the club. Steve had the money to bring in eight or nine new players and he was already talking to three or four players' agents.

He had watched the game on TV, and been impressed with the way Clooney put himself about and the way he took that goal. He explained he was confident that a young Premier League striker was about to sign but the boy would need a big, experienced target man to play off if he was going to get the goals to justify his fee. Goddard believed George could be that man. The team had the makings of a good side with Irish international Sean O'Malley in goal and former Norwegian international centre back Torr Neilsen partnering tough Aussie Mark Wybonga in the middle of the defence. Steve assured Clooney he could be the missing bit in the jigsaw.

George was both flattered and interested but he was prepared to leave the details to Allstar Allsports to sort out. A two year contract on just the basic being offered was twice as much as he had been getting. But he would have to go full time, the club were not happy at the prospect of him having another job to take his attention from the football.

He couldn't really say no yet he asked for time to think it over, which was granted. He agreed he would go through a preliminary medical now just in case there was a problem. It had been provisionally arranged for him to see the club doctor at the nearby BUPA hospital at 4 p.m. After shaking hands George departed for a medical while Steve, having received Clooney's permission, was in talks with Fraser Wiltshire about the contract.

The medical was thorough, heart monitors, body scan, eye test, full examination, urine samples, blood samples. He was there for over two hours of non-stop prodding and poking it seemed, but finally, at just after 6, he was able to take a taxi to the station for his trip to London. The hospital had generously agreed, he thought, to guard his car overnight. What he didn't realise was that would all be going on the bill to the club.

He picked up a *Four Four Two Magazine* and saw himself on a page, so when he sat back in his compartment for the short journey he had plenty to read. Checking the Blackberry again there was nothing of major importance. Just confirmation from Fraser Wiltshire that they were in talks with Watford. They also wanted to know when they could they expect to receive the promised CV. "Shit!" Clooney thought, he had forgotten that. So he ignored his reading matter and got on with it.

It was exactly 7 p.m. when he left the train. He found the hotel within ten minutes and after a quick loo visit was propping up the bar while waiting for Miss Thresham with time to spare.

Amanda arrived exactly five minutes late. Each recognised the other instantly. If you have been in the papers and featured on the internet, the whole world knows you. In the flesh so to speak, she was the double of her sister and yet not at all like her. A contradiction. She had the same dark hair, eyes, nose and skin colour, was a similar height and build yet altogether different. She stood proud, tall and self -assured, her lipstick and makeup more vibrant. Somehow the clothes she wore were casual, but expensive. A summer dress from one of the top designers no doubt. Her handbag was outrageous in size and colour. When they shook hands he was the one to feel intimidated. He ordered her the white wine spritzer she asked for and a red wine for himself. That was nine drinks now in thirteen days, probably the most he had ever consumed in such a short period in his entire life.

They made small talk. She asked him about his future in the game. Journalist or not he wanted her to be honest with him so he answered her truthfully. He told her about his meeting that afternoon with Watford. She told him about her life as a writer. She had been employed by the *Daily Express*, then become a freelancer. She still contributed articles to her old paper but also wrote regular articles for various women's magazines he had never heard of, as well as producing press releases for her charity clients.

Amanda's pet subject was the exploitation of women and she produced hard hitting fund raising propaganda for a woman's refuge, an anti-slavery charity and for a battered wives appeal. She was currently writing a book about people smuggling and in particular about how eastern European women were forced into the UK sex trade. She certainly wasn't the type he usually came across in the closeted world of professional football.

He asked her if she would like to join him in a meal. "Not yet," she replied, "I will decide shortly." That knocked him back, but he took it in his stride, she was refreshingly open and proving to be more pleasant company than he had imagined possible.

With another drink in front of her she was prepared to discuss the reason they had met. Jessica. She wanted to know all about his meeting with the girl who claimed to be her sister. He told her everything, except for what happened in the pub car park. She queried his motives, was he hoping if it really was Jess that she would suddenly come out publicly and confirm his story, or was he genuinely interested in her as a person? He answered yes to both.

Of course he would like the world to know he wasn't a liar but he had also really taken a liking to Jess and would like to see where that took them and he would like to put one over on Thresham again.

At the mention of her step-father she shuddered, but said nothing. What did he want from her she asked?

But then before he could answer she said yes to

dinner. Did he like Italian food? And upon a positive reply she phoned her favourite Trappatoria Juve and made a booking. Then after she had visited the ladies they climbed into a taxi and were whisked away to her favourite, favourite eating place. She told him Paulo Medini the owner was a fanatical Juventas fan whose restaurant was a shrine to the football club and an oasis to lovers of real Italian food and wine.

She kept up a non-stop dialogue about the place until the moment they arrived outside its hallowed doors. She paid the cab as he was buying dinner. "So no going Dutch," he thought! The owner personally greeted them, making a huge fuss of Amanda before welcoming George, his greeting was pleasant if not as enthusiastic. He was sure that as a lover of the beautiful game Clooney would enjoy the surroundings and he was honoured to have him as a guest. "So he knows who I am," Clooney thought. It still astounded him the power of the sport. He had bathed on beaches in Australia, been on safari in Kenya and ridden horseback in the Caribbean but there was always someone there who had conversed about football, wherever he had been. It truly was the world game.

They were settled at a small intimate table. They could still hear the live music but were able to talk above it without shouting. They ordered a set menu that the owner recommended and settled down, he with his sparkling water, she with her Italian wine. He had forgotten the question she had posed in the hotel bar so she reminded him. He came straight out with it. He couldn't believe her sister had managed to evade recognition for a year without help and somebody to provide money and shelter. Logic said that someone was her. Rather than answer she threw him by saying he hadn't even proved he had met Jess.

He produced the photos he had downloaded. "That proves nothing," she said "You could have been mistaken." But she knew all the facts about their life he argued. "A con woman or someone who was a fantasiser would do," she told him.

"Alright," he said playing his final card, "and how many women do you know that have a tattoo of the dove of peace holding a poppy in its mouth on their right breast?" He had never been one to kiss and tell and he hated himself for saying it, but he didn't know what else to do that could possibly prove his argument.

Amanda didn't flinch. In fact she didn't speak at all, just sipped her drink and chewed her food. He waited for a reaction but she threw him, just as earlier in the bar when she had suddenly booked this restaurant in the middle of a conversation. "Let me tell you about the book I'm working on and about one girl's story in particular," she said. "Then we can talk some more about my sister and your mystery woman. It will take some time so please indulge me and carry on eating or your food will go cold." This woman seemed to have the power to make him obey instantly; and he started to eat, while listening avidly to the story she told.

Karrina was Romanian. Blond with a great figure and a warm smile. But the family were poor and could not afford for her to go to university although she was extremely clever at school. She started work in a dress shop and her mother really appreciated the contribution she made to the family budget. Many rich foreigners came into the store and she envied their lifestyle and their wealth. When she was nineteen her cousin Gregor came to visit. He told her about how he was recruiting girls to work in England and he showed photos and letters of the girls he had helped. Karrina was desperate to go, her mother for her to stay.

They argued and they cried but neither would give in.

Gregor came to the shop. He said he would advance her the fare if she wanted to go. She could repay him out of her great earnings. The temptation was too great for a girl with nothing, living in the poverty that was their life in Romania. She ran away leaving a note for her mother, with a dozen other girls, all attractive and excited about their new life. She was smuggled under the floor of a huge vehicle. After many days and an unpleasant sea crossing they arrived in England. The vehicle was driven into a wood and the girls were allowed out to relieve themselves and stretch their legs before they were split into smaller groups for the next part of the journey.

At least now they could sit up and watch this new exciting countryside pass by. For most of the previous journey they had laid wearing nappies beneath the floor of the moving vehicle, with just a water bottle and a bag of mixed nuts and fruits to sustain them. They had not bathed for some time and knew they smelled. They felt sore from the nappies and couldn't wait for the chance to wash. After a couple of hours the car pulled into a building on an industrial estate and, once inside, the girls were allowed to use the facilities. The unit had showers, baths and toilets, there were combs, brushes, deodorants, perfume, make up and clean clothes. They spent a happy hour making themselves pretty again.

After some food and lots of water, for they were all dehydrated from their ordeal, they were taken to a building in London. All of the girls spoke some English and they were able to read the road signs and the advertisements as they completed their journey into the centre of the nation's capital.

The journey ended in an old garage where they

disembarked and were led upstairs to their accommodation for the night. There was more food and drink and a television in the main lounge which they all were drawn to. Their fears appeared unfounded and they began to relax.

Soon the combination of tiredness, drink and relief began to have an effect. Some of the girls fell asleep, others got loud and silly, eventually everyone had enough and they wandered off to bed. Tomorrow was a whole new day and the beginning of a new exciting way of life.

There were breakfast cereals and fruits on the table when the girls rose, with fresh bread, drinks and cheese available. The perfect start to a perfect day, perhaps. A group of men arrived with a lady photographer, the man in charge named Boris told them they would have to have their pictures taken for their identity papers and then some of them could audition for modelling and acting jobs. It was all a scam of course. The girls were being photographed in various states of undress, then topless, then nude. There was extra money for a bit of lesbian fun and then that was it. Later the girls were shown their details and photographs on the web and they started their new careers working as escort girls or in massage parlours but it all amounted to the same thing.

If you objected you either got hurt where no one could see or they started you on drugs. Once hooked you would do anything for your next fix.

Karrina put up with it for three months. She had managed to stash some cash, her English was good and she fled after serving some punter in his hotel. She grabbed a taxi, the tube, a bus and finally the train to Luton where she turned herself in to the local Red Cross. They of course alerted the authorities and she found herself banged up in prison in Bedford. Once the police started investigating her story Boris and his gang got word to an inmate to take care of her. A warden spotted what was happening and saved her from being knifed. Her assailant claimed Karrina had stolen a book and had threatened her so she was just retaliating.

A temporary holding hostel was her next destination, pending deportation. But she escaped and made her way to Wellingborough where she obtained work in a hotel for food and board. For cash she begged on the streets and did whatever casual work came her way, or worse.

One day a big car stopped and a businessman offered her a job in a casino waiting at tables. The outfit was skimpy, the tips were big and she was paid in cash. She did well and stayed out of trouble. Then one day the man offered her another job. More money as well.

She was to keep house for him, babysit the children and provide him with sexual favours when requested. That man was her step-father Matthew Thresham.

By now the food on the table was cold, but who felt like eating anyway. Clooney was lost for words. Amanda wiped away a tear, composed herself and poured another drink. She was visually shaken by the ordeal of repeating Karrina's story and for quite a while neither spoke.

Then she took up the story again. One day Jess came home from a morning shift at the hospital. A fierce argument was going on between her mother, Thresham and Karrina. Mum thought Karrina had misplaced some of her jewellery. Thresham called her a thief and wanted her out of the house; and Karrina was protesting her innocence between the sobs.

"Jess brought Karrina to me. I cared for her, arranged new papers, don't ask how, and she is now in Scotland with a partner, house and job and she is safe and happy. Jess returned home but couldn't hack it. After a week she just got up one morning and left. And that Mr Clooney is the truth, the whole truth and nothing but the truth."

A wisecrack would have been inappropriate. To say sorry meaningless. So George just sat there silent, tense and deep in thought. She ordered coffee and brandy for them both and they skipped desert, hunger had left them. Again he was surprised when she finally broke the quiet to ask him if they could maybe finish the conversation at her place. He readily agreed, Amanda paid the bill - a surprise - and then it was off to Highgate by taxi.

Both sat alone with their thoughts as the cab driver, recognising Clooney, gave them a lecture on football as only a taxi driver can. His ramblings improved a difficult journey and George tipped him generously. When they arrived at the new house which Amanda rented for a mind blowing amount, George discovered another side again to his companion.

Inside a very feminine stylish modernistic lounge Clooney struggled to find a comfortable chair, finally settling for one of the two-seater settees while his host stretched on the floor. She produced more brandy and coffee and, when George declined the booze, commandeered both generous glasses.

Amanda struck again, surprising him by asking what he had thought of Karrina's story. What did he think of girls like her? He didn't know how to answer and he stuttered and stumbled a reply. Of course he thought it appalling, it made him sad and astounded by his fellow men. As for the girl, Karrina, he could only wish her all the best in the future - she had earned that.

After that Amanda told him figure after figure about the numbers, lives, fate of all the girls like Karrina who were forced into virtual slavery here in this wonderful country he loved. He felt compelled to fight back. He wasn't to blame, had never used prostitutes and would never treat any woman badly, certainly not use violence towards them.

She surprised him yet again when she concluded she knew that he was a good man and she hoped one day it might work out with him and her sister. At first it didn't register what she had said, then the penny dropped, yes she was admitting his mystery woman was indeed Jess.

"So where is she?" he demanded to know.

"Not yet," she whispered, "it's not safe for her to reveal herself." But she's sorry for what had happened, missed him and would tell him everything herself soon.

He was elated with the news, tired, depressed, happy and sad all at the same time. But it was to be the last of the questions and answers for that night. Amanda's speech was slurred as she started to fall asleep, but before she passed out she offered Clooney the use of the spare bedroom with en-suite, which he gratefully accepted.

"What a day!" he thought as he lay in her comfortable if small single bed. The guest room, like the rest of the house had been arranged by a woman for women and some of the things in the bathroom he had never seen in his life before. But nothing mattered, he wasn't going mad. Jessica Thresham was the girl he had met that night after that match, although it all seemed so long ago now, and he was going to see her again. With happy thoughts of what had been and what might be, George closed his eyes.

Chapter Eleven

Amanda rose first, slightly the worse for wear, how much had she drunk last night? After three strong black coffees and several pain killers she felt well enough to sit and reflect upon the night. She could see why Jess had fallen for him, handsome, swoony, sensitive and well mannered, he was a rarity in her experience. During the night she had woken once for a bathroom visit and had to admit had been tempted to offer herself to George. Only the loyalty she felt to her sister and fear of rejection had dissuaded her.

She heard him sigh and composed herself and soon they were breakfasting together as if they were old friends, not two people who had met for the first time last night. All he wanted to know was where was Jess and how could he contact her. For one brief moment she almost hoped her sister had no interest in him, then she might have had a chance. But she quickly vanished such wicked thoughts from her head.

Later that day she would be speaking to Jess, she told him, and it would be up to her sister then to contact him.

His mobile rang, it was Kettering director Dave Evans wanting to meet as soon as possible and had he signed for anyone yet? Clooney said yes to a meeting and no he hadn't signed, although he was talking to Watford. They arranged to meet for lunch at the Falcon Hotel in Castle

Ashby. Dave would make all the arrangements and meet him there for lunch at 1 p.m. Clooney was going to have to get a move on.

The hotel was a small former coaching inn dating back to the 16th century. The only other time Clooney had been there was for a posh wedding. He sensed this visit was going to be very different.

Amanda was working from home that day so saw him off with a kiss and a hug and the promise to talk soon. She also told him she thought he was an all right guy and that Clooney and Jess made a great pair. He felt elated when he climbed in the taxi to the station. Checking his messages he was in great demand. Both his solicitors wanted to talk and Blister and a hundred others. But it was Dave Evans's call which held his attention. He couldn't fathom why the multi-millionaire builder would be really taking time out of his busy day to see him. Still, all would be revealed shortly.

He picked up his car from the BUPA hospital at Watford after the short train ride from London, then it was foot down and on to Northamptonshire. As usual the M1 was busy and he began to think he wouldn't make it. But he pulled up in the car park with a full ten minutes to spare.

At reception he was told that Mr Evans had a private room booked and they would phone him to see if George should go up. Dave obviously said yes, for within minutes Clooney found himself knocking on an old oak door. Feeling a bit like he had at school if he was told to report to the head, well at least Dave couldn't cane him or if he did Clooney was big enough to sort him out.

Dave Evans, dressed in a very business-like pin stripe suit but no tie, welcomed him in to a large bedroom meeting room with a table set for lunch, comfy arm chairs, sofa and coffee table. Light streamed in the mullion windows and Clooney could appreciate the colourful fabrics and ambiance of his surroundings.

Evans sat him down in an armchair, they drank tea and made small talk. A waiter brought a lunch menu in, then waited patiently while they made their selection. Both settled for the venison pie, no starters. Evans spoke, George listened intently. Dave looked a bit like that detective on TV, Gene Hunt, from *Life on Mars* and he was as scary.

Evans told him how as a boy in Cardiff he had played football when most of his friends played rugby. His father had been capped for Wales at rugby and always claimed his eldest son had shamed him. But Dave knew his old man was secretly proud of him. He came to so many games over the years. After being released by the Bluebirds at eighteen Dave almost gave up the game, but when Swansea called he grabbed the chance to show his hometown club what they had missed. Indeed a few years later Cardiff City did try and buy him back. "But you never go back," Evans believed.

He did eight years at Swansea, then four with Newport, before signing for Cheltenham who were then in the Conference. A couple of years later the thirty-two year old was approached by Kettering. It was his dad ironically who urged him to join. By then Evans The Builders Ltd was doing business all over the South West of England, Wales and the West Midlands. His dad had wanted to establish a base on the eastern side of the country for some time so here was an opportunity. Dave signed, and Evans the Builders became almost as familiar a sight in the East Midlands, North East and the rest as it was in Wales.

It was the reason he had learnt to fly and got the helicopter. So he could get round the country better. Last year they had expanded into Scotland and that was a journey, Kettering to Aberdeen, he preferred to do in the air rather than on the ground. Besides he got far less speeding tickets now, he joked. Then last year, at his annual medical, they had picked up very high blood pressure, he would have been surprised personally if he hadn't had it with his lifestyle. Unfortunately like a prat he had told Diane, his "second and current" wife as he liked to introduce her, and she had gone ape shit.

She wanted him to retire, stay at home or take holidays, they had really fallen out, but in the end he agreed to look at the other options which he had.

Their venison arrived with fresh vegetables, parsley mash and a rather delicious red wine. "Got to stop drinking," George thought as he tucked into a most enjoyable meal. When the food was gone they sat back as the plates were cleared and coffee was served.

Dave started talking again; it had been his wife Diana's idea apparently, why not go part time at work, with a view to retiring. Then buy the football club as an interest. After all football had been his life and he was hopping mad with Thresham and that little shit of a manager Bradshaw over the way they had treated Clooney. The more he thought about it the more excited he had become. Contacting his lawyers and other local businessmen, in less than seven days he found out all he needed to know about the support there was for such an idea. Then bingo! The icing on the cake! From very good sources he was informed that the Football League was concerned about Thresham's involvement with the club, given his reputation.

With that last piece of information Dave knew he had to do it. He reckoned Thresham would sell for the right money and he was prepared to pay it to get him out, put the club on a proper financial footing and take it forward to wherever it might go. Perhaps one day Premier League, maybe even Europe, who knows?

George couldn't help being excited himself at the thought of a successful businessman who had been a player controlling the club; but he still never saw what came next.

"I want you to be my player manager," Evans told him. "A three year contract with bonus scheme, double current wages, car of your choice up to £35,000, free health, travel and life insurance and I'm prepared to discuss with you an expenses package and anything else you might need, so what do you say?"

Knocked out, flabbergasted, call it what you will, Clooney was blown away. What could he say, yesterday he had almost agreed to join Watford, now this out of the blue. He couldn't answer, was he ready to be a manager? Could he do it? Did he want to? Eventually he spluttered out his thanks for the offer, explained how surprised he was and asked for time to think about it.

Now it was Dave Evans's turn to look surprised, he must have thought George would jump at the chance. The jovial atmosphere changed instantly and Evans became the hard businessman again. "Sure," he almost snarled, "you have until Friday and I would appreciate you signing this confidentiality agreement I've brought with me, basically if you disclose anything we've discussed today I'll sue the arse off you ok?"

George was sorry the meeting had taken this turn, he duly signed, they shook hands and as he left Clooney promised to call him by Friday at the latest.

Back at the apartment block Blister was waiting for him. Too much had occurred and his emotions were so intense he couldn't concentrate on what the old soldier was saying. Realising this, Blister agreed to leave it for now and catch up later. They agreed for a meet at 9 p.m. at the flat.

Checking electronic mail, phone messages and snail post took George another thirty minutes. His mum had phoned to remind him they were leaving on Tuesday but could cancel if he needed them. As if. Amanda had phoned, both his lawyers, his agent, Pernod and Wethers had sent texts and so on and so on. "Have to get a secretary soon if this carries on," he thought. But still no contact of any kind from Jess.

After a toilet trip and a cold drink he called the journalist. Amanda's news was a non-event really. Jess was glad he was safe, would contact him soon herself but for now preferred keeping her location private. It really pissed him off that after what he'd been through because of her she could still keep him at arm's length. They agreed to keep in touch and George got round to contacting everyone else on the to-do list. In no time it seemed Blister was knocking on the door and Clooney knew he owed the old guy the courtesy of listening.

He quickly told Blister of what had been happening, excluding the meeting with Dave Evans. His guest was delighted for him. But he had exciting news of his own and over a pot of tea he filled George in.

They were planning a raid on some of Thresham's empire. 'Doors' Dawson had got six ex-para's in on it, Scowcroft four marines and with Blister's six ex-SAS men they had a little army of eighteen very, very experienced fighting men, plus half a dozen footballers as backup if needed. Because of contacts they had been able to get access to the RAF camp at Grafton Warren which they intended to use as both base and a holding camp for prisoners. Weapons and equipment had been a piece of piss.

George listened with a mixture of fear and

astonishment to the outrageous plan. Blister's men would split into four teams of four and each would hit a target at precisely the same time. A brothel in Northampton, illegal casino in Corby, massage parlour in Kettering, illegal club in Bedford. They would go in and grab computers, and any other items that might provide information, then they would seize money and goods before bringing prisoners and plunder back to base. Two men would control operations from there. They expected to seize enough cash and goods to pay for the operation and with witness statements and hard evidence to be able to present Burns and the authorities with all they needed to move officially against our common enemy.

When he paused for breath he looked at George for congratulations and approval but found neither. Clooney seemed to spend most of his life now dealing with one unexpected shock after another, but this was the worst yet. A group of old men playing at war games with organised criminals, possibly getting hurt in the process, was not the best news he had heard this year. By God there had been some happenings of one sort or another, but this beat them all.

Clooney ignored the constant calls and texts that were coming in, this really was the most scary thing yet. He thanked Blister for planning to do this for him but begged him to cancel the operation. He would never forgive himself if any of them were hurt on his behalf. "Leave it to the law", he argued. He'd heard Thresham was running scared, his time was running out anyway he was sure. He was too ashamed to add, "And it would be bad for me right now when I've got an agent, two job offers and one of my solicitors is hoping to get me a nice pay off from MotorGiant."

Blister couldn't be convinced otherwise. This wasn't just about Clooney now, he said, they were doing this for themselves and everyone else who had suffered at Thresham's hands. This was something they should have done before and there was no turning back. Every argument George put forward was knocked back, the die was cast and they weren't for turning.

By the time the old soldier left at a little after 11 George was in a state of panic. Not knowing who to talk to, or what to do, he didn't really know why, but he phoned Amanda and over the next hour or so he explained everything in the hope of help and absolution. Amanda though thought it a good idea, she would ensure it got the right publicity. Rather than help him find a way to stop it, she supported the raid.

She argued that the police didn't have enough on Thresham to be able to put him behind bars. But this plan of Blister's might find the evidence to make it happen. In any case the publicity, and there would eventually be some she would see to that, would all help to push Thresham, perhaps to the brink. An exhausted Clooney left it at that. It seemed he was doomed. Every day now bringing its own fresh different problems. Maybe he would just get a one way ticket to Canada, stay with his Aunty Cynthia and start a new life out there, it couldn't be any worse than what he was going through here.

After a restless night George forced some breakfast down before changing into running gear and pounding around the fields in an attempt to shake himself, get fit, clear his head and maybe find a way forward. It didn't help though. After a shower and change of clothes he still felt no better. He spoke to his agent and told him to wait on the Watford deal; that was fine with Fraser as he was talking to other clubs as well. Allsports also had a potential boot deal but were annoyed when Clooney said Demon Photographic hadn't been in touch yet. Promising to follow that up Fraser rang off. Eventually Gary came through, he had put George on call waiting. MotorGiant had emailed a proposal which he thought Clooney ought to see, then they could discuss it. Though, when pressed by George, Gary's opinion was: "Don't accept it, we'll get more."

Chapter Twelve

He met Wethers for lunch at the George Hotel in Kettering, thinking sod it, if any fans gave him aggro he was in the mood for a punch up. Wethers had been staying there while house hunting when he came to the club. He was one of those people who got on with everyone and the hotel now gave him the staff discount whenever he appeared, so it was a cheap but very good lunch that the guys enjoyed.

Wethers told him the latest gossip from the ground. There were apparently lots of unofficial meetings going on between various directors. Bradshaw was talking to no one and looked scared to death all the time now. All sorts of rumours were circulating about a possible takeover of the club or even how they might not be accepted into the League because of Thresham's involvement. George felt bad about not coming clean with his mate but dare not. He had to admit Dave Evans scared him as much if not more than Thresham. Wethers was joining some of the lads for a game of golf but Clooney declined, he needed some space and time to do some serious thinking.

He checked his mail and his messages, nothing earth shattering. Someone called Saul at Demon Photographic was desperate to talk and he sounded it. So George put him out of his misery by returning his call. They agreed to meet tomorrow at 11 a.m. at Clooney's flat as he would need access to his clothes. Was he doing a fashion shoot or porn pictures? Clooney wondered. But he gave the man directions. Blister was his immediate worry - a military strike on Thresham's empire scared George shitless. But what could he do?

His mum emailed from Aunt Cynthia's to say they had a great flight and were safe and very well looked after, but everyone wanted to know when he would be there. "Tomorrow if I had any sense," he thought before going back to his mind games. What did he really want? That was the question. Not what would earn him the most dough or what people expected him to do. He thought of Jess and her sister, his parents, Blister and his gang, his mates and that bastard Thresham.

If he was going to be his own man again, walk tall and without fear or recrimination, something had to be done about the bloke who was the problem and he couldn't let a group of guys as old as his dad do his fighting for him. It was settled. Just as he knew he wasn't going to leave Kettering, whatever deals he was offered. It was time like in the old westerns his dad watched when a man had to do what a man had to do. He would say yes to Blister and Dave Evans. Mind made up. No going back. Only forward; finally he was ready. Hopefully Jess would come back into his life and they would have a future together.

But if not it wouldn't be for want of trying on his part. He felt like events and other people had dictated his life for too long, he was taking charge of his destiny and tomorrow's future started now, today.

Blister answered his mobile after only two rings. Good reactions still, despite being stood in the British Legion surrounded by a dozen loud, thirsty mates. As soon as Clooney said "Yes, I'm with you, what's next?" the old soldier knew he was committed to the cause, the strength of the voice told him all he needed to know. He urged George to stand by his bed as he put it and they would be with him in thirty minutes. Not quite knowing what to expect Clooney made himself a mug of tea and waited for the onslaught.

Three minutes before the expected time of arrival Clooney answered a knock on the door to be met by Blister's army, a sight which he had never seen before. The group marched into his room military style before assembling parade ground style in a tight square that filled his lounge. Blister barked out an order to stand at ease, then instructed them to find a space and in seconds a dozen super fit, tanned group of sixty year old men were sat silently looking at him, for inspiration it seemed.

Blister issued another command and one by one each man stood saluted Clooney, gave his number and sat down seamlessly. It was, George thought, a bit like a scene from the movie *The Great Escape*. He should know, he thought, him and his dad must have seen that film a dozen times at least. Blister introduced Clooney then it was drinks all round which fortunately Blister had brought up from his locker in reception.

Blister had briefed the group earlier. But now for George's benefit they ran through the plan again. The mission code name Crook Rattler (work it out) was planned for 0200 hours Saturday morning which meant the team would assemble at Grafton camp at 2200 hours Friday night. Supplies, equipment and weapons were there, already under a guard consisting of Paul Scowcroft and four ex-marines. Meeting the men and seeing the way they behaved, listening also to the organisation and planning, Clooney was now most definitely on board and couldn't wait to receive his orders for the job ahead.

That was another kick in the teeth though, not for

him a place in the attack teams as Blister told him, pulling no punches, he was too well known and too much of an amateur to be risked. No, he was to stay at base and assist where necessary and he was to be made up to conceal his features in the hope that no one was able to tell Thresham who had cooked his goose.

You didn't argue with your commanding officer, so George accepted his role with good grace despite his disappointment. There was final discussion about the mission, then Blister brought the evening to a close by ordering the men to return to barracks. Where that was Clooney wasn't told. His orders were a good night's sleep then present himself for duty 2200 hours tomorrow. He was almost tempted to salute, but instead gave Blister a huge grin, a warm hug and farewell wishes before, following orders, he settled down for the night.

An early morning run was followed by a message check, shower, shave, dress and breakfast then at precisely 9 a.m. he phoned Dave Evans to tell him yes he wanted the job but Dave might not want him after the weekend but he couldn't say why. The builder laughed, then told him, "You won't embarrass me George, the fact you phoned on the dot as promised and you are warning me things might get rough just confirmed my thoughts about you." Clooney remained silent, puzzled.

"Don't you see?" Dave said. "A real bad egg wouldn't have phoned and bothered to tell me. He either would have got a job elsewhere and the first I would know about it would be when I opened the paper or he would have taken my offer said nothing and let me sort the shit out when the balloon went up. No, you are a good man Clooney and you will make a great manager I'm sure."

He explained that as at the moment he had not got

control of the club he couldn't offer the job as manager anyway. George was confused, had it been some kind of trick or cruel joke? Realising his predicament, Dave continued. "So the contract will be with Evans the Builders until such time as the club can take you off my hands," he laughed. A relieved George asked him what would happen next. Dave told George to get his agent, manager, or lawyer to give him a ring and they would sort out a meeting next week. A draft contract would be electronically mailed to Clooney today that he in turn could forward to his advisors. But, in essence, from the beginning of June he would have a new job. So no problems paying the mortgage then.

Demon Photographic phoned with apologies and rescheduled, which suited Clooney fine, he was more in the mood for soldiering than modelling. It sounded good and when he met Gary later he was able to show him a hard copy of Dave's very generous offer. "At first glance it's an amazing deal," he was told, though Allstars Allsports and Gary's partner Danny Matthews would obviously have their thoughts on whether it could be better.

But Gary was concentrating on the MotorGiant offer. He had compiled a reply for Clooney's approval, seeking damages for embarrassment caused and a payment in lieu of George not pressing a claim for constructive dismissal. Clooney couldn't believe it, Gary was asking them to pay him two years' wages plus any bonus or commission due. Before he could register a view Gary told him sadly they would never agree to that much but he was sure at least twelve months' was gettable, which considering George had only been there five months and was on a month's notice each way was a deal worth having in his opinion.

Clooney agreed and left for a spot of training, feeling like his life was back on track though he was slightly nervous as well as excited about the evening's planned jaunt. The gym and pool at the Kettering Park were excellent and he felt better for a real work out, then it was home, change into dark jeans and a black top with dark trainers. He didn't know why he chose the sombre outfit but it seemed appropriate for the mission ahead.

A quick check of all messages, an email to his folks hoping it was going well and the promise he would be there soon. He checked on Canadian flights and gave some thoughts to Dave Evans's plan. He had direct control of 25% of the shares in the club, other directors, friends and contacts had pledged a further 35%; with that Dave legally had sufficient support to call an Extraordinary General Meeting in the minimum of twenty-one days' time. That being the case and with no job at MotorGiant to worry about there was nothing to stop him heading across the big pond. It still bugged him that there was no word from Jess and he texted Amanda. She phoned him back almost immediately.

She was more interested in the raid than anything else and wanted to be there with a cameraman. Clooney gave her his commanding officer's number, for that was up to Blister not him. When he told her about Canada she suddenly clammed up, said she had another call and would get back to him, which pissed him off. Still it gave him a chance to eat, try and relax and prepare for the night ahead. A couple of the lads rang and he chatted with them before he realised Amanda might be trying to get him so he rang off. There were no voice messages so he watched a bit of TV - or rather he flicked channels like crazy as he couldn't concentrate on anything - and then it was time to go.

The old disused RAF base was hard to find in the dark but George eventually found himself at the locked main gates a little before the appointed time. As he sat there wondering what to do there was a knock on his side window. He could just about make out the features of Paul Scowcroft, though he hardly recognised him in his camouflage uniform and darkened disguised face. Paul opened the gates, waved Clooney through, where a similar dressed soldier invited himself into the passenger seat of the car and proceeded to direct George to where all the vehicles were hidden. He then escorted George, with just a small torch to show the way, further into the base and the building that was to be their H.Q. for the duration.

"It had probably been the gym at one time," Clooney thought, looking at the wall bars. Now a group of what to him appeared to be very organised professional soldiers were spread out in their teams over the space. They were checking equipment, including their weapons, they had face paint ready to apply, and the smell of restlessness in the room was there for all to experience. That these guys meant business and could do it, Clooney had no doubt. Blister appeared, George was tempted to salute him he was so obviously in charge. He was shown his operations room, a side room off the main hall. Loads of gear, including mobiles, field phones, radio, computer and, for a touch of normality in the lunacy surrounding him, there was tea and coffee facilities and biscuits there.

'Doors' Dawson, rough old bugger that he was, had been shot on active service in Iraq. The bullet had been removed from his back but there had been some nerve damage. At one time there were even fears he might be paralysed. Thankfully he had made an almost full recovery, though the injury restricted his ability to lift things and it was for this reason he was being left behind to handle H.Q. business.

He quickly explained that after the teams had left

they would cleanse the gym of any evidence and prepare it to receive the prisoners as a giant holding cell. Then each group would take a different set of captives for interrogation. He explained the less the hostages knew of any particular captor, the harder it would be to ever identify them. Also different questions from different troops might provide more answers. It would certainly confuse their guests as to how many people were holding them, which helped convince them not to try to escape and made them feel more vulnerable and hopefully more talkative.

It was all a new experience to George, but the guys didn't seem fazed at all. They sat, cleaned weapons, played cards, smoked, no political correctness here and some even slept. He had never felt more awake in his life and he was staying behind to man the office. They had a light meal at midnight, then ablutions, war paint on, weapons loaded, and they joined their squads for Blister's final briefing before it was time to go. The first team away headed for the illegal gambling club in Bedford, under the command of Sergeant David Davies, still a serving soldier with the 1st Para's.

The second team converged on the brothel in Northampton. Their leader was 'Dinky' Dawson ex-SAS. He was exceptionally tall for the regiment, being around six feet two. Not so easy to blend into the background when you were built like the proverbial 'brick shit house'!

Team three had the pleasure of hitting Corby, often jokingly referred to as the Scottish capital of England, on account of there being so many relations of those who, fifty years ago, had left their homeland to work in Corby's then thriving steel industry. The team was, appropriately enough, under the control of former Sergeant Colin McRae, an ex-Royal Marine Commando.

The massage parlour down the road in Kettering

was to be the target of Brendan Shiels' team. Brendan was still on the staff of RAF Yeovilton, though now in a civilian capacity.

All groups had to be in position and ready to go by 1.50 a.m. The vehicles to be used were old transit vans, bought for cash from various scrapyards. An unnamed military vehicle depot had carried out the necessary repairs and improvements required for the exercise. They were using long wheel base models and each one had received extra sound proofing and padding before a steel cage, which fitted the space between the roof and sides, was added. All should provide some comfort for the expected prisoners and be virtually escape and sound proof.

All the target venues had been well researched and near each one a motorbike, fitted with fake number plates, had been stashed so that a team member could follow the van, taking action if there was any pursuit.

Clooney took up his contact duties, wondering where all the equipment came from, and who had paid for it? Upon arriving at the venues the teams would radio in to confirm they were in place and ready to go.

Now it was all about the waiting. Nothing to do, but everything to worry about. One by one the teams phoned in, confirming they were in position and ready for action.

The Bedford team opened the attacks. A mobile phone blocking device was activated. Main phone lines, alarms and security cameras disabled. Then the lads went in behind a cloud of tear gas. The front door blown off its hinges. It was chaos everywhere. Staff made a grab for the money on the tables, punters scrambled to get out. Within minutes twenty selected prisoners were in the van, still coughing and spluttering from the effects of the gas. Their mobiles were taken from them as they were led away. Dave

Davies managed to load computers, a filing cabinet and as much cash as he could grab into the van. Finally, he lit a small fire to keep the authorities busy, then, as the van pulled away, he changed into appropriate motorcycle gear before following his troops. They had suffered no casualties, there appeared no sign of pursuit and, as he departed the streets of Bedford at a legal speed, various police, fire and ambulance vehicles passed him as they headed to the scene.

Around the same time 'Dinky' Dawson carried out a similar operation on the brothel in Northampton. The young girl on the desk ran for it, but was quickly overpowered. There were a dozen or so people, men and women in various states of undress on the premises, and with no time to find their clothes, that's the way they were marched into the vehicle! Dawson grabbed a computer, various files and a huge collection of mobile phones. Again, just as in Bedford, the raid passed without serious incident.

All that was to change though with the Kettering and Corby operations. The casino in Corby was located upstairs in a popular local pub. At that time there should have been few, if any, people downstairs in the bar. But this was Corby, a town with a reputation for hard drinking. So around thirty young and not so young lads and ladettes were still singing bawdy songs, laughing and shouting obscenities at each other as the team made their way up the stairs via the fire escape.

Explosives took the door of the casino off and they were in. Frenzied fighting ensued between the team, the gamblers and the drinkers who had now joined in the fray, but the civilians had no chance against the super-fit mix of serving and former soldiers. But the team were aware they were past their time limit. With too many prisoners to transport McRae selected twenty, who were escorted, with difficulty, into the vehicle. The rest were locked in the main function room downstairs. As the last man climbed into the van, a taxi pulled up behind them and quickly ascertained that this was not a normal night, so took off at high speed.

McRae decided to raise the stakes and hopefully buy them some time. He stayed behind and as the van drove away he returned to the now deserted casino and let off smoke bombs before setting the half dozen cars left in the car park alight. "That should keep everyone busy," he thought, as he scrambled onto the motorbike and took off into the night.

Team four had little trouble in the Kettering massage parlour. Only eight voluptuous looking girls were on duty and only three lucky punters were being worked on. The attack went too easily, with punters, girls and equipment in the van in no time at all. As the rear doors of the van were being closed a group of six local lads appeared on the scene, obviously having enjoyed a long night of drinking and looking forward to the relief a massage might bring. They were not impressed to see what they thought might be a raid on the massage parlour and an end to their enjoyment.

Stupidly, they decided to get stuck into the team, and the unfit, intoxicated lads were unable to keep themselves upright, let alone make an impression on the super-fit strength of the soldiers; but it had slowed the operation down and, conscious the police might suddenly appear, Brendan pulled his gun. The mob fell back in stupefied amazement and was forced at gunpoint into the recently vacated premises. Brendan wedged the front door before signalling for the van driver to go.

Just as he was preparing to get the motorbike going the law arrived in two cars, lights flashing. Realising he would have to think quickly, Brendan decided to take off at high speed in the opposite direction to the one the van had taken, hoping the police would follow, which they did. He knew he couldn't possibly outrun the law unless he could get into the centre of town and lose them in the maze of narrow alleys. However, he was some miles from town and in the middle of countryside, so while the two cars were still at a safe distance he took a sharp bend at well over the safe speed limit and turned immediately into fields, fortunately surrounded by trees and high hedges. He took off across the land towards Northampton, stopping at a safe distance from the road, just in case the law picked up the throb of the bike's engine. How grateful he was for the benefit of forward planning. Blister had arranged for various troops to take up standby positions in case of just such an emergency. Brendan sent a coded text to Blister. The reply was a map reference and he cautiously made his way to Broughton, a small village just outside Kettering.

He hid just outside the entrance to the village church and fifteen minutes later a petrol tanker loomed into view. Johnny Cander, a retired old soldier and now in need of some excitement, was driving the tanker. He whistled, badly, Colonel Bogey's march from *The Bridge on the River Kwai*, by way of recognition. A very relieved team leader hauled the bike and himself inside and out of sight. Johnny had 'borrowed' the vehicle from his employers and needed to get it back before 6 a.m., so they enjoyed, if that was the right word, an unexpected ride back to base. They saw plenty of activity by the police and other emergency services, but no one stopped them and in no time at all they were back at headquarters. Johnny dropped Brendan and bike off at a reasonable distance from the main entrance and went on his way.

Last one home and everyone safe.

Clooney and the boys at base had cleared the rooms of anything incriminating, not that anyone had left anything behind, and waited for the vehicles to return. All of them wore gloves and had disguised their faces with camouflage paint. Over their shoes they wore plastic bags so as not to leave footprints. The Bedford team had entered first, the prisoners were in shock and easily bound with the American plastic ties George and his group had been provided with. Eventually all of the groups had returned and there were now over fifty prisoners of both sexes in various states of undress taken to their respective interrogation rooms. There, guarded by different troops from those who had snatched them, they were searched. Interesting items like mobile phones were taken from them and each was in turn individually questioned. Those requiring toilet visits were escorted to the rest rooms and guarded until they were returned to the group.

Blister warned the group to prepare to leave, then he informed the prisoners that they would shortly be locked in for the night but that he and his team would be outside and woe betide anybody who made any noise. With that it was lights off and away. What the poor souls left in the darkness there, manacled and confused, must have thought, heaven knows.

Chapter Thirteen

It was after 6 when Clooney climbed into bed, but the excitement meant sleep was hard to come by. He must have succumbed, because the next thing he remembered was a loud knocking on his door and the voices of not just Blister but Amanda Thresham as well. After throwing on a white towelling dressing gown he had nicked from a hotel, he opened the door to his guests, one of them a most unexpected visitor.

The three sat sharing a pot of tea. Blister explained how he had invited Amanda to the airfield where she had taken photos and interviewed some of the captives. Then she had stayed on when a large police presence, tipped off anonymously by Blister, had shown up. According to his son-in-law Burns, some useful statements had been obtained, two wanted criminals found amongst the group, and at least four of the women held were illegals in the UK. It would take weeks for the police to read all the documents seized and probably the same again to go through the computer stuff.

Amanda had been at the site with Blister since 6.30 a.m. and was now looking to George to return a favour. She needed some sleep before returning to London and, as it was now noon, wanted to get her head down. Clooney put fresh towels in the spare bedroom and she was away in minutes.

Blister, who had not slept since Wednesday night,

still seemed to be full of energy. Being back in action was obviously what he'd needed. Burns unofficially knew who was involved in the action but was going to pretend he didn't. The troops had scattered, leaving hopefully no trace, and Blister urged George to do the same. Thresham was going to be after revenge big time; that made him dangerous and Clooney was an obvious target.

George promised the old trooper he would take care, he had some business to do on Monday but he would probably make for Canada on Tuesday, if he could get a flight. Blister thought that a great idea and asked George if he needed any cash. It seems they had grabbed over one hundred thousand pounds of Thresham's loot in the raids. The cost of equipment with travel, guns, hotels and sundries had come to less than half of that amount. Clooney thanked him for the offer, but declined, he wasn't short of cash and besides he was sure Blister could think of worthier causes than him for the old man to spend his money on.

When he left, George checked out timetables. He was able to get a charter flight from Birmingham to Toronto on Tuesday, but he decided to hang on until he had spoken to Amanda, his parents, Dave Evans and his lawyers before doing so.

It was 6 when his guest rose, joining him in the lounge as he finished packing. Wearing one of his dressing gowns and little else, she sprawled decadently across the couch. Clooney suggested they order in a Chinese which she agreed with. Then inevitably he asked again about her sister. She changed the subject as usual, asking him why he was packing. When he told her she smiled and asked him to give her some contact details, phone, email, not in his name, where she or Jess could contact him. He duly obliged by supplying her with his aunt and uncle's relevant numbers.

Then she told him about what had happened after he had left. The police arrived within thirty minutes of the team's departure, Blister told her. She had been waiting off base as agreed with the old soldier and she followed them in, using the pretext that she had seen the huge police convoy on the road and tagged along. Quite by chance, oh yes! Burns had been in the office meeting with an informant, very convenient and he had joined the task force. The threat of being interviewed by her and photographed for her paper had scared several of the punters to talk. She had interviewed some of the girls and, like Karrina the Romanian girl she had told him about, they had been misled into coming into Britain and a life of prostitution.

Burns had confided in her that though of course the police did not approve of what had happened, neither would they have been able to do something similar without warrants, which they probably would have never got, and they believed enough evidence could be presented to the powers that be to enable them to really have a go at Thresham's empire. So the raids had been a success and if all else failed there might be a case of tax evasion for him to face. After all that's how they got Al Capone!

They enjoyed good food when it arrived, some soft music and then, fed and watered, they returned to the subject of Jessica. Amanda explained the only reason her sister hadn't contacted him was that she was out of the country, under cover and helping her with an assignment which might also help them nail their foe. Clooney still didn't see why she couldn't have got in touch, but, after extracting a promise that it would happen, he let the topic go, for now.

Amanda was heading back to London; she had a meeting with another kidnapped girl later when the youngster had finished for the night. She was seventeen and had been working the streets for two years, ever since being brought to the country from the Philippines. So she left at 9 and George emailed and texted all and sundry to let them know he was going on holiday, though he only told his folks his arrival time and destination. A night's TV, finish packing, do some washing and ironing - now that was a Saturday night.

There was no lie in that Sunday. He felt so unfit at the lack of exercise he ran for five miles before finishing off with a sauna, then lunch with the lads. They had an unofficial arrangement; anyone on their own for Sunday lunch, meet up at the Italian down from the ground. They had a private room, Mrs Luclerra looked after them personally and the food was amazing. Wethers was there, a couple of the Northampton players, Scotty, Tick Tock and a number of blokes he didn't know. All the talk was about what was happening at the club. Most of the lads hoped Dave Evans would succeed in taking over, he was well liked and they repeated the fact he'd been a bit useful as a player as well. Clooney daren't say anything, he just listened, but was relieved when the talk turned to the usual; money, women, holidays and scandal.

Just relaxing reminded George of the time before that goal, Jess, Thresham and everything else that had happened. The hard bit was he didn't like keeping the truth from the others and wondered how they would feel if everything went according to plan. He wouldn't be one of the lads any more, except on the pitch. Could he do it? He didn't know.

Back home TV, radio, internet were full of rumours about Friday night's raids. Some said it was vigilantes fighting back against organised crime, but everyone seemed in agreement with the actions taken. A night catching up on the messages, housework, and holiday arrangements followed, then, knackered, he called it a day.

Monday started with phone calls to Dave Evans and solicitors, everyone said they would get back to him. Blister brought a couple of newspapers in for him to read, they were all full of the events of Friday night though short of facts. Except for the *Express* of course. Their special correspondent Amanda didn't use her own name on the article, she had a real scoop there. Morning television had experts in discussing it and one ex-SAS bloke seemed to be pretty near the truth, either through experience or inside information.

Blister wasn't a bit worried. As far as he was concerned it was all going according to plan and the publicity should bring more informants out of the woodwork to help move the case against Thresham along.

Just before the allocated time the man from Demon Photographic arrived. Saul Rivers was just what Clooney had expected, he was young, bearded, casual open necked shirt, blue jeans and he never stopped talking. His assistant, a pretty young blond who looked about twelve to George, "must be getting old," he thought, brought in equipment, three cameras, lighting kit, screens and various outfits. Saul told him that in order to appeal to different clients they needed to show George at his best in football kit, dinner jackets, casual garb, overcoat and in his underpants. So perhaps it was a porn shoot after all. Sam the twelve year old looking blond handled hair and makeup, and then George spent the next hour of his life in a variety of outfits having his picture taken. When they left he was ready for the break and then lunch, but Dave Evans called.

Dave thought it a great idea the trip to Canada and

he took contact details from George. The AGM would take place in the club restaurant at 11 a.m. on Tuesday the 18ᵗʰ May, he would need Clooney to help in the days before the vote, so that gave George the chance to have a week or so in Canada. More support was coming Dave's way all the time and the strange events of Friday night were doing his cause no harm either. The contract for Clooney was with George's solicitor and Evans told him he would like that signed and done before he left if possible. Clooney promised to try. They wished each other well and agreed to meet at Dave's home upon George's return.

Gary Wicks asked to meet him that evening and he was happy to come to the flat about 5 p.m. if that suited, which it did, so Clooney took time off from the chores to go for a run followed by a message check and a call to Amanda. She was happy, very happy, her fame was spreading world-wide on the strength of the story and she hoped to make some serious money as well. She was going to keep the pressure on her step-dad and promised to contact Clooney in Canada. Reminding him before he could ask that Jess would most definitely be contacting him there.

He finished his preparations for the trip and moments later Gary arrived.

They talked over tea and biscuits, how terribly civilised. He had taken part in a conference call with Danny Mathews and Fraser Wiltshire. Obviously only matters appertaining to football contracts had been discussed with Fraser. But the two lawyers had talked long and hard afterwards and it had been agreed that as Clooney was off to Canada it would be best if he was brought up to date on events.

The first item on the agenda was an invoice for George for legal work done to date that seemed amazingly reasonable to Clooney. A settlement had now been reached with MotorGiant. One year's salary to be paid, half now and half in six months time providing George had not commenced any legal action against them or defamed them in anyway. The black Saab convertible he was currently driving he could keep as a gesture of their good will and best of all they wanted to talk to Fraser about paying George to do some publicity work for them. A brilliant result, Clooney thought, he was now richer than ever and he needn't shell out for a new car. The next bit of news was about the contract with Dave Evans which in Gary's opinion was one of the fairest he had ever seen and just confirmed what everyone thought about the man. He recommended Clooney sign it which he did and Blister, who was working late, came up and witnessed it. The old boy seemed ten years younger. Friday's fun must have been good for him. But he declined to stop and have a drink, he was baby-sitting for his daughter. A bit of a contrast from the other night perhaps!

With regard to commercial activities, Fraser had reported lots of interest, but all of George's advisors felt it would be better to wait until his position with Kettering was resolved before he committed himself. As Dave Evans appreciated, Fraser had to be told what was going on, but all of them were sworn to secrecy. Gary hoped Dave would be successful in his takeover of the club. He was sure it was the right thing for everybody. After listing Clooney's contact details in Canada in his phone he wished him well and they said goodbye.

Clooney confirmed the flight details he had on reserve, booked a car parking space and hotel, then emailed Canada to let them know when he would arrive. It was as cheap for him to stay at an off airport hotel and park there as it was to just turn up on the day and use the main car parks. So, ever the thrifty, he prepared for his drive. He had to be at the check in desk for 7.30 a.m. so better to be on the spot than risk being late. He had a last look at the TV and the internet, the story of Friday night was still making headlines around the world, and with pleasant thoughts about the future in his mind he set off at the start of his next adventure. He was looking forward to seeing his family and to hearing from a certain young lady again.

Chapter Fourteen

Anyone looking in the car as George drove to Birmingham would have thought he was a madman. He listened to the radio phone-ins hearing them talk about Friday and laughed himself silly at some of the crackpot ideas being put forward. It was the National Front, Al Qaeda, communists, the Christian right, a new form of vigilantes - but whatever the opinions it meant people were talking about it and it must be increasing the pressure on Thresham.

There were no major traffic hold ups and he found himself checking into his hotel less than an hour after leaving home. The Sentinel was a pleasant if quiet little place to spend a night, and after an excellent dinner in the hotel's near deserted restaurant he retired to his room to watch TV, catch up with his messages and plan what gifts he should buy at the airport to take with him. He had stopped at the services on the way up and bought a thriller to read on the plane; he was a fan of a writer called Greg Isles and he spotted his latest. So, with that and his copy of *Four Four Two* football magazine, he felt ready for anything.

Now he had time to think he reviewed his feelings about Jess. He hardly knew her, she had caused him grief, she hadn't been in touch, why was he even thinking about her? He promised himself that if she didn't make contact and come up with a good explanation he would come back from Canada, get on with life and he wouldn't give Miss

Thresham another thought. He meant it as well, and once Clooney had really made his mind up on a course of action that was it!

Breakfast was good, so was the service, then it was the courtesy coach to the terminal, check in and the journey to Canada had begun. Once he had handed over his luggage he decided to get some pre-flight exercise, so, dodging the crowds, he did some fairly fast walking through both terminals and the short term car park. It was going to be a long flight, thank goodness he had an extra leg-room seat.

In duty free he bought some *Opium* for both his mum and aunt, he knew it was their favourite. Brandy for his dad and Cuban cigars for his uncle. He didn't know if you could buy them in Canada or not, or was it only the States that banned them? He picked up a *Guardian*. His folks, great liberals that they were, had taken the paper all their lives so he was used to it. It would put the world into perspective anyway comparing their view of it with the *Express* which he had bought for himself. The special correspondent for the latter had a piece on the front page and both middle pages were given over to her as well.

Amanda had written a hard hitting story about the tide turning against those who corrupt with drugs and gambling, who illegally import innocent girls to use in the sex trade and so on and so on. A well-known Kettering businessman was suspected of being the leader of the crime gang that was targeted on Friday. She really was getting close to home there. The vigilantes were well meaning citizens faced with no choice but to take the law into their own hands. In the last paragraph she urged anyone who knew anything about the crooks to contact their local cop shop. Reminding them they could do so anonymously and there might be a reward. It was powerful stuff and should keep the heat on her step-father.

He locked his mobile in the car so Thresham couldn't track him. On the plane he was relieved to discover no one was allocated the seat next to him. He wasn't normally reticent of company but today he wanted to just read, think, eat, sleep and maybe watch a movie. The new *Robin Hood* with Russell Crowe was scheduled to be shown. "Be interesting to see just how bad the accent is," he thought.

When they landed in Toronto the weather was hot compared with the UK. Which was more than he could say for Robin Hood's accent. But it had been a good flight and as he entered the main arrivals lounge, suitcases in hand, he looked around for his folks amongst the mass of humanity congregated there. He heard his mother before he saw her. She and her sister were screeching his name. It was so long since anybody had actually called him Jason he wouldn't have turned his head if he hadn't recognised his mother's voice. There were lots of kisses and hugs, then he was away in their giant Ford pickup on the road to Burlington. Everyone was talking at once, he had only met his Aunt Cynthia on a few occasions but she was so like his mum he couldn't not get on with her. Local time was 10.30 a.m. The same almost as when he had left home. He could expect a dose of jet lag later he thought. The Queen's Highway, as they called the motorway, was busy, but Clooney was surprised how slowly they drove compared with England. Every car had sidelights on, the law apparently out here.

Burlington was a pleasant town by the lake and about halfway between Toronto and Niagara Falls. His parents had been on the *Maid of the Mist* and urged him to do the same first chance he got. Lunch was in the garden of his aunt's spacious plot. Their home was a three story house with pool and the basement had a home cinema, a table tennis table and a bar. In the first tour of the property he took before chilling out on a lounger, drink in hand, he was seriously impressed by his aunt's home. Though just for one brief moment it brought back memories of Perth. A place he hadn't thought of in a long time.

His aunt's husband Ross McKinlay was a Canadian of Scottish descent, who had served in the air force and whilst on a tour of duty to the UK had met, fallen in love with, and married mum's sister Cynthia. The doom-sayers had predicted it wouldn't last and maybe they would be proved right, but they had been together for over thirty years, so they must be doing something right. Ross was about sixty-eight now but could have passed for fifty plus. He was tall slim and fit, with a military style crew cut. He spoke little, had a bizarre, Sheffield, Glasgow, Canadian accent and yet his friendly manner made everyone feel at ease.

The barbecued steaks he made were out of this world, and with a fresh salad and huge jacket potato he and his wife produced a meal fit for a king. Dad provided the drinks, mum her special raspberry, bananas and ice cream dessert.

After what was lunch for them but dinner for Jason, according to his body clock, he presented them with their gifts and sure enough, as the afternoon heat, the food and the jet lag took effect, Clooney fell asleep.

He enjoyed a good two hours in the garden before waking up and joining the others in the house. There were lots of holiday snaps to peruse and then he had to bring everybody up to date on what was happening back in Kettering. He'd sensibly remembered to hang on to the two English papers he'd bought. No doubt they would be scanned later for every bit of gossip and news. The family had got into the habit of having their supper/dinner around about 7 so the ladies retired to the kitchen to begin preparations. Ross invited George and his dad to join him in the study.

It was a room big enough to take the old fashioned writing desk and the two big comfy armchairs easily. Ross wasted no time when they were seated in informing George he had received a number of emails for him. An intrigued Clooney logged on to see that, at last, Jess had been in touch. She was in New York, had provided him with a cell phone and email contact names and numbers, and prayed he would call. Wild horses wouldn't stop him, he was severely pissed off with her and looking for an explanation. Danny's email was to confirm that contracts had been exchanged and the deal with MotorGiant done. He was now rich and unemployed. Not a bad day's work!

The men left him to make his call to Jess in private, she answered on the second ring and for a moment he was thrown. They hadn't spoken since that night, and he was, for a moment, dumbstruck. Jess filled the gap, telling him she was desperate to meet, anytime, anywhere. She had missed him, had so much to tell him and wanted to say it in person. She had been in New York since the Tuesday after she had failed to arrive for dinner with him. That seemed a hundred years ago but her sister had kept her up to date on events and she knew how fantastic he had been and could they meet soon? George knew that much as he wanted to, he couldn't just go so soon after arriving. So they arranged to meet on Sunday in Niagara at the landing stage for the *Maid of the Mist*. A trip down the waterfall would be par for the course for him at the moment.

Then, if that wasn't enough of a surprise for one

day, she asked him if he fancied staying overnight with her. Did he? He said he'd book them in to a nice hotel, she offered to pay at least half. He declined; when they met he would explain his newfound wealth.

After saying goodbye he logged onto his emails again. Pernod had sent a message to say rumour had it that Bradshaw would be fired if Dave Evans took over and that Clooney was tipped for the player manager's job. Did he have any comment? Shit how did he deal with that? There must also be a leak. He texted and emailed Dave Evans immediately to inform him and receive, hopefully, some guidance.

Jason was never a good liar and he always showed his feelings, so the minute he walked into the kitchen they guessed there were problems. As the family discussed the news over drinks, it was Ross for once who was vocal. "Meet the girl," he said, "don't worry about us and if it's going well bring her here, I'm sure we would all like to meet her". His dad spoke next, regarding the football, "Do nothing till you've heard from Dave Evans," was his advice. "Also remember," he told George, "you've done nothing wrong so let's all relax and pray we don't die of starvation before that meal arrives." Mum threw a cushion at him and Cynthia followed suit, which caused laughter all round.

The next meal was as good if not better than the last. Southern fried chicken, sweet corn, mash and gravy, with a fresh fruit salad to follow. All washed down with Canadian wines from the Niagara region. Shades of Australia again! Ross and Cynth suggested some of the tourist sites he could take Jess to. Mum tried to plan what they could all do tomorrow. Sadly the party mood was broken when the phone rang. Ross informed him it was Dave Evans from England. George raced to the study to answer without interruptions.

Dave wasn't surprised about the rumours and suggested, subject to agreement with Clooney's advisors, that they offered no comment on the news. As George was outside Britain he promised to contact them and ask them to fill George in on what they decided, he believed it would be unfair to current manager Bradshaw to act otherwise.

After small talk and the exchange of common courtesies Dave rang off promising to call Clooney's advisors straightaway. George could only guess about him keeping the news from his fellow players. They, by and large, had stood by him, and it would appear that he was not returning that loyalty.

If it all came good, and Evans had control of the club, would the players respect him now? He could only guess.

As they tucked into the splendid feast he briefed them on Dave's call. But it created a tension in the air as they waited for one of George's advisors to make contact. Ross lightened the mood by talking about winemaking in the area and the excellent ice wine which was popular in Japan. It was picked in the early hours of the morning, when there was still a frost, and it produced a powerful dessert wine that had won awards the world over. He was very knowledgeable about the locality and suggested vineyards George and Jess might like to visit. He had just about restored the mood when the phone rang. It was Gary Wicks. All of Clooney's advisors agreed it would make sense now not to acknowledge the offer, but say something like Clooney was flattered and if the chance ever came he would take it, but for now Kettering had a manager and he Clooney was on holiday, destination unknown but believed to be in Australia. George agreed and he texted and emailed all his mates reminding them not to believe everything they read in the papers and he promised he would be in touch.

Feeling better now it was sort of out in the open and he was being a bit more honest, everyone was able to enjoy the rest of the evening without being disturbed.

Bloody body clock! He woke at 4 a.m. Canada time. After an hour or so of struggling to get back to sleep he showered, dressed and took a coffee into the garden. It was just after 6, light, warm and very pleasant; coming awake with a shock, he must have dozed off, there was Ross with a second mug of coffee that day for him. For a while they just enjoyed nature and the coffee, then Ross spoke to him with information that was another surprise. His uncle had done some checking with friends in the Canadian police force and the more he had been told about Thresham the less he liked him. He admired Amanda for her crusading work and was sure that Jess must be a girl of great character as well.

George had forgotten that Ross had worked in security when he left the forces. But he promised Clooney any help he might need, for he had both the contacts and the expertise if required. George thanked him and their talk switched to more mundane matters until the rest of the household joined them. Cynth cooked a big Canadian breakfast, Clooney thought the bacon fatty and nowhere near as good as home but didn't say so. They all helped clear up, load the dishwasher, then it was get ready to go and be tourists. Before that Clooney checked for messages and mail but there was nothing worthwhile.

They decided to start the day with a walk by the lake, then on to a little vineyard Ross knew that did the most amazing lunches. They had a great day, George insisted he paid, and they were a tired and happy group on their return that afternoon.

That evening they went to the movies, which in their case meant down in the basement with sweets and popcorn. They watched the Nicole Kidman film *Australia* and not surprisingly George found himself remembering his time there. Since Lara there had only been a few one night stands and no one special in his life until Jess. More and more he regretted his decision to wait until Friday to meet her. He wanted her, here and now. The plan for tomorrow was a visit to the Royal Botanical Gardens, lunch then a walk along one of the nature trails along the Niagara escarpments. Exciting it you were sixty plus, less so if you were half that age. But he felt he owed them that, he could sense his mum was disappointed he was leaving so soon.

Ross showed him the website for the Riverbend Inn and Vineyard at Niagara-on-the-Lake. He and Cynth had weekended there a year ago as a birthday treat and he raved about it. Clooney equally fell for the whole package and booked a room for Friday night for Jess and him. "If she turns up," he thought. He whipped his dad at table tennis, beat Ross but only just after three demanding games, and after checking his messages decided he needed an early night. All of them had suffered jet lag at some time or another so no one was offended when he called it a day.

Up at 6.30 a.m. that was better, but he felt unfit so he ran for forty minutes before returning to find everyone preparing breakfast. Seemed the excitement of the day had woken them all early. "Oh well maybe when I'm their age I'll feel the same," he thought. He passed on the cooked breakfast, couldn't face that bacon again, but told everyone it was part of his staying fit routine to just have cereals and toast from now on, which they all accepted. Cynth had this amazing juicer machine, so he enjoyed three glasses of fresh orange with his food and he felt good.

The gardens were vast, interesting and even he had to admit worth the visit. They had lunch at the Turner Pavilion Tea House, salads and fruit, before hitting the shop. His dad had to remind his mum not to buy half the things she wanted or they would need their own plane to get home, he joked. She had bought rose hip jam and rose water perfume for just about everyone she knew. They did a twenty minute online guided tour of the garden before taking off on a walk of their own. The sun was really hot now and they cut it short to head back into the coolness of their air conditioned home.

Everyone had to change into respectable clothes for the evening. It was his folks' treat, they were taking them to Spencer's restaurant at the Waterfront. Cynth had told them all about it. The panoramic view across Burlington Bay and with floor to ceiling windows throughout apparently every table had a view of the water. Ross arranged a cab for 7 p.m., they were eating at 8, so that was that sorted then.

The place was as good as promised, if not better. For dinner Clooney had *Pepper Porano Gnocchi* as a starter, a dish he had never heard of, and *Roasted Yukon Arctic Char* for his main dish, it was wonderful. He passed on the sweet but did consume two glasses of wine. He was going to have to watch it. Seeing the way the two couples behaved, their closeness and the obvious affection they felt for their partners made him feel quite lonely, or maybe it was the wine. But he knew he would kill Jess if she let him down again.

It was a very merry, very content group that made its way home that night. Ross and Cynth had another surprise for him in the garage, a most pleasant one as well, Cynth had a red 2007 Lexus, automatic of course; she had arranged insurance so George could use it. He had planned to hire a car the next morning but this was a most unexpected gift and another money saver for him. As a car salesman, or as he was now a former car salesman, he had driven loads of different vehicles every day so he could anticipate few problems and he thanked them both sincerely.

Amanda had emailed him with details of an article in the local Kettering paper in which he had been named as the potential new manager if Evans got control of the club. A number of players who wished to remain anonymous had told the reporter it would be the best thing that could happen and would have their full support. On that happy note he said his goodnights and excused himself.

Chapter Fifteen

Breakfast was a sombre affair. Both couples had drunk a lot last night and were feeling the effects. His mum was sad at his leaving and worried that he might be hurt again. George tried to keep everyone's spirits up with his false enthusiasm and at 10 he left in the Lexus with everyone waving goodbye and the two women crying.

The car was a dream, air con and sun roof, so he decided not to pollute the atmosphere and had the roof open as much as he could. The sound system was excellent, though he knew few of the Canadian and American artists on the CD player. The deep leather seats were comfortable, the satnav worked a treat and at 11 on the dot he drove up the drive to the magnificent Riverbend Inn. As he drove through the vineyard he was reminded again of Australia, but that didn't matter anymore. The old house had been superbly restored. He checked into a large double room with every amenity, unpacked his gear and wandered around the grounds, partaking of morning coffee in the lounge before checking his messages again and calling the folks to tell them how he had arrived with car in one piece.

He drove down to Niagara Falls and was shocked at the contrast. Niagara-on-the-Lake was a classy historical village, the town of Niagara Falls was like the worst tackiest English seaside resort, the only difference being the crowds.

He heard the falls before he saw them, the power

of the water threw up spray. It was only then he realised there were two falls, the American one and the world famous Canadian one. After parking his car he had walked nervously down the hill to where the boats were kept. In his ignorance he had assumed there was only the one vessel called *Maid of the Mist* not half a dozen. He watched as the leading craft made its way to the falls and back, even from the shore it looked quite an experience.

At the landing stage there were tourists from all over the world, particularly the Far East it seemed. Some queuing to board, others disembarking. Many wore the ponchos issued to prevent getting wet. He was twenty minutes early for his meeting so he sat on a grassy bank and did some people watching, looking at the heaving masses around him he felt quite thin; the size of some of the Canadians and Americans was outrageous.

He felt a touch on his shoulder and turned to see the sight more than any he had been waiting for, Jessica Thresham in person. She gave him her biggest smile, he rose to his feet, did they shake hands, hug, kiss on the cheek or what? Fortunately Jess took the initiative. She threw herself into his arms, gave him the biggest kiss of his life and for a few moments it seemed they were the only people in the world. It was only when a group of tourists started to applaud them that they realised they ought perhaps to move on.

Hand in hand, then arm in arm, they clung to each other, neither speaking as they joined the queue for the boat. Clooney broke the silence by asking her how she got here. Jess told him she'd taken a plane from New York to Buffalo then a coach to Niagara. Her luggage was in a locker now in the bus depot in town. Sometimes, when there is just so much to say, you don't know where to start, and that was the case for them. So for an hour or so they just behaved like any other tourists enjoying the sights, people watching and moving ever nearer forwards to the front.

They huddled together on the boat. For one brief moment, such is the majesty the power of the falls, you can't help but think what happens if the engine breaks down. Will this be the shortest reunion in history? The moment though that would live with George forever, and he discovered later for Jess too, was when the skipper of the boat halted as near as was sensible to the mighty water and above the roar and the spray he said, "Ladies and Gentlemen this is Niagara Falls." It was like being at an outdoor cathedral and the effect was to suddenly make you and all your little problems seem very small. On the way back he noticed Jess was crying. She saw the worry on his face and lightened up. It was then she confirmed that, as it was for him, for her the whole experience had been quite emotional.

They collected her belongings from the bus depot and realised it was almost 2 p.m. and neither had eaten since breakfast. At his suggestion they drove to their hotel, deposited her things in the room, then sat on the veranda and prepared to talk. Although they were too late for lunch their hosts did them proud with salad and cold chicken, French bread, orange juice and wine from the vineyard. So they certainly wouldn't starve.

Jess felt she should go first, so she told him all that happened that seemed relevant since he had waved goodbye to her that night. She desperately wanted to see her mother, was so worried about her and it had been playing on her mind, the torment she must be going through. She still had her key and she knew the alarm code so her intention was to slip in quietly, sleep in her old bed then, after Thresham had gone to work the next day, give her mum the surprise of her life. But there had been a light on in the downstairs study.

Suspecting Thresham might still be awake she tiptoed up to the window and peeped in.

Thresham had on a dressing gown, he was stood staring across the room, still, almost like a statue. Then she noticed, kneeling in front of him, the naked body of Olga, the girl who had replaced the unfortunate Karrina. Her sister had shown her pictures of the girl, but not like this, giving her step-father a blow job.

She was disgusted, poor mum betrayed by that bastard. Feeling sick and angry she made her way to the summer house where she and Amanda had sometimes slept as kids. Letting herself in, she made up a bed from the sleeping bags that were still there and cried herself to sleep. When she awoke it was 10 a.m. He would have left for work, but she had to be sure. She phoned her mum and they both cried after her mum confirmed Thresham had left. But her mum wondered why it bothered Jess, he'd been such a wonderful step-father! In anger she told her mum what she thought of him and about what she had seen just a few hours previously. Her mother called her wicked and a liar refused to believe it, and, in her confusion, either accidentally or by design, cut the connection.

At that point she knew she had to get away. She walked the mile or so to the road, then at a petrol station she tidied herself a bit before hitching a lift to Kettering railway station and a train to London. She had actually gone past his flat that morning, George thought, but said nothing. Amanda had met her off the train and taken her home with her. After much talk and many tears both agreed she would need to remain undercover until they could present their mother with cast iron proof about the shit she was married to. There was no way of patching up relationships until they did.

When Jess had first left home, taking Karrina with her, she had been persuaded eventually, for mum's sake to give it another go. But she could only stand it for a week. She loathed Thresham so much that she had phoned her sister for help and Amanda had arranged accommodation and cash in hand work for her, so then she disappeared. At first she had hoped it would be for only the shortest of times. That she and her mother could make it up and go from there. But every time Amanda had tried to explain matters to her parent it only provoked further fury.

She had been staying in Amanda's flat for just a few days, carrying out research for her sister involving missing girls. Using the phone and the internet she was in touch with organisations and people all over the world and she was becoming as committed to the cause as her sister. Then Thresham turned up at the door, she hid in a wardrobe and Amanda dealt with him. He made some veiled and some not so veiled threats to her and only left when she started to call the police.

Amanda worked closely with a part time actress, a model who also was a freelance journalist. A bizarre mix but it worked. This girl Sophie needed a flatmate to help with the bills so Jess moved in with her. Amanda realised she was being followed from work one day, and had noticed the same car outside the flat on too many occasions for it to be coincidence.

She was sure it was Thresham's doing. By splitting up at least one of them could be safe from him so that's what they did. Amanda arranged fake ID and she became American. It worked well for nearly twelve months. Jess dyed her hair, changed the style, different clothes, make up, and always wearing built up shoes had helped make her unrecognisable to the casual glance anyone might give her.

Amanda told her she made an important team member, she and Alex the girl she worked with in New York got on well. But she missed her mum. When you have had only one parent for most of your life and they've always been there for you it was impossible not to think about them. But it was Clooney's fault really that she had risked returning. He looked amazed.

"The match," she told him, "the match." As a fan she wanted to be there the night they clinched promotion. She came back from the shadows specially. It was also her mother's birthday on the Sunday and she had this crazy idea that she would go home after the game, she and her mum would embrace, eventually she would return to England permanently, carry on the project from there and on Sunday they would celebrate mum's birthday as everything was okay. Amanda would come up on the day and they would all be together again. She had even warned Alex, the girl she worked with in New York, she would be away a while. It was all planned. Then in the after match excitement she had met him, then gone back and caught Thresham out, so it was back to London again and her return stateside.

She was so upset she didn't know what to do. Then Amanda got her some more fake ID. A ticket back to New York and that's where she had been living since. She felt so bad about letting him down, getting him involved in such a mess and as more and more ills befell him her guilt trip was such she couldn't do anything. Amanda had told her about his visit, she thought he was fantastic as well and he'd definitely made a fan there and not for the football either! She read about him on the net, followed his exploits through Amanda's updates, and was in the process of writing him the biggest "I'm sorry" letter in the history of the world when Mandy told her he was coming to Canada.

So now she had been able to sit down, tell him everything and say sorry to his face.

She looked at him with big sad eyes, would he tell her to sod off or what? But she didn't need to worry as he took her in his arms and for the second time that day they embraced as if the world would end if they broke apart. Without a further word being spoken, they both seemed to know what the other needed and they walked arm in arm to their room.

Jess wanted more than anything for this first time to be special and it made her nervous. So she asked him to close the blinds, get into bed and she would join him after a visit to the bathroom.

Clooney's thoughts were still on the story she had told him and his heart went out to her for the hurts she had suffered. He was determined also to make this first time special and he hoped in the excitement he wouldn't come too soon. He undressed, folding his clothes over the chair, and positioned himself on his back on the left side of the bed and waited for her to join him. The thick drapes coupled with the blinds effectively cut out most of the light but there was still enough to enjoy watching as she crossed the room to join him. She had the body a man liked, slim but busty, a great shape, a real woman, not a skinny model looking more like a pre-teen than a grown female.

She snuggled into him, he was very conscious of her bare flesh. Jess told him she wanted to enjoy pleasing him, kissed him again and reached for his cock. As she stroked him he nearly passed out. Then sucking her breasts he used his hand to caress her hair, feel her shoulders, face and finally he delved between her legs to bring her pleasure and prepare her to take him. Buried inside her he managed to make the moment last by thinking about what the future may hold for him, for her, but hopefully for them. Days later he discovered she had done the same. Almost miraculously they climaxed together, then in the post coitus afterglow, both of them feeling this was so right and so good, fell asleep.

His watch now on Canadian time said 4.30 p.m. and he realised she was also awake and watching him. They cuddled together, then he suddenly remembered he had booked dinner for 8 p.m. that night at the Skylon Towers restaurant. It had a revolving platform so they could see over the Horseshoe Falls and various parts of the Niagara region. Ross had told him it was not to be missed. Jess was excited but begged for time now to get ready, so he checked the internet for news while she used the bathroom.

Nothing earth shattering from home, except the rumour that Bradshaw the club's manager was having talks with a Middle East side with a view to leaving Kettering. "Classic case of jumping before he was pushed," Clooney thought, but he'd wait and see. It could just be a ploy, to get the board to back him and pay him more. Lots of others had done it. Still right now England and football were the furthest thing from his mind. Jess came out of the bathroom, a giant bath towel wrapped around her. He kissed her and immediately felt aroused again. "Later, tiger!" she told him, as she commenced her make up. A contented George showered, shaved and dressed ready for the big night out.

He decided if he was splashing out he might as well go the whole hog. He asked reception to order him a stretch limo, "No problem!" they said. It was collecting them at 7.30 p.m. so he needed to hurry. But hell, compared to a week ago life was really looking up.

They made the perfect couple, him in a white linen jacket and shirt with black trousers and shoes. Jess in a black flowery dress with red roses. It seemed a shame to leave their magnificent suite and king sized bed but they would be back there later. As they waited under the mock Grecian porch canopy for their ride Clooney suddenly remembered he hadn't, as he had promised, let the folks in Burlington know how things were. A quick text said it all. 'Jess and hotel beautiful, falls awesome, going for dinner as suggested to Skylon.' At least they wouldn't be worrying now.

It was a huge stretch by British standards, a ginormous white monster with a crazy bar in the back lit up like a disco. It was based on the Lincoln town car but how many had been chopped up to make this was anyone's guess. They sprawled in the sumptuous seats, more like a five seater couch at home and just enjoyed the experience. The Skylon Tower was the tallest building in Niagara and the revolving eatery rotated at one revolution per hour the driver told them. They thanked him, arranged to call him later, then used the elevator to take them to their table. The view was truly amazing, looking out across the Horseshoe Falls and the Niagara region. It was said that on the clearest of days you could even see the CN Tower in Toronto.

Their meal was long and leisurely, which suited them. Service was not fast, so it was a good job they were in no hurry. They held hands as if they were in a real relationship, not on what was their first real date. They talked about touristy things like places to visit; he wanted to know how New York was panning out, she wanted to know about his aunt in Burlington and three hours later they were back in their suite.

Jess texted Mandy to let her know they were well. They tried to watch some TV but the number of adverts made it almost impossible, they sipped ice water, talked about tomorrow, but then it became that time again and she once more headed for the bathroom first. In bed they quickly, comfortably enjoyed their second round of lovemaking that day. Afterwards they told each honestly their sexual preferences and the no go areas. Jess believed such frankness might prevent problems in the future but whether she was talking as a nurse, a woman, or through bitter experience George wasn't sure. The next day they planned a walk around Niagara-on-the-Lake; the pretty village, not the ugly town at the falls. Then perhaps a drive around the area and, best of all for him, Jess had agreed to stay for a few days or longer if that was all right with him? He didn't even bother to answer, just kissed her, then stroked her until they fell asleep.

Waking up with someone else in bed was an experience Clooney had almost forgotten. But as he lay there, listening to the sound of her breathing, he remembered just how good it was. As noiselessly as it was possible he made his way to the bathroom. He relieved himself, washed his hands then debated what to do next. Jess called to see if he was alright and he re-joined her in the bed. She told him how well she had slept, feeling safe beside him. Then, when she realised he was gone, she had momentarily panicked. Looking into her face he realised what a vulnerable girl she was, but also just how fond of her he was becoming.

Breakfast was superb and afterwards they visited the tourist shops of Niagara-on-the-Lake. The little town, big village, he wasn't sure which, was as different from its namesake as it possibly could be. This place oozed class, history, everywhere was clean, the shops were different, the hotels timeless. They had coffee in a quaint little place with a picture of the actor Nicholas Cage who had apparently been there while making some movie called *Escape to*

Xmas or something. When the waitress saw them looking at the photo she came over with more coffee and told them how the filmmaker chose here because it looked just like small town America. Only problem they had was it didn't snow much that winter and they had to pump the artificial stuff in instead.

As planned they spent the afternoon visiting a couple of the many wineries in the area. Neither of them had realised what a major industry it was in this part of the world. Then it was back to the culture shock that was the real Niagara, their ice wine bottles safely stowed in the trunk and hidden. It was that kind of place.

The 'Journey Behind the Falls' as it was called provided them with a free poncho for viewing without getting wet, standing behind the massive sheet of water really was something else. Certainly far more exciting than Clifton Hill, Niagara's version of Blackpool. Hunger was beginning to kick in so they grabbed a table at the Key Steakhouse at the top of the falls and ate and talked and laughed whilst watching the water begin its descent through the giant plate glass.

It was around about twenty minutes back to their hotel. Both were quiet, a combination of deep thoughts and tiredness perhaps or maybe more? They enjoyed a drink on the patio of the Riverbend Inn gazing at the vines, lost in the moment. Jess spoke first, typical woman. Throwing questions to him and the air. What did he want to do from now? Where were they going? Did he want to get back to England?

He had to think for a moment so many questions, so little time. But truth will out. He told her straight, how yes he wanted the manager's job in Kettering. He hadn't been sure at first but now he was. In the ideal world he would like her to move in, see how it turned out. The way he felt, he was sure it would work. But like her he had been hurt and time was the great healer and the great test of what they might have together.

Jess was surprised at the answer. The obvious honesty as always with George. But the sentiments tore her apart. She explained why.

Though she didn't as yet like New York she had only been there a few months, she owed her sister who had gone out on a limb for her. Mandy was working with The Human Trafficking Centre, based ironically in his home town of Sheffield. It was Europe's first centre to help the victims of this evil trade. She also had ties with the Poppy Project which provided support and accommodation for women who had been trafficked. They had helped Karrina start a new life. Mandy was an honorary PR consultant to Stop the Traffic, a global coalition working to help stop the sale of people. It was one of her sister's contacts in the States who had got Jess the job with the American State Department office to monitor and combat trafficking. If she walked away now after such a short time she would be letting herself and so many other people down; she didn't think she could do it.

There was a long tense silence. Then Clooney spoke, he told her he admired her for her beliefs, it actually made him love her more. Realising what he had said he blushed, paused, then continued. He had his job, hopefully, and she hers. But that didn't stop them spending time together, holidays, whenever they could, and she would be able and welcome to stay with him anywhere as far as he was concerned. Jess thanked him for being so understanding, well just for being him she told him and they left it there for now.

In the bedroom the atmosphere had changed, she no longer undressed in the bathroom, they really were a couple, even if that meant they were going to be separated by the Atlantic Ocean for the foreseeable future. Now their love making was different, each pleasing the other but equally relaxing and enjoying their own pleasure. He came, she followed, they shared a box of bedside tissues. Then with a thousand unanswered thoughts racing across their minds they found sleep. During a restless night both of them made bathroom trips, each of them was finding sleep hard. There was no easy solution to their problems but both of them tried their best to think of one. Eventually, each realising the other was awake, they made tea and sat like an old married couple enjoying the quiet, the togetherness and their thoughts.

Clooney had a week or so before returning to England. Jess told him she would like to spend some of it with him. She suggested they should really visit his folks and he was delighted she thought so. He phoned them, they couldn't conceal their excitement and suggested dinner that evening. Rather than put Jess under even more pressure though he told his mum they would book into a Burlington hotel. Ross suggested the Holiday Inn it was probably the best and had an indoor pool. His father said they would sort out the booking, "Just be here for 6," - and that was it.

It was going to be quite something introducing her to the family, for all concerned. They had a late breakfast, settled up and headed back towards Burlington, stopping on the way at three more vineyards and enjoying lunch at the largest of them. It was now after 3 and pleasant though the day had been they both needed to talk again. They were in total agreement with what they should tell his family. Yes they were an item, but she would possibly be working in New York for the foreseeable future though they would be in touch daily and see how it goes. He gave her an up to date thumbnail guide to the four strangers they were going to meet, then, as if it was the most natural thing in the world, they indulged in some heavy petting in the car before continuing their journey.

Chapter Sixteen

Both took a deep breath then knocked on the door, George's mum was out first, she threw her arms around Jess and hugged her. The rest of the clan followed, as excited as his mum but controlling it better. Then through to the garden for drinks, everyone talking at once. But the genuine warmth in the welcome she received soon put Jess at ease, despite her nervousness. She was invited to join with the women in making the evening meal, which meant a chance for them to get her on her own and give her the third degree.

The men stayed outside talking. His dad, as he had forecast, was totally knocked out by Jess. She reminded him of a young Catherine Zeta Jones, so no surprise there. Ross agreed, toasted their future happiness then led Clooney down to his study where emails had been arriving thick and fast. Leaving George to his work he returned to sort out the drinks. Home and football seemed like a distant memory but Clooney was soon brought bang up to date.

Bradshaw had gone, the rumours had been true; he was now the manager of some unpronounceably named side in the Middle East. All the speculation was that Clooney would take over. Allstars Allsports and Gary Wicks needed a conference call ASAP. Danny Browne and half the lads at Kettering needed to talk - and Amanda sent a message saying what a wonderful couple they were and could she be a bridesmaid? Bloody cheek.

He answered Fraser at Allsports and Danny Browne was saying he would make himself available at a place and time to suit them. The UK was about six hours in front so it was about midnight there so no point calling anyone. Instead he asked Gary to contact him in around fourteen hours time on the house phone. They would just have to come back for the afternoon, he thought. He sent a round robin email to all the lads at the club explaining how difficult it was for him to comment at the moment, but promised they would be the first to know when he was able to speak. He did advise them though not to put pen to paper for any other club before he got back. None of the media enquiries for an interview or statement he acknowledged. But he couldn't resist replying to Mandy. On the lines that both of them were at the present concentrating on their careers and that she shouldn't believe everything she read in the press!

When he re-joined the men he brought them up to speed on events. Dinner was served properly in the dining room. No al-fresco evening or TV dinner tonight, on such a special occasion. George presented his hosts with wine purchased that day and Jess had a bunch of flowers for the ladies and a bottle of a local style brandy for the men.

The drink flowed, the food was devoured and the conversation never stopped, a good night was had by all. Playing safe, the younger couple climbed into a cab for the short journey to their hotel. His mum whispered in his ear "You've got an absolute treasure there, guard it." Then it was time to go.

As soon as they had waved their goodbyes, they sat back to enjoy the ride and Clooney asked her how she thought it had gone. To his relief and great pleasure she replied it had been one of the happiest nights of her life. She loved his mum, thought Cynth a hoot, fancied his dad and would eat anywhere with Ross. He was thrilled, relieved and able to tell her truthfully the effect she had on them. He hadn't had the chance before to tell her the news from home and about her sister's cheeky message. She roared with laughter at his reply to Mandy and they checked into their new hotel and new room in great spirits.

They literally threw themselves on the bed this time and made love still partly dressed. It was as good as before and afterwards they showered together until he was naughty again so Jess fled into the bedroom. In bed they talked more about the evening and their plans for tomorrow, before Jess spoilt it for him by reminding him she would have to leave on Thursday, but why didn't he visit her in New York for the weekend? A very good idea which he quickly agreed to. They fell asleep watching TV, a good time had by all.

Jess joined him in the pool wearing a borrowed costume. He won their swimming race so she had to pay a forfeit. They were having breakfast in the room and she had to eat it in the nude, "Little things amuse little minds," she thought, but if it made him happy so what. When they had eaten he had other plans but she reminded him it was look not touch.

His mum phoned. She and Cynth were getting the express into Toronto for a day's shopping and they wondered if Jess would like to join them? Both were in two minds. They wanted to spend every minute together but were going to have to get used to being apart. He had work to do and Jess wanted to please him and his mum, so in the end she joined them. They picked her up to travel to the station, dropping George off at the house. He joined the men in a session at the golf driving range then had a run before lunch. Ross prepared another barbecue and, while they settled down for an afternoon snooze, Clooney sat in the study and waited for his call from England.

He checked messages while waiting and read the Kettering paper online. Dave Evans had done an interview with Trevor Wolfe, he had set out his vision for the club and his hope that Clooney would become player manager.

When the call came through there was a time delay so there was always a pause before anyone replied. Fraser wanted George to confirm it was Kettering or nothing, as he had some interest from other clubs wanting to talk to him. Clooney confirmed it was. Allstars AllSports had clients from the world of fashion, men's toiletries, motors and retailing interested in deals. He ran through them all in detail. Clooney deferred to Danny Browne who thought they were a good business and could see no problems with them. Then there was a tricky one, Fraser could make a lot of money for George from the media if he would give them the rights to negotiate an exclusive. That meant no more giving Amanda the scoops for free. That one he wanted time to think about. After all she was nearly family! A number of charities were keen for Clooney's endorsement. There was no money in it, though it was good for his profile. He thought for a minute and then declined, there was another charity he planned to help and what was that old saying, "charity beings at home"? He explained his fairly sudden decision to help the organisation devoted to stopping people trafficking and the rehabilitation of those rescued from its clutches.

There was a real pause this time, not just because of the time delay. Eventually Fraser replied, he thought it brilliant. As soon as George could be specific on who he was helping, what his commitment was and when he would be starting they would get maximum publicity for that one. There were some more routine matters to discuss then they all wished each well before ending the call.

Gary was waiting to hear from him and delighted with all Clooney's news. His new work contract with Dave Evans was signed, sealed and in Gary's safe, the cheque from MotorGiant with it. He reminded George, he hadn't made a Will and they agreed to meet and organise it. But it was his last piece of news that was the most interesting. Francis Collins, the club's solicitor, had resigned; he was known to work very closely with Thresham but was opposed to Dave Evans's takeover plans. Gary had been offered the honorary post but before accepting felt he should speak to Clooney.

George was thrilled to have such a potential ally and didn't hesitate to say yes. That being the case it was explained, if the takeover was successful Gary felt it would be more ethical and less problematic if Danny handled affairs for him, if he didn't mind. Clooney would be sorry not to have him as his legal advisor, but he could see the logic of it and agreed. That was it - calls done he returned to join the two sleeping beauties in the garden.

His dad woke first and he told him what he had done. He was proud of him and told him that after mum had explained about the work Jess did they were going to help as well. Miss Thresham had clearly had an effect on the Clooney family.

His father told him how impressed everyone was with Jess and they were keeping their fingers crossed it would work out. George mentioned that he might take off for New York at the weekend. His dad laughed and said what a good idea. Ross was alive again and joined them, they shared tea and biscuits on the lawn and talked about football, politics, the weather and all those other important things you can waste time discussing as if they were vitally important. It's what holidays are all about.

It was nearly 7 when the girls arrived, but as news was transmitted and shopping examined and put away Clooney realised how much he'd missed Jess and wanted to get her on his own. She seemed just as pleased to see him and had bought him as a present a shirt by a top Canadian designer..... it must have cost a packet. But he felt very proud to try it on for everyone.

They ate al-fresco in the garden, wonderful salads, wine, bread and cheese. All rustled together by the ladies within an hour of returning from their shopping spree. The next day Jess was returning to Toronto with Clooney to do more tourist things. Easier, now the shopping trip was out of the way. At last, duty done, they were able to leave, though any outsider looking in would probably have assumed this happy family had been together years, not less than forty-eight hours.

Toronto was big brash but still slightly different from New York, Jess told him. They did the CN Tower, "like the Skylon, but without the falls," he thought, but an impressive view of the city nonetheless. They wandered through St. Lawrence market, tasting some of the fantastic food en route. They had lunch in Chinatown, which was definitely bigger and more exotic than the London version. They behaved like silly kids at Wonderland theme park and finished their day at the Eaton Centre Shopping Mall. Jess had spent most of yesterday there. Clooney had enough after an hour and wanted to get her back to Burlington.

On the trip back they talked more about what the future held. She was proud of him but also stunned when he told her about his intention to help the cause, but the thoughts of her leaving in the morning cast a dampener on their spirits. Ross met them off the train and they returned with him to say goodbye to everyone before leaving for Niagara or to be precise the Riverbend Inn, Niagara-on-the-Lake.   Her choice, to return to the first bed they had ever slept in together.

The food was excellent but dinner was not good. A cloud of melancholy had descended over them and they returned to their room in near silence.   Even their love making was affected; at the end Jess burst into tears, so much had happened, in such a short time.

Both woke early, Jess reached for him and they started this last day together with some wild fantastic love making. It must have given them an appetite because they wolfed down breakfast like they were starving. All these Canadian pancakes and maple syrup were not helping Clooney's weight or fitness - he was going to have to get down to some serious training soon.

Saying goodbye at the bus depot was one of the hardest things George had ever done.   Jess sobbed and sobbed to such an extent that he, embarrassingly for him, joined her. As she waved goodbye through the disappearing vehicle windows he felt as if a little bit of him had died. He collected Cynthia's car from the parking lot and headed towards Burlington feeling as miserable as he'd ever felt.

The family soon changed that though.   Perhaps deliberately, for they knew him and had surmised how he would be. But certainly with feeling, they crowded round him for the first real conversation together they had all had since Jess had visited. The unanimous verdict. They were made for each other.

This was to be their last day as a group. George was flying to New York the next day. He would return to Toronto only to catch the plane for Birmingham on Tuesday. They were all heading for Vancouver and planned to continue their holiday with a seaplane visit to Vancouver Island, a trip on the Rocky Mountain train and a stay at Lake Louise. But it meant they could travel together to the airport and at least prolong the time together a little bit.

Over lunch, barbecue again but he wasn't complaining, they took his mind off things with tales of the two women growing up in Sheffield that he had heard before but laughed at again. Later he made himself do some work and with the blessing of all decanted himself to the study where online he was able to read his mail. He had the facility on his borrowed phone, but found concentrating easier if sat at the big desk with the somewhat bigger screen.

The letters page of the Kettering paper was full of the takeover and his appointment, with ninety percent of the writers glowing in their support. But it was funny how the ten percent could hurt though. He was going to have to toughen up if he was going to be a manager.

On Tuesday he would return to England. That would give him a week before the club's AGM to work with Dave Evans on whatever was needed to get the result they both wanted. Everyone for different reasons was as excited as kids as Ross drove to Toronto. Last night had been devoted to packing bags and clearing up, today was holiday time again. When the time came for him to board his flight everyone was quite emotional. Ross told him he was welcome back anytime. Cynthia that he was "a lovely lad". Hardly at his age! His mum just cried and his dad hugged him and told him he loved him. Clooney thought to himself he'd probably cried more this last month than any time since he was a kid. But he could handle it.

His flight was on time and as he disembarked into the arms of Jess it was as if yesterday had never happened. They were together again. She told him all she had planned for them, hoped he wouldn't mind her tiny apartment, described how sad she had been on the bus to Buffalo and the flight home. Then, as they say in the song, she did something really stupid and she told him how much she loved him and at that moment George was the happiest man in the world. For he also had come to realise how much he was in love with her. They embraced long and hard, much to the amusement of passers-by, before departing for his first ride in a yellow cab.

Her one bedroom apartment was at 400 West 37th Street, the midtown area. It was the Big Apple's most popular tourist area, at the hub of the local attractions. With no car, it suited her for work and leisure. She felt reasonably safe there, it had 24 hour concierge and security. The residents had their own gym and laundry and it was fully furnished with TV and all mod cons. Mandy had promised the owner free publicity in the English press and in return Jess had a reasonably priced short term base. As they only had three days, and two of those she had to get some work done, Jess had planned the time with a precision Blister would have been proud of.

As a change from cars or flights she had booked them on a dinner cruise that evening. Sunday, after a suitable lie in, they were to join a walking tour of the city and Sunday night she had obtained tickets for *Jersey Boys*. No other place to see it really but Broadway.

But the afternoon was unplanned, she told him, as they entered her apartment. Which was just as well, for within minutes of being there she was naked and they were in bed. The first time since they had declared their love for each other and the best yet. Afterwards they showered together again. But this time it was more relaxed. Apart from wanting to continuously wash her boobs George behaved.

After an afternoon spent exploring the apartment and each other they dressed for dinner. Their cab took them to Chelsea Pier, where eventually they boarded their ship, *The Spirit of New York*. The three hour trip included an all you could eat buffet and they saw such attractions as the Brooklyn Bridge, the Statue of Liberty and the Empire State Building. Jess had booked a table for two, complete with roses and bottle of champagne, and as a take home souvenir they got to keep the champagne flutes. Over dinner a quartet sang some of the Broadway hits they knew and a couple of songs from *Jersey Boys* as a taster for tomorrow. It was a perfect evening. There was a photographer on hand and they now had their first photographic memories to treasure.

Sunday was even better if that was possible. The walk was well organised and interesting, being the quietest day for traffic also made it easier to get around. They stopped at one of the many Italian restaurants for lunch before going back to make love, change clothes and head for the show. Broadway was just a short step from the apartment so they walked to the theatre. Some of the music he remembered as being favourites of his folks. He didn't really know who Frankie Valli was but enjoyed the experience.

Jess read her emails when they got back, Mandy had sent details of how the police case against Thresham was growing. The hard evidence and witness statements obtained after Blister's raids had prompted more people to come out of the woodwork. The combined revenue, customs and serious crime squad teams were unearthing more each day. She sincerely felt it was the beginning of the end for the man the girls always referred to as "that bastard" rather than their step-dad.

Following breakfast they walked to the tiny office

she shared with Alex Carson, the friend Mandy had arranged the job with. She was a tall sassy blond with a New York mouth and accent, but a great girl. It was a tiny room on the fourth floor of an old brownstone building. Without air conditioning two giant old fans blew warm heat about, to give the illusion it was cooler. Everything about it was old or cheap or both. But the girls' enthusiasm for what they were doing was boundless. Clooney had meant to just stay to say hello to Alex then hit the shops, but he became enthralled by the work. Alex subscribed to various news services which supplied stories from the world's press, be they local papers or international publications like the *Times* and *Herald Tribune*. Anything mentioning people trafficking was there. She then evaluated their possible relevance to a particular country and forwarded them accordingly, with this office as the contact point.

At first he couldn't see the point, but Alex explained that no one was necessarily going to point out to, say, the British government, that the six young girls of Indian origin rescued from a brothel in Tunisia were British citizens. Hopefully if her message hit home they might get help for the kids. They maintained a database and website of children and young women believed to have been taken. It was pretty grim stuff and almost unbelievable, except he was seeing the evidence it was true.

He treated the girls to a quick lunch, then he started shopping as they went back to work. Dinner that evening was on him; he wanted to make it special as it could be their last for some time and he was also gripped by a crazy idea as well.

Shopping done he collected Jess from work, they had a quick drink with Alex then back to base to change. "Best party frock," he told her, "for this surprise". There was just time for a quick kiss, cuddle and fondle then their cab arrived. It was fifteen minutes to the helicopter pad and Jess was terrified. He hadn't warned her, she didn't know if she could do it, but the spectacular flight over the city's skyline was another memory that would live forever.

Dinner later at the Granary Tavern could have been a let-down after that, but it wasn't. This was fine dining at its best. From the elegant *décor*, the superb service and food and drink to die for, it was the perfect ending, except it wasn't over yet. As they drank coffee, touched feet and whispered sweet nothings, George produced the *pièce de résistance*: an engagement ring. Which, much to his relief, she accepted without a moment's hesitation.

Back in bed, they phoned and texted the news to everyone that mattered to them, before engaging in the wildest sex either of them had ever known. If they were going to be apart now for a while, each would have something to remember this night for.

Amanda's call woke them at 7. It was 1 p.m. in England and she couldn't wait any longer to congratulate them, to say how happy she was, but jealous! It gave George the chance to explain about Fraser and the media. She understood perfectly and promised to have a word with the chief football reporters at the *Express* to see if they would be interested in buying his exclusive story. His mum rang, but couldn't speak, she was crying down the phone; and eventually his dad came on, wished them both all the best and asked him to phone when he arrived home. Texts and emails were coming in from literally all over the world. It made a great start to a sad day.

He walked to the office, said goodbye to her and Alex and they then said their final farewells in the street. George didn't speak once to the cab driver who, taking one look at his face, decided silence was the best policy all round. Within five hours he was on a flight from Toronto to Birmingham but he couldn't have told anyone how he got there or anything about it, he was so lost in thought. His flight arrived home at 4 a.m. UK time, Wednesday morning. He was deep down knackered and probably shouldn't have driven, but he opened every window in the car and managed to stay awake until he crawled into bed around 6.

Chapter Seventeen

Four hours later he awoke confused; where was he?

As he surfaced he recapped on what had been probably the greatest, craziest week of his life. A long shower, a week's mail and papers to catch up on, then he took his third coffee since rising, walked over to the computer and switched on.

There were millions of emails. Enough offers of Viagra to last him for ever. If he needed it, which he'd certainly proved last week he didn't. Among the mountains of junk were some little gems. Bob Carmill the boss of Perth Glory sent his best wishes, he was sure Clooney would make a great manager. Furthermore if he could help in any way he expected him to call. But the one that reduced him to tears, blame it on the jet lag, was from his *fiancée*; she was so happy to have him, so sorry to be apart. She described their time in Niagara as the happiest part of her life. He had to stop reading and concentrate on more mundane matters, it really got to him. He phoned his boss because that was what Dave Evans was now. He was flying both virtually and actually. He was in his helicopter on his way from Scotland. The building business was going great and he had lots of good news on the football front as well. He intended to clear the decks of everything but football matters that day, so they could both really start on it in the morning. It was agreed they would meet at Evans the Builders' office in

Wellingborough at 10 the next morning.

Blister was manning the reception desk when Clooney staggered down a little after 11, they greeted each other warmly and the old man congratulated him on his engagement. It was his lunch break in half an hour and they agreed to share a natter then. George tried to exercise, but anything but a slow walk was beyond him. He needed a night's kip. But he had to keep going for another twelve hours before the chance of that came along.

Blister offered to share his sandwiches but George wasn't hungry, so he thanked him but declined. They sat outside in the warmth, the sounds of traffic on the A14 nearby occasionally forcing them to speak up. It was an open secret that Burns was feeding his father-in-law information, but both pretended it was local gossip.

"The police believe," so Blister said, "that the raid had been carried out by well meaning citizens with some military experience." Well, they were right there, however because their actions had proved so useful in the ongoing enquiries into other matters they were not searching particularly hard for the culprits. One of the prostitutes saved that night had given evidence of her experience and named Thresham as the boss of the Northampton brothel. One of the croupiers working at the illegal casino in Corby was being offered immunity from prosecution for the evidence he had on the crime boss. Experts were still digging through the mass of information obtained, but if all else failed they would have him on tax evasion charges.

This tied in with what Amanda had told Jess.

Blister reckoned any day now the law would swoop, grab Thresham's assets and publicly everyone would know the game was up. They would ask for seizure of his passport, and if they couldn't bang him up to await trial he would certainly be under constant surveillance on bail. So the local gossips said! George then brought Blister up to date with all his news and the old boy was whistling contentedly as he returned to work.

George had to close his eyes. It was now 8 in Canada and he should have been eating dinner; forty winks, which were actually one and a half hours, saw him wake up feeling much better. He spent the next twenty minutes on the blower to Amanda, Jess, mum and dad, players and friends. He had to keep going for he had arranged to meet Danny, Barry and Fraser at the Northampton office of Watson Greene that evening at 6. He finished reading the email from Jess. Wolfe at the local paper was desperate for an interview and kept leaving messages, but George knew that would have to wait until after tonight's meeting.

It was drinks all round as the four of them convened in the board room in Northampton. One of the Watson Greene staff even asked him for an autograph, it made him feel good. All congratulated him on his engagement. Fraser told him not to plan the wedding without involving him. Allsports would be able to get him a deal on the hotel, and for whatever else he needed. He reckoned he might be able to get one of the celebrity mags to cough up for an exclusive. Football manager and runaway girl wed. They would love it. Amanda it seemed had been a busy girl and he had a contract if he wanted it from *Express* newspapers. The *Sunday Express* and the *Daily Star* had joined together to offer him a package where he always spoke to them first and was available to comment on any issue they brought to him. It was £300,000 up front for the year less Fraser's commission, and George and his legal team all said yes - Barry was now his lawyer, Gary formally handing over to him. The appropriate documents were signed and witnessed by Fraser. A draft Will had been prepared for Clooney to look at, but bearing in mind his sudden engagement he might like to change some of it Barry thought. He took it away to revise it.

On the charity side they really needed to know if he had made a decision. He told them he wanted to support the work of the Poppy Project but he was available to help in any way any organisation or service working towards helping those who were effectively modern day slaves.

They were all impressed by his integrity and his sincerity, Fraser was sure he could capitalise on this on behalf of his client. Clooney was shown the photos from the session with Demon Photographic, he had to sign on the back of the photos he liked to show his approval. There were various other items to cover but then it was meeting over and he finally could head back to Kettering. Blister had left some of those pills he had taken the night he was beaten up, hopefully they would keep him asleep long enough to be fit for his first day at work.

They did, he had ten hours asleep, waking refreshed and ready to go. He was able to report early for his first day with Evans the Builders. His now boss Dave Evans led him to his new office, explained how he had a copy of the shareholder register for the club and from that his secretary had managed to find out the contact phone numbers of the thirty or so people who had shares. A number with red stars against them were known Thresham allies - and one of course was the man himself.

Dave wanted him to call the rest, introduce himself and ask them if he could explain anything prior to the meeting. This was obviously to get them on side and Evans supplied Clooney with a list of answers to the questions he might be asked. They practiced a bit of role play with Dave being the shareholders. Evans was impressed. Two years of selling cars and the training he had received coupled with Clooney's natural charm convinced his boss this was going to work. They were to meet again at 5 for George to report. If there were any problems he was to contact Evans immediately; otherwise it was get making those calls.

Of the twenty eight he attempted to contact he only managed, for various reasons, to speak to fourteen that day. But the results were most encouraging. Many of the shareholders had been gifted their holdings by relatives. In the main they themselves were over forty years old and had the time and the inclination to chat about the club, Evans's plans, Thresham and George himself. By the end of the day ten had guaranteed their support, two were still undecided and two unhappy about the whole business.

Evans proclaimed it a great result when they met. He had a whole raft of reading material for Clooney to work on. A proposed budget for the next three seasons, current balance sheet for the business and details of the players contracts and a breakdown of the costs and income relevant to the club. He had arranged for his company accountants to meet with George at noon the next day in his boardroom. Before then he wanted Clooney to read up all the background and have questions prepared so as not to waste Alan Barnes's time. There were still fourteen shareholders to contact as well, so George was going to be a busy boy.

He stopped at the Kettering Park hotel on his way home; a session in the gym, followed by a vigorous swim, made him feel good. There were plenty of messages. Fraser had arranged for him to meet the *Express* team in London the next day. He confirmed his attendance. Then he read a message from Mandy inviting him to stay with her after the meeting, which she would also be attending, to cover the big story of him and her sister. He sent a message to Jess, one to his parents, opened the post, then without any enthusiasm whatsoever, spread the wadge of papers Evans had given him out on the dining table and started reading.

As a player you didn't have a clue how the club was run, nor did you care. You just tried to get the best deal you could for yourself and that was it. So it came as a shock to George when he realised how little, if any, spare money the club had. To make it easier for him Alan Barnes had provided notes and useful explanations of what the figures meant. In winning the title last season the club had made a surplus of half a million pounds. But for the previous five years their losses were three million and, loathe him as he did, George had to admit that without Thresham's funds and guaranteed support there would be no club. Dave Evans was not taking over a money making machine that was for sure.

About 9 he realised he was hungry, so he made himself some food before carrying on his work until the early hours. He had realised fairly quickly that being a manager took a lot more than he had ever realised.

After a morning run he phoned Jess. It was late in New York, she was already in bed, but delighted to talk. Quite by chance they had stumbled on a possible American link to her step-father and she was working on it. A routine police check of vehicles in Washington had resulted in a people carrier being impounded and the six occupants being interviewed. The vehicle had been reported stolen some weeks previously and was in a poor state mechanically. The driver's paperwork was false, he turned out to be an illegal immigrant, but it was the five females who were the most interesting of all, for many reasons. The leader of the group was a known prostitute and a madam with convictions. The other girls were of East European descent, spoke little English, but had all been brought into the States on illegal passports. Translators were brought in, who were able to help and determine all the girls were from Romania. One of them was a sister of Olga, the girl currently attending to Thresham's needs. It was another link in the intelligence that was building bigger than ever against her step-father.

She wished she could be with him and Mandy. Tonight she reminded him that as yet the three of them had never been together even once. She also told him to behave and they promised to speak soon and meet when they could. Then it was off for another day at the office that would probably end with the world and its mother knowing about him and Jess.

He managed to get through to another six shareholders that day. All of them promised their support. His meeting with Alan Barnes was an eye opener. Alan pointed out the difference between operating profit and a real profit. When loans, player sales and tax were taken into the equation the club had actually made just £100,000. Two players out of contract and talking to other clubs were skipper Tommy Ferguson and goalkeeper Paul Hodgkinson. Evans had discussed both with Barnes in case of the deal falling through and they were agreed they wanted to keep them subject to the manager's approval, so it was Clooney's call.

Now it was beginning to hit home what it meant to be the boss. Did he want them? What should he pay them? He cared for both as team mates, their experience as former League players could be invaluable next season. Yes, he wanted them on board, the planned budget for next season would give him the seventh highest payroll in the division so he couldn't complain of lack of funds to pay wages. But there was no money to buy players, though there was £100,000 available for agents and signing-on fees. It hadn't occurred to George that the so called free transfer signings all entailed the club sweetening the deal for the player with a generous signing-on fee. It made him realise how cheap he'd sold himself when he joined the club.

He examined the various income streams, gate revenue, sponsorship, perimeter advertising, programme advertising, player sponsorship, merchandise and gate sponsorship, revenue from the League, media and non-football activities like the clubhouse bar, car parking, replica kit; it was all Greek to the prospective player manager.

On the train to London Clooney continued to read the many documents he had been presented with. The emails and texts continued to pour in and Allsports Allstars confirmed they were now holding on to twelve commercial contracts pending the news about Jess, George and Kettering United breaking. Amanda met him from the train - they kissed, hugged, laughed and cried as if they were the loving couple and they made their way to the waiting car arm in arm.

At the headquarters of *Express Newspapers* the football writers for the three papers were there to greet him. Over drinks and snacks he was interviewed and photographed. Several company personnel came to meet him and finally pictures were taken of him and Amanda together. Then Mandy sprung as ever her own surprise, there was a phone call with Jess who gave her version of events without mentioning Thresham's name. When questioned as to her reasons for fleeing the family home she pointedly stated she couldn't answer at this time as it might affect an ongoing police operation. This was all dynamic material and by the time the evening broke up everyone concerned was extremely satisfied.

George and Mandy returned again to her favourite Italian. They couldn't stop talking as each tried to bring the other up to date on events. Mandy had spoken to her mother that day, she felt she owed her an explanation rather than let her read about it in the morning paper.

Her mother had been furious. To discover that for a year Jess had been safe and that Mandy had known all the time, she had slammed the phone down on her daughter. Mandy felt bad about it but didn't believe she had done anything wrong. The conversation then inevitably turned to Thresham and the police investigation into him. Burns had told her that the FBI had taken over the investigation into the incident in Washington that Jess had informed him about. The outcome of that, plus the final information obtained as a result of the raids, would lead to the arrest and conviction of her step-father any day now.

"Which means," Mandy warned him, "extra care needs to be taken." The cornered rat might turn, so she was warning him to be vigilant. They enjoyed, as before, a great meal with excellent service. Mandy explained how the paper's front page would carry the Jess and George story and the back page the Clooney and Kettering story. To complete a clean sweep Dave Evans had done a piece on his plans for the club and the financial pages were covering the proposed takeover. After tomorrow George would probably be one of the most famous faces in the country, for a short time at least. Dave Evans sent an email that he was to join him at the Kettering Park hotel for a briefing before the press conference at 10. Fraser's text confirming it followed.

They left the restaurant and took a cab to a private club favoured by the media where Mandy was a member.

Latest copies of the world's newspapers were there to peruse. Old leather chairs invited you to relax and read in quiet corners. It could have been an old fashioned gentleman's club except for the high proportion of young females present. The place was full of television personalities, executives, PR personnel, journalists, photographers.....all busy drinking and, judging by the noise level, all talking at once.

Clooney recognised one or two faces from television and Mandy seemed to know all of them! She introduced him to the investigative journalist Sue Pinnock, the girl whose *exposé* of the exploitation of British dancers working in Japan had been headline news worldwide. Sue herself was attractive and intelligent with the most warming of smiles, and soon George found himself talking quite freely with her.

Sue's big story had come about when her sister Lucie had returned early from a dancing contract in Tokyo. She had been disappointed and upset as it seemed that the booking, which appeared in every way to be perfectly above board, was anything but. Lucie had flown out with three other girls to be part of a spectacular concert in the night club of one of Tokyo's top hotels. However, 'escort duties' and much more was expected from the girls, if not demanded.

Soon the formidable Ms Pinnock was on the case. She discovered that over a thousand British girls every year were working abroad on dance contracts that were really something quite different. Sue's subsequent delving and hard hitting story had produced outrage. There were even questions in Parliament. Equity, the actors union, stepped in and, belatedly, the English and Japanese police. She went on to win an Industry Award for her troubles, and a powerful reputation as champion of fair play.

The women Clooney was used to, Jess apart, were very different from these powerful ladies. Many of the girls he had met through football were quiet, shallow and vain and would certainly never have heard of female exploitation, never mind fought it! George was grateful that his parents, with their liberal politics, a house full of books, the *Guardian* and *Observer* papers, had made him a different person than the type of men these two were slagging off.

The conversation ranged from why every business should be run as a co-operative to how women could get equality, fair play and satisfaction. The latter discussion making him blush as never before! The girls laughed at his discomfort and the evening ended back at Mandy's place, drinking coffee, each trying to outdo each other with jokes and hilarious stories.

Tonight had been a rare chance to relax with a member of his new family, a person he would be working with more and more in the future, but with the 7 a.m. train beckoning, it was time for each of them to hit their own beds.

Chapter Eighteen

The train was full, but Mandy had paid for first class seats for them so they were able to relax. Dave Evans sent a car to collect them from the station; as a result they were sat sharing a coffee with him by 9.30. Fraser brought along a colleague, Lindsay Paterson, who would be responsible on a day-to-day basis for handling commercial enquires for George and organising business appointments for him. Danny Brown was also there for him and Gary Wicks for the club's prospective new owner.

He barely had time to talk with Dave about the tactics for the day before the media started to arrive. Wolfe looked at him with some resentment, probably thinking he should have been told first. He laughed when the Kettering radio people tried to approach him. He hadn't forgotten, nor would he, how they and the local paper had treated him. Mandy was constantly at his side reminding people he was under contract to *Express Newspapers*, while Lindsay Paterson let the media know just who they had to speak to if they wanted any commercial advantages. It seemed like a circus to George.

Dave Evans called the meeting to order, thanked them for attending and assured them there would be press packs distributed at the end containing all relevant information. Then quickly, confidently and smoothly he addressed them. Reminding them that he had been a player at Kettering, then a supporter before he had become a director, he proceeded to bury Thresham. Dave told of his concern that possibly the wrong elements had control of the club, how it was starving of real investment, without a manager and in danger of becoming a laughing stock despite achieving League status for the first time.

For these reasons he was attempting to gain control of the club and if he was successful he would be appointing Jason Clooney as manager. When he finished the questions came flying in. Dave answered them all with charm, belief and sincerity. It was a master at work, George thought. On the television monitors he could see and hear how well his boss came over.

Then it was his turn. As agreed with Dave he told them how honoured he would be if he was granted the job. He answered questions as honestly as he could but constantly reminded them it would be wrong to say more until or if he ever was appointed the manager. Everyone had seen the *Express* articles that morning - now they wanted their take on it and again Clooney found himself the centre of a media swarm as everyone wanted clarification on the story.

At last Dave Evans called the meeting to an end. He left Clooney accompanied by Fraser and Lindsay to make their way to a conference room where George was available for further interviews, subject to payment. It was mid-afternoon before the whole side show ended. Over a late lunch in a private room the team discussed how the day had gone. A total triumph was the unanimous decision and now they needed to keep up the pressure until Tuesday's meeting. Mandy was staying the night with her brother-in-law-to-be, and they left the hotel to collect his car from the station. Dave drove them there, at the same time inviting them to be his guests for Sunday lunch, which they quickly agreed to.

Keen though he was to know what people had made of his performance he resisted the urge to read the emails on his phone. All messages could wait 'til they were home. Mandy seemed to have enjoyed the day as much as him and she chattered the whole way back.

After a drink, TV and messages check they phoned Jess. She was delighted that they were pleased but wished she'd been there. Hopefully in a way it was just her being paranoid, she told them, but Alex had been questioned at the office by a journalist for the New York Times and they were getting phone calls from various media sources now. Amanda couldn't hide her concern, it was her fault, she more than anyone should have realised the press and others would stop at nothing to find her sister now the story had broken. That was the problem when you were too close to something. All she had been concerned with was using the Clooney and Kettering story to help bring down Thresham.

Her stupidity had endangered Jess and could result in criminal charges against her for procuring illegal papers for her sister. Jess would have to come back, it was the only answer. She needed time to think, so she left George and her sister whispering sweet nothings and put her thinking cap on.

Clooney's parents had sent Jess a long letter and a card wishing her all their love and welcoming her to the family. It was such a beautiful letter it had made her cry, she told him. While the two of them talked Mandy got cracking on the mobile, calling in favours from all over the world. Over the years, because of her special project, she had received help and got to know many people. Serving police officers, social workers, public employees and passport and border guard personnel. Now she needed some of them to help her big time. She also thought of the contacts she had with business people like Richard Branson - but who could help her with this one? She didn't know.

Jess felt alien, lonely a little scared and she missed him, she told Clooney. Kettering was obviously the place where the action was and she wished she was there and part of it. A heart-torn George didn't know how to console her. He couldn't depart before the meeting yet he couldn't leave her suffering in the situation she was in. Both of them were saved further trauma by their very own fairy godmother, Mandy.

This is the plan she told them. Jess had to get to Toronto airport as fast as she could, Mandy had arranged for a hired plane to be on standby at a Buffalo private airfield from 10 tomorrow her time. Today she needed to let Alex and no one else know she was fleeing the city. To protect Alex it was better if she had no other details - then Jess was history. One of the tourist helicopters that flew to Niagara Falls had agreed to transport her to a hotel close to the plane. When she finally arrived at Toronto airport she was to page Alice King of Canbrit Charter Holidays. She was going to give Jess a very basic crash course in the work of an airline steward.

Jess would be working her passage to Glasgow, disguised as cabin crew. The checks on crew at every airport in the world were so haphazard there should be no problem getting her back to Britain. Karrina the Romanian girl they had helped would meet her there, give her shelter and provide the cover when the story broke that Jess had been there all the time. The paper was funding everything, though it knew few of the details. Management would have gone mental had they known what they were paying for. But with the scoop they were going to get they wouldn't be complaining about the cost. Although Jess was more interested in hearing about her escape route and being with Clooney, Mandy also reminded her that as a key part in the story she would be able to extract serious money from the media for the details.

Phone calls ended they discussed their next steps and drank some wine while Mandy planned the press conference for her sister's homecoming. They watched TV, more to see what news they featured in rather than the programmes, then called it a night.

Clooney rose early, morning run, shower, usual stuff. Mandy joined him for breakfast, just coffee and toast as they had a lunch date with the boss. They really were becoming firm friends both realised and they couldn't wait for Jess to make up the threesome. But for now they speculated on Dave Evans's motives for the lunch invite and tried to guess what lay ahead.

Chapter Nineteen

The beautiful man-made lake that attracted so many tourists was Evans's home base. His house overlooked Rutland Water, with its own moorings, helipad and parking for God knows how many cars. It truly was a country mansion anyone could be proud of. Clooney and Amanda were both very aware that they were about to be in the presence of real wealth and in Clooney's case the man who had the power to affect his destiny.

A very relaxed Dave Evans opened the door of his home to them and his welcome made them feel like VIPs. Dave's wife Dianne came to meet them, immaculately turned out she still had the model looks that had attracted her husband twenty years ago. The foursome made their way through the house to the sun terrace, with its views across the water. Other guests were there in all their finery, enjoying drinks and the ambience. Amanda and George were introduced to them: Colin Thompson was a kind of banker, something in the City, and his partner Simone was a lawyer. "I feel right at home here," George thought to himself sarcastically. Tony Barlow and Clooney had met before - Tony was Vice Chairman of the football club and a successful shoe manufacturer to boot. No pun intended. He and his wife Celia were the oldest couple there and slightly more formal or maybe more self-conscious than the rest.

The eight of them enjoyed the sunshine, the drinks

and the small talk until they were summoned into lunch. Presumably Mrs Evans had a cook, for she seemed to have little to do with the food's preparation. The long dining table seated them all with ease; George had Simone and Celia either side of him and he worried he might struggle to hold a conversation, but both ladies were charming and interesting in their separate ways and the meal was a most enjoyable experience.

He learned quite a bit more about his fellow guests, as they did no doubt about him. The international law firm Simone worked for had its main office in Zurich, Switzerland. One partner provided free legal advice for the International Red Cross in Geneva. She herself was planning to assist the charity sector in England to help improve the image of lawyers and in particular her own company. Celia was actively involved in church matters as well as the Women's Institute and as a school governor in Northamptonshire. She told him her husband Tony was keen on rotary, the church, golf, business and football but not in that order. Simone's partner Colin was the director of several City based companies. "Private bankers, equity raising, buy-out and new business funding," she said. Clooney nodded, though in reality he hadn't understood a word she was talking about. Apparently Colin was helping with the financial side of the football club buy-out and future financial structuring. Still none the wiser George chewed on his venison and sipped at the wine.

They retired back into the sun lounge for coffee and chocolates, brandy and liqueurs at the end of the meal. Huge armchairs and sofas, the sun beating down over Rutland Water, it was going to be a fight to stay awake Clooney thought.

As the drinks and chocolates were being enjoyed

their host got up to speak. He hoped they had enjoyed the food as much as he had enjoyed their company and everyone spoke at once complimenting him and Diane on the day. Then he asked them if they would allow him the opportunity to say a few words. Which nobody could or did deny.

He reminded them of his humble beginnings, of the struggle to play, enjoy and succeed in a sport his home nation regarded as inferior to real football. Rugby football! He told them what it was like as an amateur player, the camaraderie, the committee members, the ladies making tea and sandwiches, the fund raising activities; everyone, players, fans, committee men, all meeting for drinks in the social club which many of them had helped build after the game. How it was so different in the full time professional world and how he would like to take the game back to its roots to grow stronger and better as it went forward. When you think back that greats like Sir Stanley Matthews used to travel to play professional football on the bus or the tram with the fans. How professional football really only came into being because working lads sometimes couldn't get Saturday off and daren't be injured as it would have meant no pay. How players lived alongside ordinary fans; when they retired they bought newsagents, pubs, or sport shops in the same community. A totally different world from the multi-millionaire young footballers of today, who were as remote from their fans as if they lived on another planet, which in a sense they surely did.

His vision, when, being positive, he controlled the club, would be to return it to the people. Ordinary fans would be invited to buy shares in the flotation he would make happen. A representative selected by the Supporters' Club would be allowed to join in board meetings. His five year plan for the ground, the club, the team would be made available to everyone and anyone upon request. Players would be contractually obliged to attend supporters' functions, visit hospitals and carry out charity work.

He had met with people at Premier League Aston Villa who had explained to him how their club's sponsoring of Acorns Children's Hospice had worked. Of the good it had done for all, fans, players and the kids. It had changed minds, opened hearts, made people think, care and do something for others not just themselves. That concept he was going to pinch, copy and refine. Kettering United shirts would proudly bear the name of a charity for free - not a commercial sponsor's name for reward.

The group had hardly had chance to voice their approval before he was off again. A free office would be made available at the ground for a charity coordinator. After that it would be her job, because he already knew who he was going to offer the post to, to make it happen. That person would work tirelessly to fund raise for charity. They would ensure maximum positive publicity for all concerned. There would be a place and a person to turn to when in need and they would report their results to the football club board as a courtesy, not to be managed or criticised by anyone at the club. The job would be as big as the person made it and they would have his tireless support.

While the group took time to take all of this in he hit them with another bombshell: the job would be unpaid! There was an immediate explosion of noise. Evans just smiled like a friendly head teacher might do, then when silence fell he handed the floor to Mandy. Clooney dropped his coffee cup with surprise. Fortunately it was empty.

Mandy rose, smiling at her astonished brother-in-law elect before she floored him again when she announced that she had recommended her sister for the job. Again everyone started talking at once. Taking her cue from the way Evans had handled them she just smiled and waited until they stopped. She then explained how Jess had worked with her on charity liaison, had given practical help to those in need, obtained commercial sponsorship and was after all both a qualified nurse and one of the few people with a high profile living locally who would be prepared and could afford to make that commitment without remuneration.

The room was again in uproar. Clooney felt all eyes on him, but he was as flabbergasted as anyone. Nobody had pre-warned him about any of this. He was angry that Dave Evans and Amanda could just drop this on him and he wondered if Jess knew any of it.

While people settled down Amanda asked for time alone with him and the pair of them ventured into the garden. Clooney let rip, his language was disgusting and a part of him could easily have smacked her, except she was a woman and he was above that. When he paused for breath Mandy explained. Dave had told her of his plans over lunch so she had no chance to tell George. Evans was going to ask Simone if she could recommend anyone from her company to help and he planned to ask Tony and Colin if he drew a blank there. Mandy had to get in quick. She believed Jess would be perfect for the job. With the book, TV and magazine deals she was planning to get her sister, she expected Jess could make a million pounds or more. Dave Evans had assured her that with the proper mix of investments, properties, ISA's, bonds, gilts and Jess should be able to make £30,000 a year after tax without ever touching the capital. That's more than she was taking home as a nurse, she wanted to give her first chance so she had stepped in before he told anyone else. Her sister could still turn it down or Dave and she might not get on, but she had done it for all the best reasons and she was sorry if he saw it differently.

Clooney calmed down. Inside he was still seething but he could see the logic of what she said. He agreed to smile, go back inside with her and behave, which he did. Dave looked him straight in the eye. Clooney returned the look, smiled and nodded. Everything was fine by him.

Their host took centre stage again, mesmerising his audience as he shared his hopes and dreams of making the club a major force in football and the community. How it would succeed because everyone would be working for a common good. New stadium, new manager, new philosophy, new finance, new beginning. They were all sold on his vision. Mind you, so persuasive, believable and charming was he that he could have sold oil to an Arab, Clooney thought.

Afternoon tea was served on the lawn and talk turned to Tuesday's meeting, Thresham, next season and even non-footballing matters eventually. When it was time to leave George's mood had improved, largely as a result of all the positive stuff he had heard and the positive people now on board. When he said his goodbyes Dave asked him to meet him in the office for breakfast at 7.30 a.m. the next day. There was still much to do before Tuesday's meeting.

Amanda never stopped talking the whole way home. George drove as Mandy had enjoyed her fair share and more of their host's booze. But neither could wait to tell Jess all that had happened. It was nearly 6 when they got back; after checking for messages they phoned the USA. Jess was still aboard the helicopter and it was difficult to converse. She promised to phone from the hotel later which gave Clooney and Mandy time to get on with their respective chores. She spoke to Karrina, receiving assurances that all was in place for her sister's arrival in Glasgow. George spoke to his folks and was amazed to discover they had only a few days left of their holiday. How time flies. He phoned Blister, but he was "Out, doing granddad things," his daughter told him.

They were both still so full from the food at the Evans's that they had tea and toast and called it dinner. Mandy felt it could sabotage the coverage of the AGM if Jess put in an appearance before Wednesday. Clooney agreed, but he was desperate to see her and be the one who brought her back home. Mandy suggested he speak to Evans at their breakfast meeting about getting some time off. Then they prepared themselves for the next day whilst waiting for the call.

Jess phoned, she was in her hotel. When they told her of Evans's job offer she couldn't believe it. It sounded perfect to her as long as George approved. All three agreed she should go for it and he supplied her with Dave's contact details. Reluctant though all parties were to prolong the separation, they all could see the sense of Jess staying in Scotland until Friday, then flying down to either Birmingham or East Midlands airport where Clooney could collect her. Then the two of them could have a quiet weekend together, while Mandy would set up a press conference for Monday in London. The football club issue would be resolved by then and Clooney should be able to have a couple of days off. It was also important that Jess build her cover story. With Karrina's help she could immerse herself in the Scottish neighbourhood she had supposedly lived in this last year.

Mandy left them talking as she started the planning process for the media frenzy that would be sure to follow her sister's reappearance. Clooney and Jess talked about their future; possible obstacles that might get in the way.

Then about life in general. Jess had spoken several times to his mother now and looked forward to visiting them in Sheffield. She said she would sort out the plans for Friday as he had enough to do and he suggested maybe they stayed at a romantic hotel for the weekend. But Jess was keen to see her new home and promised him just as romantic a time there as in any hotel.

Chapter Twenty

The breakfast business meeting with Dave Evans occupied his mind that morning. He was nervous and a little unsure of himself when he knocked on his boss's office door. Dave was his usual welcoming self, attired now in a suit rather than the casual look of yesterday. They made small talk as they worked their way through bacon sandwiches, orange juice and copious amounts of tea.

Dave had heard from Jess and was meeting with her next week. He asked George how he felt, in all honesty, about his wife working at the club. Clooney admitted how shocked he'd been when it was sprung on him. His real concern though was what happened if he left the club, "Would Jess have to go as well?" Evans took his time replying. He had thought about it too it seemed. In his vision of club, community, charities working together, it was the perfect scenario: the manager's wife with her role and George with his. If she didn't deliver it would be a shame but it wouldn't have cost the club anything in wages. Both of them had to accept, he believed, that George would probably not spend the rest of his life there, yet start his managerial career at the club. He would either be so successful that a bigger team would come in for him, or he would make a pig's ear of it and Evans would fire him! In either of those cases, and Dave hoped neither would happen, only Jess could decide whether she should go as well. But being the confident man he was Evans believed there could only be great results for both of them ahead.

Feeling infinitely better George was able to then concentrate on the plans for the day and tomorrow's date with destiny. Dave explained how with the shareholding he now had he was legally obliged to inform shareholders at the assembly that he now owned the largest stake of anyone in the club. Colin Thompson had pledged his shares and support and with the non-attendees that Clooney had contacted committing themselves to the cause, it was a done deal.

But Dave, being the man he was, wanted all or as near as damn it all of them to buy into his vision of the club's future. Three directors, Thresham, Collins and a man called O'Mara who George didn't know, had resigned and agreed to sell their shares to Dave so he anticipated no problems there. Collins would chair the meeting and the intention was for Evans to be appointed the club's new Chairman as well as being majority shareholder before the day was out. He was sure the real football fans in the audience would want to grill the new manager, but he recommended Clooney deferred on the grounds that it was too soon and would be inappropriate to say too much at this stage. "Just tell them how pleased you are to have the chance and that your hopes and dreams for the club match mine, or something like that," his boss said.

Then, while Dave combined his role as a builder with that of a prospective football club Chairman, George got on with his homework. He still hadn't totally mastered all the stuff he had been given but vowed to meet up again with Alan Barnes and seek clarification.

That evening he met up with Blister, who was thrilled to hear all the news. He also looked forward to meeting Jess who he now knew all about. Mandy had booked herself into the Kettering Park Hotel for the night. An evening of drink and debauchery with her fellow media reporters would set her up for tomorrow's big day. Clooney found himself missing her; without either of the Thresham sisters he felt a lonely man. After a catch-up on messages he made himself a meal from the freezer and prepared to phone Jess. Her plane was due to land in Glasgow at around 11 British time, until then he concentrated on his homework, took himself off for a training run and put on some washing. "What a glamorous life I lead," he thought.

Her flight was early and she phoned him. Karrina had been there to meet her and she was ready to start her familiarisation homework just as he was concentrating on his. She was tired, jet-lagged and "couldn't wait to be with him," she told him, wishing him all the best for the big day. She piled into a car with Karrina while Clooney settled down to work. He couldn't see how any of the shareholders could ever make any money out of the football club investment unless it was sold. Trying to make sense of the accounts, he realised only the players made money from a football club, a fact he had never appreciated until now. When he was player manager things were certainly going to change!

It was a little over five weeks since that game, that goal. Since then he had been physically attacked, verbally abused, fallen in love, lost his job, become engaged and was possibly this day going to become player manager of Kettering United F.C. At least he couldn't complain of boredom! In best suit and tie, the one he wore for funerals - hopefully not an omen - he met his boss for breakfast again, though this time at the hotel rather than the office.

A few tables away a group of journalists were talking loudly, among them Mandy, who gave him a wink and blew him a kiss. Dave did not seem in the least concerned about the day ahead, talking incessantly on his mobile while dishing out last minute instructions to George. Colin Thompson joined them with Gary Wicks in tow and the men exchanged pleasantries over breakfast before getting down to the serious business of the day. They moved along to the room in the hotel Evans was using as his headquarters before making their way to the ground. The restaurant had been turned into a meeting room for the day and all costs were being footed by Dave, not the club. By the time they were ready to start, the venue was full of shareholders and media representatives. But no Thresham and gang.

At 11 a.m. on the dot Colin Thompson brought the meeting to order and opened by reading a statement prepared by Gary Wicks. Basically it informed all present that, by virtue of the shares he held in his own name, Dave Evans was now the largest shareholder in the club. Then it was explained that at his instruction and expense this meeting had been called. He went on to explain about the three directors' resignations and to advocate the appointment of the said Dave Evans as Chairman.

When he finished speaking there were immediately figures on their feet, demanding the right to speak. One after another they praised Dave, damned Thresham and urged the meeting not to waste time, but to appoint him as Chairman, now. It was a total anti-climax, no dissent, discussion, just the unanimous approval of all that Dave should take the chair.

After the vote had been noted and recorded Thompson handed over to Dave. He was as always magnificent for the occasion, grateful but not servile, strong but not arrogant. Soon they all shared in his vision and his speech earned him a standing ovation. Ever the diplomat, he assured them he wanted to hear their concerns and he invited questions. Soon the inevitable was asked about whether Clooney was taking over as manager. Evans again displayed his skills as an orator. Reminding them all how the club would not now be a League side were it not for that goal, he mentioned, but only briefly, the appalling treatment George had received from some of the media and a few supposed fans. But he quickly moved on to Clooney's playing ability, the respect other players had for him and how, with his contacts and his ability, he, David Evans, had no doubt that George was the man to help make his dream come true.

This provoked a second standing ovation, followed by chants of "Clooney, Clooney," more familiar to the terraces than a company meeting. Evans signalled for George to speak.

Following on from Dave Evans was an almost impossible task. George lacked his style, experience or confidence. But he was a born salesman, as well as being honest, committed and in his own way a good talker and a good listener too. He soon told them what he knew they wanted to hear, but also because he believed in what he was saying. He praised the lads on the field who had got them into the position they were now in. He praised all of those off the park who had worked to make it happen. He assured them of his total commitment and belief. The future could be all that they dreamt of and more, with a slice of luck, a bit of money and a mountain of hard work. And he couldn't wait to get started. It produced the third standing ovation of the day and probably the loudest. After a few further questions and answers the meeting was brought to a close.

George was mobbed by the media and the share-holders immediately after. It was all so positive and everyone was so happy, Clooney felt he was ten foot tall, 'walking on air' would describe the elation he felt. Mandy kissed him, full on the mouth, hugged him and burst into tears of joy. People clapped him on the back, promised support and if he had accepted even a quarter of the drinks he was offered, he would have been flat on his back in no time.

At the end, snacks and drinks consumed, questions answered, vanities smoothed, only the diehards were left. Mandy was heading back to London but would keep in touch. She told Clooney she had never been happier. He was to do an interview for Wolfe and a down the line one for Kettering radio. Evans was handling questions from the more serious media, *FT* and *Daily Telegraph*, *Guardian* and *The Times*. Clooney found a quiet corner and sat down with Wolfe. There wasn't much to add to what had already been said but Wolfe, as the local football reporter for the local rag, had to pad it out. He was genuinely sorry for the way his editor had treated Clooney, and his apologies were received in the spirit with which they had been given. It was still frosty with the radio station though, they hadn't liked Dave Evans calling them in public. "They will get over it," George thought. It was strange being interviewed down the telephone line, he always thought. It seemed more like you were just talking to a mate than being heard by thousands of people. A couple of other journalists asked for a word and he even did a piece for Sky television sports news before his boss summoned him.

"Just rescuing you," he said, then they joined Colin and Gary for celebration drinks and a late lunch, before George was told he'd done well. "Now go on home and relax and enjoy the moment while it lasts."

Clooney was buzzing, the adrenalin high, there was no way he could just go home and sit in an empty flat devoid of people, not the way he felt. So he moved into the office, the manager's office. It was 4 p.m. and the club was still buzzing with people, action, and life. Everyone greeted him warmly, congratulated him on the day, and it helped keep the magic going.

He phoned Jess, she had been desperate to hear how the day had gone. Watching television she and Karrina had seen him. Karrina thought he was gorgeous and so did she. While he was big news everywhere, she was learning by talking to Kat about life in Scotland, sorting out flights for Friday and immersing herself in the false history she might need to keep herself and Mandy out of trouble. They talked for almost an hour, about nothing for lots of the time, but it was important stuff for absent lovers. Eventually they finished with Jess reminding him to phone his folks and give them her love. Which like a good boy he did. He was enjoying being so much a part of another person's life and of her being so important in his. Having someone, particularly this woman he loved, give him orders was a pleasure not a chore. His folks were packing for their return on Thursday, his mother told him. Why do it two days early was beyond him. They had seen him on television in Canada, what a surprise, though it was only brief.

Everyone wanted to know all the news, his life was so amazing they thought. From what they said they had certainly had a great time there but were looking forward to getting back now and excited at the thought of welcoming Jess to their home. She surrendered the phone reluctantly so that he might have the briefest of words with his dad, Ross and Cynth. Promising his folks he would be bringing Jess to visit as soon as he could, he finally got off the call. He dealt with his voicemail and emails before finally and reluctantly again attempting to make sense of the notes Alan

Barnes had provided.

Dave Evans popped back into the office around 6.30 and was surprised, but pleased, to find his *protégé* hard at work. Over drinks they talked future strategy. From tomorrow George should base himself at the ground, "Forget the office and Evans the Builders," Dave told him. It was time to make his presence felt and with Tony Bradshaw's departure the club had been without a manager long enough.

Evans phoned Colin Thompson, who agreed to meet George at 9 the next day and work with him as required, for as long as was needed. Colin was sold on Dave's plans for the club and would do whatever he could to help them succeed. The truth was he felt a bit guilty as Vice Chairman that he had not stood up to Thresham more.

Clooney was now the boss of Kettering United, a fact he was going to have to get used to. He sat that evening at home contemplating how he would tackle it. The players he wanted to keep, get rid of, obtain. The coaching staff, the training, working with the directors, fans and others, he was going in at the deep end. "Sink or swim," he thought, management training for himself he would need to organise, thank God through boredom he had taken all his coaching badges years ago. It was all a blur. For relief he phoned Mandy, but she was out. So he trawled the net for information whilst eating, again, a freezer meal.

Blister phoned and then came round for a drink. He offered his and the lads help with pre-season training. They might all be around sixty years of age, but he reckoned they could still teach pampered footballers a thing or two. Clooney thought about it and said he would run it past Dave. That drew a long hard look and a sigh from the old soldier.

When Blister had been in the army, he told George,

all the blokes looked up to the N.C.O.s. They might not like them, but they respected them because they had proved what they were capable of. Whereas the young commissioned officers, wet behind the ears and straight from college had only read about it. A bit of stick, a bit of carrot and they soon fell into line for Blister and his like, as they would for Clooney he reckoned, if he proved himself the boss. But, if he kept running to Dave Evans all the time, the players and everyone at the club would do the same. He had to take complete charge and he had to do it straight away. Everyone seemed to believe in him, but himself.

Clooney thought about it and could see the other man's point. He promised himself that, from tomorrow, he would be the man in charge and not a yes-man, doormat, subordinate.

Jess phoned and they talked at length again. It was going to be about 3 when she arrived at Birmingham airport on Friday and it couldn't come soon enough for either of them. Mandy phoned to say everything was in place for next Monday's press call. It was at the Café Royal at 11.30 a.m. and she wanted two hours at least with them both beforehand, to discuss the plan of campaign. Jess was going to try and see her mum on Sunday night. She didn't want her reading all about it in the paper first. Lindsay from Allstars Allsports would be at the event as would Simone and Colin, while Dave Evans had promised to be there if work permitted.

He grabbed yet another frozen desert, cleared up, ate when it defrosted then planned his first real day as the player manager of Kettering United. He was on the point of turning in when the phone rang again and he was surprised to hear from Blister's son-in-law Burns.

Apparently Thresham had fled the country, they

didn't know how, but he had, leaving Mrs Thresham home alone so to speak. The police were now applying for warrants for his arrest and the right to search his home and businesses. He just thought George might like to let the girls know. They chatted briefly and he rang off, leaving Clooney to consider his next move.

Chapter Twenty One

After contacting both girls, who wanted time to consider what to do regarding their mum, Clooney had slept. Now it was his first day in charge and he had woken early, gone for a run before an early breakfast and heading for the stadium. The ground built just off the A14 dual carriageway was ultra-modern in appearance, with a six thousand capacity. But the clever design allowed for additional tiers to be added-on relatively inexpensively, to raise that to ten thousand if attendances warranted it. The club had so much land that it could expand further with ease and George had to admit for a first start in management he could have been at far worse places.

Colin Thompson had been at the club since eight that morning, so when Clooney arrived he was able to brief him straight away. The first players would arrive just before ten for training. Being the closed season there would only be a few of them who bothered to stay fit. George had decided last night he would contact all the playing staff and invite them to meet him for open and frank discussion about the way forward. Judie Green the company secretary, head of administration, typist, receptionist and general dogsbody, agreed to contact the squad for him.

Judie was a true fan, who had supported the club all her life. Now aged fifty and on her own, the club was her reason for living, as well as her employment. She was a jolly, pleasant woman, probably a looker when she was young, but with the years taking their toll and an expanding waistline she was more mumsie than supermodel, though everyone liked her, for her constant commitment, energy, humour and devotion to the cause. She made him and Colin coffee before leaving them to get on with her work, which was essentially the day-to-day running of the club excluding the players, training staff and Clooney.

When the first few players Pernod, Tick Tack, Bobby Davidson - a young reserve player - and Kevin Slipermaker, the club's most expensive signing, entered the changing room Colin Thompson greeted them warmly, then handed over to George and left. Clooney explained he would be getting all the lads together as soon as it could be arranged, but he was glad to see them and that he would join them for training. If any of them had any questions they were to go ahead and ask now or see him privately any time. No one spoke as he changed with them, but as they left the room Pernod stopped him to tell him how he had the support of all. They felt for him, for what he had been through with Jess, understood he couldn't tell them what was happening until it was finalised and were sure he would be a great boss. Clooney was elated, even when Pernod finished by telling him he was a lucky bastard though and a crap footballer. With that George knew there were no hard feelings and this situation would work.

After training he worked on the relevant list, getting Judie to fire off letters to those players they had options on, exercising the club's right to extend their contracts and for those players he saw as key men he offered extended and better terms. There were several he wanted to sit down with and discuss their futures. If there wasn't a big change in attitude they would be out.

Agents and players had emailed the club details and some had sent DVDs. He needed to look at them all to make sure he didn't miss a gem, although more likely it would be more a case of finding the proverbial needle in the haystack. Several hundred people had contacted the club recommending players, or the players themselves had written in. All needed to be checked out.

His mobile rang. It was Mandy, she was meeting her mother that evening and wondered if she could stop over. Clooney didn't just agree, he decided to get spare keys cut for her and Jess so both could come and go to suit. That call made him think of his *fiancée* so he called her, to discover how concerned both she and her sister were about their mum. He would have talked more but Dave Evans arrived and after promising to phone her later he sat down for the first time with his boss in his office, the manager's room, Clooney's lot.

Dave was all smiles and pleasantries, but George knew he would also be assessing if his new manger was up to it. A quick recall of Clooney's morning seemed to please the Chairman and they both went off for lunch at the golf club courtesy of the club's new Chairman.

Over salads and steaks and a big bowl of chips for the boss they discussed potential future signings, releases and even next week's press conference, which Dave was hoping to get to. Clooney explained his idea, gifted by Blister, to bring the three ex-soldiers in to toughen up his troops before the start of the new campaign. "Pure genius," Evans thought. A good start then, Clooney expressed to himself, it meant George had six weeks before pre-season training began. In that time he had to sign a squad of players, organise his coaching staff and scouts, work out the tactics for next season, set up pre-season friendlies and closed door trials for interested wannabees. That being just playing matters. He had then to attend board and Supporters' Club meetings, meet with the media, help season ticket sales, start his final coaching badge qualifications, try and grab a holiday with Jess, spend some time in Sheffield with his folks and sit down with Blister to formulate the pre-season strengthening programme. "Not a lot then!" he thought.

Back at the ground he started watching the DVDs and YouTube clips, assessing potential. After two hours he realised there were only three he would like to look at closer and he made a note of their details. The club's assistant manager and head of scouting under the old regime had been Mark Norman, a former player whose own career had been tragically ended at the age of twenty-nine, when he received such a kicking from an opponent he suffered a double fracture of his right leg which to this day had left him with a pronounced limp. He was well-liked by everyone, talked a lot of sense and at thirty-five was young enough to be able to communicate with the lads on their level. Clooney wondered if he would follow his predecessor or stay with the club. "Only one way to find out," he thought, and phoned him.

Forty-five minutes later they were sat drinking coffee in Clooney's office. Mark was slightly shorter than George and as blonde as Clooney was dark, a good looking man, he was married to a local girl and had a couple of kids. Originally from the North East and a former model pro with Middlesbrough, Derby, Northampton and finally Kettering, he would be the ideal number two, Clooney thought.

Mark explained he wanted to stay with the club and in the area. He had declined to follow his former boss when asked and had been approached by three other clubs who he was prepared to name if needed, but he'd turned them down as well. He enjoyed the role he had, but for the foreseeable future had no interest in the manager's chair. Clooney knew instinctively they would get on. Shaking hands on it they told the Chairman before alerting the local media to the club's first new signing of the new regime, even if it was an old favourite.

He briefed *Express Newspapers* first, as agreed in his contract. Then, just after 4, he took a call from Wolfe wanting more details on Mark Norman's position. "News travels fast," he thought. Talk inevitably turned to Thresham, about when the story was about to break internationally. Another down the line interview followed with the local radio and he gave the full story agenda to Bob Fletcher at the Rutland and Nene Valley Press Agency who would no doubt circulate it to all and sundry. After a brief chat with Judie, it was time to bring his first day as the gaffer to an end. So he drove home a very contented man.

Only sixty emails to wade through, though half were junk, then voice messages and within an hour of his arrival his beloved came on the line. Mandy had just phoned her from their mother's. Mrs Thresham was in quite a state and desperate to see her daughter, so if Clooney didn't mind she was going to arrive a day early and spend some time with her mum and Mandy, who would not be staying at Clooney's now.

How could George mind? He immediately offered to collect her from the airport but her mum and sister were going to do that. They did though want him to join the three of them for dinner, and Jess would come home after with him if he wanted. That was a resounding yes on both counts and after much love talk they both said goodnight happy. George decided to celebrate by ordering an Indian takeaway while he prepared the flat for the visit of his lady.

Next day, like all his days now, this one flew. He had a long conversation with football agent Kevin Holmes, who represented amongst many others Paul Wilson, the midfield player Clooney was interested in. They would both attend the ground the next day for a look around, discussion, and if agreement was reached, a medical for Wilson. He brought Mark Norman up to speed and they agreed that Mark would organise trial games for a week on Sunday when they could look at further possible acquisitions.

Jess phoned to say she had arrived safely and was on her way to mum's and looking forward to seeing him later. He asked if he should bring anything and was told quite firmly, just himself. Getting back to work he sat for over an hour going over things with Judie Green, fired off letters and emails to fans, agents, sponsors, the media, local companies asking for support, various players, well-wishers, friends and people trying to sell him something. He realised they would soon need to organise some formal training sessions. Players were wandering in for an hour or two doing their own thing then clearing off. He made a mental note to sort that out with Mark. From Monday he would have an assistant, the first ever in his life and it couldn't happen quickly enough.

Finally it was time to head home, a run, a shower, more emails and messages, then prepare for his first meeting with his prospective mother-in-law. He wondered how that would turn out.

He turned off the A14 to go left for Loddington, then thinking better of it proceeded around the traffic island back onto the dual carriageway and almost immediately into the filling station. He nearly hadn't noticed how low the diesel was. After filling the tank he bought a box of chocolates, a bottle of wine and a bunch of flowers. Something for each of them as there was no way he could just turn up empty handed.

The gates were open so he drove straight in. Strange to think that just over a month ago he had dropped Jess off here the first night they met. So much had happened since. As he exited the car she came racing out of the house. There were tears in her eyes, but a smile on her face. She kissed him, held him, hugged him, felt him, squeezed him, laughed and cried all at the same time. He followed suit. Never had he felt this way about another person. Then Mandy joined them, slightly more restrained but otherwise the greeting was the same, and as he stood there with two beautiful ladies in his arms, a third, older but stunningly attractive, walked towards him.

Mrs Thresham was as tall, slim and as attractive as her girls, but twenty-five or so years older. A younger Sophia Loren she could have been. He wondered why he always categorised people's looks by likening their appearance with that of a movie star. Another thing to talk to a shrink about!

Paula Thresham *née* Granger shook his hand in welcome, her girls had their mother's smile and she greeted him warmly, just as her eyes betrayed the stress and sorrow she was suffering. In the house, which was as magnificent inside as you would have expected from the commanding exterior, he accepted a glass of wine and perched on a two seater sofa with Jess sprawled all over him.

Mrs Thresham spoke at some length, grateful to have him joining them and glad to meet him at last, having heard so much about him, particularly in the last twenty-four hours from the girls. She asked him to call her Paula, for now. She confessed to having no knowledge or interest in football, yet she managed to understand clearly all that was taking place at the club. When the girls were dispatched to finish dinner preparations she continued, apologising for the incident with Thresham, a man she did not want to talk about this evening. She questioned him pleasantly but firmly on his past and his future interests, particularly towards her younger daughter.

Clooney took a swallow of wine then a deep breath, he told her what he had never told another person, how he had fallen in love with Jess, how they were just so right for each other, how his parents and everyone who had seen them together felt they were just made for each other. Finally he personally guaranteed her that he would never hurt Jess, nor would he allow anyone else to.

Then he paused for breath because he was emotionally drained from his diatribe. She crossed the room, kissed him on the cheek and told him how she was in no doubt herself now, having met him, why her daughter had fallen for him and she was sure he would always cherish and protect her. On that note they joined the girls at the table for dinner.

The dinner was memorable for many reasons. It was their first together, the food was superb and the conversation never let up. Time seemed to fly, always a good sign, and when it was over, time for Jess and George to leave, Mandy laughed and made some sexy remarks about the first night the couple would be spending in the flat. Her mother hoped they would return soon. Goodbye kisses and a few tears later the pair left.

Driving home together for the first time was not just a new experience, it was exciting, thoughtful, scary and yet another beginning of which there had been so many. Conversation was loud, not forced, both of them were making the journey together, but alone with their own thoughts, fears, hopes, love as individuals as well as a pair. Clooney carried her case in, Jess admired the masculine *décor* and then fears and inhibitions aside they were in each other's arms. Overcome by passion, fear, love, they tore at each other's clothes, made love naked on the rug in front of the fire and afterwards George carried her to what was now their bed and they enjoyed each other again.

He woke about 7 a.m., the sun shone and the most beautiful woman in the world was next to him. What more could anyone want? Jess stirred, they cuddled, they became aroused, they made love for the third time in their new home, an experience, Clooney couldn't help thinking, he could not have imagined a few short weeks ago. She made breakfast, he tidied the bed. Together they enjoyed the food, each other and the moment. Jess was going to come into work with him, meet Dave Evans, then spend the day with her mum and Mandy. He had to get some players signed and was meeting Holmes and Wilson at 11.30 a.m.

As they drove to the ground together, another first, they talked about the weekend, parents, food and before they know it they were there. Dave Evans met them at the entrance and after introductions and small talk wandered off with Jess, leaving Clooney to get down to the day's business. Judie Green as usual had already sorted the post, drafted some letters which if he approved, he could just sign and she would do the rest. He couldn't yet still believe the volume of daily mail. Fans wrote offering well wishes, opinion, recommending players he should sign; businessmen offered their services; agents offered players; charities wanted him to attend functions; the Professional Football Association circulated details of players who were unattached and therefore available for free, except for whatever generous offer they could negotiate for signing for you rather than anyone else. The League wrote with rule changes and general rubbish. There were letters from the Football Association, the bank, the auditor, the solicitor, the police wishing to meet to discuss matters relating to crowd control, and so on and so on.

He hadn't even finished going through half of it when Jess appeared. He introduced her to Judie who welcomed her warmly before discreetly leaving. His *fiancée* was flying as high as a kite, over the moon whatever you wanted to call it. She and Dave Evans had hit it off right away, she couldn't wait to start her new job and was so happy she could cry. He embraced her and might have been tempted to go further had Dave not at that moment appeared. All three were excited about having Jess on board and then she took Clooney's car and headed to her mum's to tell her and Mandy about the job. Evans told Clooney that now, having met Jess, he was more than sure they had the right person on the team and couldn't fail.

Kevin Holmes the agent and Paul Wilson the player arrived. While Dave and Kevin chatted in the board room, Clooney showed Wilson around. Paul had been released by Everton for whom he had played eight first team games in three seasons. He was still only twenty, born in Corby so knew the area well, and was looking at all the offers open to him. Had Kettering not been in the League he wouldn't even have been there, he told George.

Back in the boardroom Dave Evans weaved his magic, selling his dream for the future, the opportunity for Paul to be part of it, and after answering all their questions he left the player and his agent to talk while he and George stepped outside. Dave wanted to know if Clooney really wanted the lad and was he sure he was right for the club? George took a deep breath, paused and then delivered his verdict. In his opinion Wilson was not as good as he thought he was, would probably never make a Premier League player and would need handling carefully, but on the plus side he was born locally so would attract fans, was part of the new image the club was trying to foster. He could certainly play above the level they were going to be in, as a Division Two side. He would make it easier to attract other class players, people would see they meant business by seeing a former Premier League player had joined, so, yes, he wanted him.

Dave's only comment was, "So let's go do it then," and they went back inside. After debate, argument and discussion a deal was thrashed out, subject to a medical. They all shook hands on it, though wily old fox Dave Evans knew that meant nothing and the player would sign for someone else tomorrow if he got a few more pounds. It was agreed that Wilson would have a medical in Liverpool on Monday where he was still living, which Kettering would arrange and obviously pay for. Then the player would travel down to announce the deal the same day.

After the pair had left Clooney phoned his new number two Mark Norman and told him how it had gone. Mark had organised the background checks on Wilson, finding out what he was like, if he was in any trouble, how did he get on with team mates and managers. All had come up okay; Evans and Clooney chatted some more before the Chairman left, and George caught up on his calls. Lindsay Paterson phoned with news of the latest commercial deals she had struck for him. She really was making him some dough. Alan Barnes spent yet another hour explaining the club's finances, then he managed an hour's training for himself before heading home.

He called his parents, home in Sheffield but still in Canada in their minds. Promising to bring Jess up as soon as possible, he had no sooner finished the call than his *fiancée* rang - dinner at the Italian with mum and Mandy if he didn't mind, as if. He arranged to meet them at eight, they had made the reservation. Blister popped in, disappointed not to have seen Jess. Seemed all the people in his life preferred her to him, he thought.

The restaurant was packed. People greeted him, clapped and some cheered when he arrived. Joining the girls in the private room upstairs he quickly realised all was not well. The police had been in touch just before they left, a body had been found in a villa in Tenerife. Their investigation showed it was owned by one of Thresham's subsidiary companies. The corpse could be the missing man and dental records and a DNA sample were being compared. Mrs Thresham would have to go there to formally identify the body. Clooney immediately offered to go with her, as did the girls. They all agreed that if it had happened they would tackle it together as a group and a family.

The meal was a subdued affair, the women were lost in their memories of the past. George was frozen, unsure what to say or do. They ate mechanically, they were honouring the booking, not really wanting to be there. Mandy was as ever busy organising but at last she grabbed all their attention. She had used her contacts, called in favours and they were booked on the morning flight to Tenerife from Birmingham, returning to Gatwick on Sunday evening, so they would still make the press conference.

What she didn't tell them was that this latest twist in the tale would certainly make them even more money. They paid up quickly and left, assuring the owners that the problem was the group's not the restaurant's. George collected his passport, clothes and other necessities from home then followed the girls to Loddington. Tonight would be yet another first, when he slept in the Thresham family home. But no one rested that night. There was a tension enveloping them all. Clooney drove them to the airport in comparative silence and only Mandy with her incessant calls and texts appeared at all normal.

Fortunately everything was on time and they had good seats. Jess fell asleep on his shoulder the moment they settled on board and the flight passed without event. Immediately upon landing they were allowed off the plane first. Local police escorted them to the municipal headquarters and as a unit they visited the morgue. Paula identified the body. It was Thresham. They completed the paperwork and by mid-afternoon it was final.

Mandy had arranged a hotel for them. She shared a twin with her mum, leaving Clooney and Jess with the delights of a double room. They were all emotionally exhausted and the heat outside made them glad they had the luxury of air conditioning in their spacious suite.

As they dozed naked beneath the top sheet Clooney's mind turned to the manner of Thresham's death. One shot to the head, gun in his hand, open and shut case of suicide, but no more. "Could someone have made his murder look like a self-inflicted killing? If it was so, did it matter?" George thought. But something niggled him at the corner of his mind, perhaps after a sleep he would sort it out.

They met up for dinner in the hotel's giant restaurant, full of holiday makers, noise and colour. The drab, sad foursome stood out like the proverbial sore thumb. To make matters worse Clooney was recognised by some football fans from Northampton and had to sign autographs while listening to their aimless chatter. In no time at all they finished up, and then retreated to Mandy's room.

All of them shared a bottle of wine. Paula was amazingly composed considering everything going on. She told them she had arranged for Thresham's body to be flown home for burial after the inquest; Abbots Undertakers had promised to take care of all the details. She had used them before, for the girls' father, and trusted them implicitly. It wasn't long before the sad group broke up and George and Jess returned to their room for the night.

The taxi collected them on time and they were back at the airport only thirty hours after they had arrived. Their flight to Gatwick was uneventful and they arrived only twenty minutes late. Express drivers and security guards met them and by six they were ensconced in the Kensington Hotel organised for them.

Mandy as ever had been busy arranging things. She was now working for both her mother and her sister, ensuring their privacy whilst at the same time making sure they would earn whatever possible from the sad affair. She would 'ghost' write their stories for them and was convinced with the interest that would be generated she would be busy for some time to come. The paper had arranged for new clothes to be delivered to their suites. Got to look at their best for the media tomorrow.

Over dinner she briefed them all on what not to say and how she thought the event might go. Afterwards Clooney caught up on his messages before the group broke up for the night. Jess wanted a touch of normality in their lives and persuaded him to join her in front of the TV, where the late garbage on offer washed over them. Michael McIntyre's show lightened their mood and an earlier night meant they had time to please each other before crashing into a deep sleep.

George woke at 4 a.m. needing the bathroom. It

was hard to believe that only two months ago he had never heard of Jess. Yet now their lives were so entangled it was almost impossible to separate them.

As agreed they met for breakfast in a private room. Mandy briefed them all again on the event. They had scheduled interviews at television studios throughout the day, collectively, individually and in pairs. Northampton police also wanted a meeting to talk about, as they put it, "the circumstances surrounding Thresham's death." Lindsay Paterson, Clooney's contact at Allsports, was demanding a meeting with her client prior to the press conference and George desperately wanted to catch up with Dave Evans. Mandy informed the group that she had arranged for them and Clooney's parents to stay at the Four Seasons hotel at Canary Wharf for the next two nights. This would protect them from the media, let them be available for her to get to television studios and generally allow her to control the group.

For a moment George was annoyed that she had set this up with his parents directly and not consulted him. But it passed. She was the expert and life was frantic enough as it was. Besides he couldn't wait for the two families to meet. So he let it go. Lindsay and Mandy were too similar and clashed over everything, so he was glad to leave it with them. Jess was looking after her mum and he was trying to remember all the instructions he had been given.

At that moment he spotted his boss. Together they shared a coffee and caught up on news from the club. "Mark Norman could do the job of covering for George," the Chairman said. If Wilson signed after a satisfactory medical, they could do it Thursday, giving Clooney time to get back for the unveiling of his first new player.

By the time the meeting was due to start over two

hundred representatives of the media worldwide were crammed into the conference room. Lindsay and Mandy were booking interviews for them, right left and centre. Then the room fell silent, as television presenter and professional media expert Paul McStay took to his feet. He was eye-catching with his looks, height 6' 5" and superb styling, but it was his Inverness accent that seduced and beguiled. All were putty in his hands. Whatever Mandy was paying him, he was worth every penny.

He handled proceedings with aplomb, in total control the whole time. The sensationalist press wanted to talk about Thresham's death and his links to organised crime, the sports press about the effect of all this on the new Kettering manager, and the women's magazines wanted to talk to Jess and her mum. It lasted nearly two hours before McStay closed the open session and the various members of Clooney's party dispersed for expensive private interviews with whoever had met the asking price.

Clooney was on Sky Sports News at 2 p.m. Jess on the BBC at the same time. Her mother was on the Six o'clock News for ITV. But all of them were on Channel 5 at various times, as the station was now owned by the *Express* group. Mandy arranged exclusives for American TV, radio and newspapers. They were asked the same questions a hundred times by a hundred different people, they were rushed from interview to interview, the whole day was a blur of people, places, faces, noise and fear, the worry of getting a question wrong, of saying something stupid, even worse of not knowing the answer.

It was almost 10 p.m. when they met again, this time in a private bar in their new hotel with its stunning views of Canary Wharf. Clooney phoned his parents' room and they quickly agreed to join the party. Though Jess and her family looked and felt more like they were recovering from a heavy party the night before, such had been their day.

When his folks arrived he introduced them to Mandy and her mum. They were delighted to see Jess again and she seemed just as pleased to meet up with them. Champagne was served, courtesy of the newspaper, then with everyone talking at once he tried to summarise events. Apparently even his folks now were being managed by Mandy and she was working on deals for them as well as everyone else. "Still, keeps it in the family," he thought. Jess sensed he was annoyed and took him to one side - she more than anyone knew what a control freak her sister was and she understood his annoyance. But she made him promise to stay cool, the pressure they were all under, particularly her mum, made her anxious that none of them should fall out.

George kissed her, promised to be good, then grabbed the opportunity to have a word with his dad. Clooney senior was not just coping but obviously enjoying the limelight. The accountant in him was looking forward to earning, whilst something in his male ego enjoyed the flattery and interviews. In just a couple of months, it seemed to George, his life and everyone he shared it with had changed for ever.

When he and Jess finally made it to bed she was amorous, funny and loving in a way that took all Clooney's negative thoughts away. In part it was her way of saying thanks, but also she had felt so proud of him she wanted him to know it.

They talked for hours, it seemed so rare they were alone together, they made up for it. Her mum had told her how she liked Clooney's parents. She could see herself becoming lifelong friends with his mum. It looked like all of them would do well financially out of the publicity; she just wished they could have a normal life whatever that was.

The two families breakfasted together before each was rushed off for another endless round of interviews, phone sessions, radio phone-ins, and television appearances. They couldn't wait for the evening, when he had top seats for *Blood Brothers* and a late supper specially arranged for them back in the hotel.

The show moved them all to tears, but it certainly took their minds off things. Over supper Clooney managed a rare conversation with his mother, before calling it a night. Mandy struck up some dialogue with him about commercial opportunities, but he wasn't in the mood and left her to say his goodnights to one and all before dragging Jess off to bed. Both of them felt shattered, and tomorrow it was back to Kettering and a meeting with the police before catching up on everything, then returning to work on Thursday. Neither needed any rocking as they unsurprisingly fell into a deep sleep.

As the train carried them towards Kettering, Clooney suddenly thought it was only forty-six days since he had scored that goal, and in thirty days time he would be leading pre-season training. Where had time gone and how was he going to find the time to sign new players and do the one hundred and one other things needed prior to the big kick off?

His folks were on the same train, but headed for Sheffield. Mandy stayed in London to keep up the good work as Jess and Clooney were going to stay with her mum for a few days. They said goodbye to his parents, promising to visit them soon. He couldn't remember his folks ever being so animated, so alive. Jess was having a positive effect on everyone.

With his car in Birmingham at the airport, they took a taxi from the station to her mum's house. Clooney phoned Blister, who willingly agreed to take him to the airport. On the way he told the old man his concerns about Thresham's supposed suicide. Blister told him to leave well alone. The kind of people he had mixed with you wouldn't want coming after you and if they had got Thresham perhaps a little bit of justice had been done. George thanked him, insisted on paying him, then drove back to collect the girls.

At Kettering police station they were told that the Spanish authorities and the local cops accepted Thresham's death as suicide and would not be pressing any further enquiries. Clooney couldn't have explained even to himself why that still made him uneasy. Back at work he had no time to think about anything but the season ahead and the next day he was to attend the first board meeting of the new group of directors Dave Evans had assembled.

The man himself took him for lunch and explained how he thought the event would go. It seemed even the club was earning from all the publicity surrounding Clooney. Season ticket sales were at record levels, sponsorship, advertising and executive boxes all selling like hot cakes and the media constantly at the ground. With the budget he had George was able to bring in more players and he discussed some of his targets with his boss, finding as ever, total support for his ideas. He finished his afternoon with some light training as he knew he was really out of shape, then met his assistant Mark Norman who had news about the trialists he had seen at Sunday's practice game. One, an Irish lad, over from Belfast on holiday, had stood out. Background checks showed he had been a youngster at Glasgow Rangers before homesickness had taken him back to Ireland. In the last two years he had played Gaelic football but the money in English football and a girlfriend in nearby Wellingborough had prompted him to join in the open trial game.

John Henderson was eighteen, tall, well built and a very gifted attacking midfielder who Mark believed could make and score a lot of goals for them, given a chance. Clooney watched a DVD of the match and after twenty minutes stopped it and told Mark to find Henderson and get him to the ground pronto, before someone else nabbed him.

Jess and her mum wanted to hear all about his day, as they ate their evening meal. Afterwards Clooney returned to his flat to pick up more clothes and his post. Playing his messages and collecting his mountain of mail, for the first time he realised just how much Jess had changed everything. This apartment, just a few months ago his dream pad, now seemed all wrong. Now he wanted with Jess to find their dream home, with a garden, a place one day to perhaps bring up kids. He realised he was getting old.

He called his folks. It seemed even his relatives in Canada had managed to earn from his story when they had been interviewed by Canadian television. His mum again told him yet again how happy she was he had found Jess, she couldn't resist asking again for the hundredth time though had they set a date yet? His dad was more interested in hearing about any actual or potential signings his son was making. Afterwards he read the long detailed message from Lindsay, setting out his earnings to date and future planned income. He was making twice as much now for not playing football as he was for doing it, which seemed like madness but it was true.

Mark rang, to confirm Henderson would be at the ground tomorrow for signing talks, which was good news. On that note George headed back to Loddington, his *fiancée* and his prospective mother in law. Yes, life really had changed.

John Henderson was also in love and had promised his girlfriend he would sign for Kettering and they would get a place together nearby. That being the case he accepted the first deal he was offered. Subject to passing his medical he would be a professional footballer by teatime.

The board meeting passed as smoothly as Dave had forecast. Financially the club was in better shape than most and all of the news coming out of the club now was positive. Everyone felt pleased with themselves. Clooney announced formally the signings of Paul Wilson and John Henderson although all the details were already known. He advised them of other possible signing targets and answered their many and varied questions. This was the bit the directors like talking about, the players, not the finances and the rules. When they concluded the day's business with a very late lunch Clooney couldn't help feeling he'd passed his first board meeting with honours.

Mark Norman brought him good news about Henderson's medical and they signed him on the spot. Though tomorrow, staged for publicity, they would go through the charade of having him sign in front of the media audience. All in all it had been a good day and it got even better when he returned home to find the love of his life waiting for him. Her mum had insisted that Jess go and spend some time with her *fiancée* and that she would actually manage without her, though she was grateful for all she had done.

Mandy was staying at her mum's for the weekend so Jess knew she could relax, not worry about her, but instead spend some time with her man. They decided to dine out in Rothwell, the restaurant where they should have eaten on their first date. The meal was good, the owner gave them wine on the house, people came up to their table and congratulated them, it was the perfect end to an amazing week. Later they made love and that also was perfect. As he fell asleep Clooney thought to himself how good his life was at present and he slept like a babe until morning. He woke before Jess and decided to go for a run, returning hot and sticky forty minutes later to be met by the aroma of fresh coffee and a kiss from the most beautiful woman in the world. While he was out his folks had phoned and Jess had agreed on his behalf that they would travel to Sheffield the next day for Sunday lunch. Sounded good to him and he showered and shaved before breakfast.

House cleaning, laundry, shopping and car washing then followed. "Oh the glamorous life of a football manager," Clooney thought. But deep down he was enjoying every minute of it. His life had a purpose and he was a very happy man. That night Jess cooked a meal for them, they talked about a wedding next year, about football, parents and Thresham's funeral. The whole spectrum of life, death and in between George thought, but wisely said nothing.

Chapter Twenty Two

Jess was greeted like visiting royalty on her first visit to the Clooney home in Sheffield. "Hope she likes turkey and vegetable pie!" George thought. His folks were celebrities in their own right now. They were going to be in one of the woman's weekly magazines and they had been interviewed on both local radio and television. Mandy had promised them lots more publicity as well, paid of course.

After lunch the two men adjourned to the study. Clooney senior was plainly excited and couldn't wait to show a picture he had found of the late Mr Thresham. It had appeared on the web, with the story of the discovery of the deceased's body in Tenerife. It had been taken at a golf club, all four men in the picture were in playing attire, gloves, shoes, clubs the lot. George didn't recognise any of them except the man himself and didn't see what his dad was so excited about. In the end his old man had to spell it out for him: Thresham was left handed.

Of course he was. George remembered the night at MotorGiant when Thresham had thrown a punch at him. He led with his left. So why use your right hand to shoot yourself? Clooney junior guessed the question, if not the answer. Had someone else pulled the trigger after all?

But why hadn't the police realised the same? If someone had killed him then who was it, and why? Was there a cover up? A hundred scenarios ran through his mind but no answers. Eventually George had an idea. Blister's son-in-law. He would know what to do - and Clooney had his number.

Detective Sergeant Burns picked up after only two rings. He listened to Clooney's ramblings, then suggested they meet later that evening at the flat. George agreed, sent his best wishes to Blister and wondered what, if anything, he should tell Jess. His dad suggested he did nothing for now. "Least said soonest mended and all that." Clooney was so quiet on the way home Jess worried and constantly asked him if he was alright. He bluffed his way through by saying he had football matters on his mind. He dropped her off at her mum's but didn't go in to see Mandy or his mother-in-law-to-be. When he sped off back to his flat he left a very concerned young lady behind, fighting back the tears as he roared away.

Arriving home, as usual he checked for emails, phone messages and he scanned Ceefax for the latest football news. He didn't have long to wait for his guest to arrive, but passed the time with a quick phone call home to his dad. Promising him he would phone again as soon as the policeman had left, which of course he forgot to do.

Vic Burns, not that Clooney would have thought to use his Christian name, arrived at nine on the dot. George showed him a copy of the image his dad had found and explained again about the fight he had with Thresham. Burns didn't seem quite his usual composed self. He asked for a drink and they both had a beer. Eventually the detective spoke.

"It was a locked room in Tenerife. There was a suicide note which Mrs Thresham read, then confirmed the writing as being her late husband's. No signs of a struggle, no other injuries to the victim. The Spanish police and the coroner were happy; and in the opinion of most decent people, it was goodbye to bad rubbish." So he was at a loss to know what Clooney expected him to do.

George knew something was not right, the detective didn't make eye contact, he looked uncomfortable and here he was being presented with potentially damaging evidence of a suicide perhaps being a murder. Yet he didn't want to know. Cover up, immediately sprang to mind - but by whom and for why, Clooney couldn't guess. But when the policeman suggested that it was best left alone, forgotten about and nothing further said he knew there was something wrong here and clammed up.

As he was about to leave Burns told him, in confidence, that his father-in-law was dying; Blister had terminal prostate cancer. The old soldier was coping well, but didn't want everyone knowing or making a fuss.

The news shook George. He had grown fond of Blister and he respected him very much. But surprising as the news was, even more perturbing was the way Burns had come out with it. Clooney determined to talk to the old man after the copper had left and, with little further conversation, Burns disappeared

George phoned Blister, there was no reply so he left a message sending his best wishes and promising to call and see him. Then, mind racing, he knew he had to talk to Jess and he made his way back to Loddington.

All three ladies were delighted to see him and Mandy brought him up to date on commercial activity. Paula talked to him about Thresham's funeral and Jess just wanted to get him on their own and find out what was going on. Mandy was working almost full time now on the story; updates for the *Express* on the lines of Thresham and the Clooneys; ghost writing her mother's book; arranging commercial opportunities for Jess, Paula and Clooney's parents - there seemed to be no end of money making schemes she had unearthed. Which reminded Clooney, he should talk to his agents and find out what was happening. Thresham's funeral was to take place on Thursday at Kettering Crem., then refreshments at the club afterwards. Paula had invited as many of Thresham's family, friends and business acquaintances as she knew, but how many would turn up was anyone's guess.

It was midnight and Jess and he bade everyone goodnight, before heading for the apartment. On the drive home he brought her up to date with everything. She cried when he told her about Blister and they had to stop the car so he could console her.

Although she was genuinely saddened to hear about the old man and confused about Thresham's death, she was actually relieved to know that this was what had been on Clooney's mind. She had begun to wonder if he was getting fed up with her. When she told him he was touched, hugged, kissed her and their love making was even more satisfying when they pledged their devotion to each other.

Afterwards they talked more about the possibility that Thresham's death was in fact murder, but agreed they were powerless to take an investigation further, given the disinterest shown by the police. Then Jess had a *eureka!* moment. Mandy, as an investigating journalist par excellence, she could make things happen - and they agreed to call her first thing in the morning. At last they could relax and sleep.

The phone rang at 7 a.m. It was Dave Evans, he wanted to see them both at the ground at 8.30 a.m. He had some great news for them that he wasn't prepared to discuss over the phone. They confirmed their attendance then contacted Mandy, who didn't seem as surprised at the news about Thresham as they were. She promised to see what she could do and get back to them. On that note they rushed around ready for the start of another amazing week in the life of George and Jess, soon to be Mr & Mrs Clooney.

The Chairman was waiting to greet them at the stadium. The news was, thanks to them though they didn't know it, International Organics the American food conglomerate were going to pay several million pounds to have their name on the stadium. In future Kettering's ground would be known as the International Organics Arena. Dave couldn't hide his excitement. It appeared the firm, which was owned by a Mormon family, had considered investing in a football club for some time, but were worried about some of the unsavoury publicity the clubs attracted. Kettering's commitment to charity had swung it for them, plus the positive press about Clooney and Jess.

Dave wanted to break out the champagne and celebrate, but George persuaded him that perhaps 9 a.m. was a touch early. The club also wanted Mandy to handle the media for them, for which the Chairman was prepared to pay. It seemed it was becoming very much a family affair Clooney thought, as Dave gave his sister-in-law- to-be a call and a delighted Jess kissed him before setting off to her office.

When Dave had finished on the phone they talked about football matters concerning the playing staff rather than off field attractions. Sixteen full time professionals were now committed to the cause. Seventeen if you included the player manager. There were four part timers and seventeen juniors making a total playing staff of thirty-eight.

George would have liked at least another three full

timers. They had no real cover for their keeper except for a sixteen year old in the juniors, and he would have liked another experienced central defender to start the season. Dave threw names at him and they checked the PFA lists as to who was available. Nobody seemed to fill the gap immediately, so they agreed to put feelers out through agents, scouts and contacts. After covering another dozen topics in the next hour, Clooney finally made it to his own office for 10.30 a.m. just as training started.

He joined the lads, the few who had bothered to turn up that is, in a series of warming up exercises, then spent an hour with them before a telephone call sent him running back to his desk. He felt so unfit, he really was going to have to get back to some serious training he thought, but as for when, who knows. The urgent call was from Lindsay, his handler at Allstars Allsports Agency. He had been offered a chance to appear on Sky Sports that night. They were covering a veteran's match for charity at nearby Northampton's ground and being close by and such a personality were willing to pay handsomely for his attendance.

He would have turned it down, but Lindsay cautioned him that it would get his foot in the door with the nation's bigger broadcasters of football, so he reluctantly agreed. She would be at the game herself looking out for him and bring him up to date on the deals in the pipeline, so no early night for him then.

He met with his assistant Mark Norman. More problems it seemed. Jack Condent, a promising young mid-fielder, had been arrested for dealing. Wonderful! He would get a short jail sentence no doubt but would not be available to play for a few months. "The dickhead," Clooney thought. Kevin Gillespie the veteran winger had asked to leave, his wife wanted to get back to elderly parents in the North East and he had to follow her or else. That was a shame because he was a good man and a good player, but there was no point trying to keep him in the circumstances. Four players would definitely miss the season's start through injury and Bobby Carstairs was a doubt about ever playing again. Mark was worried, but his mood lightened when George told him of the news about International Organics sponsorship.

They grabbed an early lunch in the club's restaurant and discussed potential signings. One of whom, Northampton reserve keeper Brendan O'Grady, Clooney knew. The Irishman and he had played together before the Australian debacle. George knew what a good lad he was, as well as a useful stopper. He would probably be at tonight's game, so he might be able to speak with him. Although O'Grady was keeping fit by training with the Cobblers, as they were nicknamed, they had not offered him a new deal, so he was a free agent. Better still.

A few of the game's top managers had sent Clooney a congratulatory note on his appointment. The legend himself, Sir Alex at Man U, had been particularly kind, offering advice if required. "Dare I ask him for some loan players?" Clooney thought. He left Mark to carry on with various matters and presented himself at Judie Green's office for a meeting with her and Vice Chairman Colin Thompson. She had drafted over one hundred letters for him to sign; replies to fans, suppliers, agents, charities, police, fire, ambulance, Uncle Tom Cobbley and all! He started straight away while Colin talked about budgets, future plans and actions required by him. By the time he returned to his own office his head was spinning.

At last Jess joined him for a cuppa and they agreed he would go to Northampton while she looked after mum.

He dropped her off at the house then made his way to the Sixfields stadium. The Sky studio was easy to find, and after a briefing from tonight's show presenter Richard Hawkins he was made up and ready. He read the background notes provided, then they did some 'dummy' discussions to check sound and light levels but also to prepare him for what lay ahead.

They game was light hearted, played at a walking pace with lots of famous names on show and lots of goals. Clooney felt he handled the occasion well and at the reception afterwards met up with Lindsay whilst keeping an eye open for Brendan O'Grady.

Lindsay showed him a photo from a Canadian magazine featuring Ross and Cynth his relatives. There were pictures of him and his folks taken on his recent trip and Lindsay assured him they had earned well from it. Spotting O'Grady he excused himself and chatted with the player and Brendan agreed to meet George at Kettering the following day. "Looking good," Clooney thought.

Lindsay had arranged a fair bit of work for him, but it meant he was going to have to make himself more available to the needs of the people paying him. She had drawn up a schedule requiring his presence every Thursday for the next few weeks. Well this week was out with the funeral, he told her.

She had done well though, a free Swiss watch worth £5,000 and £50,000 over two years to appear in adverts for them. He had to say something like, "For a player manager there aren't enough hours in a day, but I always know the right time thanks to my watch!" MotorGiant were offering him a free car and £15,000 a year for two years. Well, that one he would have to think about, given the history. Style Suits had offered him lots of clothes and £30,000 a year to promote them and there were dozens more. It all seemed a joke to Clooney but it sure was a rich one.

People interrupted them for an autograph, a photo, or to recommend someone. George was courteous to them all and Lindsay reckoned he was a natural on the box and at meeting and greeting. She said she felt inspired to find him even more work. They said their goodbyes, and George headed back to Kettering to collect Jess. Listening to his voice messages, there were lots of congratulatory ones and a message from Blister asking him to call. Tomorrow promised to be another busy day, but he was loving it.

Jess was meeting with the marketing people from International Organics so she was on the train to London, Clooney dropping her off at the station before heading to the ground. It was her birthday in August, the twenty sixth he remembered, perhaps he would get her a car as a present. After all he seemed to be making lots of dosh.

At the ground he filled Mark in on O'Grady. His assistant was mighty impressed by the way Clooney had handled himself on TV. Clooney sensed his remarks were genuine as well. George trained as hard as anyone that morning and felt better for it. Later, after a shower and a change of clothes, he concentrated on his office jobs. Several hundred emails for a start and only thirty of them spam. O'Grady phoned to see if 2 p.m. was alright, George confirmed yes, then phoned Dave Evans to let him know. The Chairman remembered Brendan from a Northants senior cup game a couple of seasons back, when only O'Grady's prowess between the sticks had denied Kettering a win. He wished Clooney well and rang off.

When Brendan arrived they got straight down to business. O'Grady was thirty-two and looking for a three year contract. He lived in Holcot, a village between

Northampton and Kettering, and would like to stay there, so he was looking for some permanency. After some debate on bonuses, signing on fees, testimonials, image rights and the rest, the deal was done, subject as always to a medical. Clooney phoned Dr. Cresswell, the club's honorary medic, and he agreed to see Brendan at six if he was willing, which he was, so with a bit of luck that bit of business could be put to bed that night. They shook hands and Brendan left.

Clooney bought some beers and headed for Blister's. He felt guilty he had not seen the old soldier for so long. On the way his mum phoned for a chat and as usual asked the inevitable: "Have you set a date yet?" Clooney laughed at her, asked after his dad, then finished the call as he arrived at Blister's.

The old man was glad to see him. He looked older and thinner but otherwise no different. After a beer, shared, Clooney brought Blister up to date on events. The old soldier thought he was doing well and told him so. When they talked about Thresham, which was inevitable, Blister shared Clooney's view that the death did look suspicious. When George queried "Why, then, are the police doing nothing?" Blister remained silent. Clooney promised to visit again, said goodnight and headed for the apartment.

Answering machine messages, emails, texts dealt with, he listened to some music, relaxed with a beer and waited for Jess. She burst in shortly after him. Happy, exhausted and full of her day. International Organics were offering all kinds of support apart from financial: secretarial equipment even, perhaps a free plug on their packs. But they needed to know exactly what was going on the players strips and they needed to know now. Jess had been talking to a charity called CFAB - Children and Families Across Borders - and she wanted to help them. Mandy was in agreement so that was alright then, and when George said yes they were able to call it a night.

Jess was involved in funeral agreements and spent the day with her mum. Clooney got the nod from Dr Cresswell about Brendan's medical and he phoned Dave Evans with the news. The Chairman was clearly delighted and asked George to get him signed that day, but hold the story until Monday. That way they would get the headlines after the media had concentrated on Thresham's funeral.

Clooney trained hard, aware he didn't feel quite so bad and was perhaps getting fitter. Over lunch O'Grady and the Chairman signed the paperwork. Brendan didn't have an agent, which made life easier. After their new player left, a hesitant George explained about his commercial activity and the probable need to take Thursdays off. He was pleasantly surprised to discover that caused his boss no problem at all. It all promoted the name of the club, Dave told him. He was also pleased to learn about the potential tie up with CFAB, promising to check them out and let George and Jess know by Friday. As the Chairman the decision, as with most, would be up to him. But at least he seemed on side.

A couple of hours in the office followed, with Mark Norman, Judie and others, before at five he felt brave enough and had the time to call Sir Alex. His secretary informed him her boss was elsewhere on business but would make sure he called George on his return. "Oh yes and pigs might fly," Clooney mused, before calling it a day.

All three women were subdued that evening. Paula put on a brave face but she looked drawn and nervous, she busied herself with everything and nothing. Jess shook, had tears in her eyes and clutched him for support constantly. But most surprising of all was Mandy. Normally loud, sure of herself, strong, she had retreated into her own private world. She hardly spoke, didn't smile and might as well have not been there for all she contributed to the proceedings.

Clooney worked hard to support the girls, making light conversation, boosting them and making sure they ate. His parents fortunately arrived at nine and they dived in. His mum and Paula disappeared for a chat. His dad tried to engage Mandy in conversation, leaving George able to devote time to the love of his life. It was a difficult time, but Clooney felt proud of his folks, who had volunteered for this unenviable task and had done it for him.

Much later, with all the females settled, Clooney and his father enjoyed a whiskey nightcap before bed. Two large glasses of Highland Park single malt with the same again of water no ice. To be sipped and enjoyed while they chatted or silently gazed into space, content with each other's company, the drink and the moment.

Emotionally exhausted, George later slid into bed alongside the sleeping Jess and pondered for a while on the ordeal waiting the next day before falling into the deep sleep his body desperately needed.

It was a dry day, but dull, making life easier for those attending the service at Kettering Crematorium. Clooney couldn't believe how many had turned out. Mandy reminded him that many were there to see Kettering's own version of Posh and Becks, not to pay respect to the deceased. He supported Jess on his arm; his dad, gentlemen as ever, escorted Paula; while Mandy as always did her own thing, one minute chatting animatedly to Dave Evans, the next on her own. He had never seen her quite like this before.

Mercifully the service was brief. If any of Thresham's blood relatives were there they didn't make themselves known. Television and radio crews shared the limited space available with journalists from around the world. George spotted several of his players in the crowd, as well as the mayor of Kettering and other local dignitaries. The police kept all of them at bay as the mourners' cars left in a procession for the reception at the Kettering Park Hotel.

Around a hundred or so shared drinks and a buffet in the private suite set aside for them. As well as supporting his *fiancée*, Clooney found time to exchange remarks with various guests as well as being interviewed by the BBC. On his way to the gents he spotted Mandy in the bar on her own; on the way back he went to speak to her. That she was worse for wear was putting it mildly. She clutched at the bar with one hand while she grabbed at a glass with the other. Clooney spoke kindly to her and persuaded her to re-join them in the main suite.

It was evening when they returned to Loddington. Clooney made hot drinks for the ladies, sufficient alcohol had been consumed to last a week. His dad joined him in the kitchen. Conversation was stilted, though when they returned to football it took a surprising twist.

The 'Owls', Sheffield Wednesday, were in such dire financial straits they had today released lots of players, juniors and seniors, and one of them the old man raved about. Amazingly, as he like his son was a lifelong 'Blades' supporter, but even a biased Sheffield United fan would have liked to have Tony Miller on their books. The former Scotland U21 defender was comfortable anywhere in the defence. He was thirty-three years old, 6'2", had very few injuries in his career and was now a free agent. George phoned Mark Norman, who agreed here was someone they could definitely use, and, given Clooney's personal commitments, he volunteered to follow up on it.

George thanked his dad for that lead and they re-joined the ladies. Mandy was still behaving out of character. Quiet, withdrawn; but as everyone else was subdued it seemed only Clooney noticed. His parents set off to stay at George's flat, while he was going to keep Jess company with her mum and Mandy.

Inevitably it was Mandy and he who were the last ones standing and she started drinking again. 'Here goes," he thought, "more trouble." But he daren't leave her so he sat back, prepared to listen.

The house was quiet. In the lounge Clooney and Mandy sat facing each other. George nursed his drink, sipping from it occasionally, while Mandy continued to pour wine like it was going out of fashion. For a while neither spoke, then Mandy couldn't stop. There were tears, pauses for breath and drink, then, like an express train, she was away again. Clooney just listened and nodded. Then, when she finished, he squeezed her hand, offering comfort, support or maybe just an acknowledgement that he understood, was not judgmental and cared.

Mandy's rambling had ranged over her hurt at her real father's death, how she missed him and how sure she was that Thresham was responsible for his killing, because from all she had learned it was not an accident. She described how one night, when preparing for bed, she had realised her step-father was watching her change and she had known from that day to be wary of him. Meeting Karrina had been the real beginning of her quest to bring Thresham to account. The more she had learned of his criminal activities, she knew she had got to free her mother from this monster. Then when she heard he had fled justice, in her anger she had sought Blister's help. The old soldier, who hated Thresham as much as she did, had done the rest. He had nothing to lose now, he was dying, she couldn't tell her mother and Jess the truth and Clooney was the only person in the world she trusted enough to share her guilt with. Now it was up to him what happened next.

Amanda was asleep and snoring. Her story told, she had been at last able to relax. Clooney covered her with an overcoat from the downstairs cloakroom and left her to her dreams or nightmares, whatever they might be.

He made himself a mug of tea and moved into the study where he sat and enjoyed the total silence while attempting to make sense of the revelations Mandy had decided he alone should share. The big question as George saw it, was should he tell the police, confront Blister and how about keeping secrets from Jess? Some people say information is power. To him it seemed a curse.

Birdsongs announcing it was dawn woke him. His neck ached and he needed a wee; as he stood at the downstairs loo he still couldn't decide what was best, so decided for the time being to say nothing. Glancing at his reflection in the mirror he was shocked how old and rough he looked. Although he was apparently making lots of money, he definitely looked like he'd paid a price. Still, "Whoever said things come easy?" he thought. He checked in on Mandy, still asleep, still snoring. Upstairs he grabbed some casuals and set off for an early morning run, hoping to clear his head, flush out the booze and help himself make some decision. He wasn't sure a slow by his standards trip round the deserted village achieved any of that, but when he got back the first cup of coffee of the day sure tasted good.

He was in his office by nine. Jess would not be returning to work until Monday. All of them were still in bed when he had left the house that morning. There were dozens of messages and hundreds of emails to catch up on and, before he had dealt with a fraction of them, Mark Norman had arrived. Tony Miller was prepared to talk to them and another twenty clubs it seemed; then he would decide who to join. As far as Mark could tell he was after a three year contract, a decent car, and the most money he could get. No different from most of the others then.

Mark had compiled overnight video footage from the net of some of Miller's games, he had spoken to one of his mates who used to play with Tony for Scotland, and generally collated all the info he could on the man. Both of them agreed he would be a fantastic signing if they could get him, and Clooney phoned the Chairman to let him know their plans.

Dave Evans said yes, yes, yes several times to show his approval. He also confirmed the go ahead for CFAB to be the shirt sponsors but he wanted it kept secret 'til Mandy could organise the details. Which caused George to forget about football for a while and consider instead what he did with the information he now had? For the moment though that was nothing. Instead he joined the lads for training, his second attempt at keeping fit that day, not bad when it was only 10 a.m.

The mood within the squad was good. It was an exciting time to be part of the club, most of the players were enjoying all the publicity and all could feel fantastic times lay ahead. He grabbed a quick call to Jess after training. She had a brainwave, why didn't they go to Sheffield stay with his folks, take them out for a meal as a thank you for their help over the funeral, and he could meet up with Tony Miller. "Brilliant!" he thought, as she went off to ask his mum and he set up a meeting with the player.

Dave Evans popped in to catch up and the rest of

the morning was spent on football matters. Tony Miller agreed to meet at Clooney's parents' house the next day and George confirmed it with his dad. Lindsay phoned, checking he was available to be in London for commercial meetings and interviews. She had spoken to several garages and obtained offers of a car for Jess, no bother. But the best of the lot came from no less than his old employers! Checking the date he realised it was now the third week of June. Two weeks before the entire playing staff reported back for pre-season assessment and training and he was still at least three players short. He reminded Mark Norman to concentrate on remedying this as they walked to the restaurant for lunch. He joined the queue for his self-service choice of food and spotted Mandy talking to Dave Evans at a nearby table. He would for now have preferred to avoid her, but Dave waved him over.

Then Julie Green burst in, phone in hand, hardly able to conceal or control her excitement. It was Sir Alex on the phone for him and it wasn't a wind up.

The whole place was quiet as he listened to the words of Manchester United's manager, one of the greatest leaders football had ever known. His help and generosity to other managers was legend, but now Clooney was discovering for himself the charm and the charisma of the great man. He knew all about George it seemed, congratulated him on his achievements and promised help and advice if required. Clooney was gob-smacked at his kindness and his interest. But he recovered in time to ask if there were any players he could borrow on loan. Sir Alex promised to think about it, invited him up to Old Trafford to watch a game and wished him well for the new season. It was unbelievable.

Dave Evans patted him on the back to wish him well done and the whole restaurant stood and applauded him, not that he had done anything, but it felt amazing nonetheless. The rest of lunch passed in a blur and he found himself back at his desk with just Mandy for company.

Over tea they said little. Then she asked him what he was going to do with the news she'd given him. After a moment's thought he told her he still didn't know, that he needed to speak to Blister and for now would not be telling anyone anything. Mandy gave him a sisterly kiss and left, saying she was sure he would do the right thing and that she was glad she had told him. With an effort he returned to the more mundane work associated with the job, putting the high drama aside for the time being.

That afternoon he decided to put the past behind him regarding MotorGiant Northampton, and he phoned Lindsay to tell her he would accept their offer as he wanted a nice little sports car for Jess. He could always get her something else for her birthday. Spend some of his own money perhaps. God, he realised, he was becoming one of those people he despised, the sort who wouldn't cross the street to help a dying man unless he was being paid. Not a pretty thought.

A fan of the club now domiciled through work in south Wales had written in about a winger formally at Swansea. A local lad called Bryn Jones, he had as a seventeen year old looked a world beater until the spotlight had burnt him so to speak and he had stupidly got drunk, crashed a car and slightly injured a pedestrian. All made worse by the fact he was only a learner driver without insurance and he had run away from the scene. The letter writer was the boy's uncle, through marriage. He assured Clooney this was totally out of character for the lad and the six months he'd done inside had marked young Jones to such an extent he'd never break the law again - ever.

Clooney didn't remember the story or it had never reached Australia but out of instinct he phoned his Welsh Chairman Dave Evans for guidance. His boss was very familiar with the details and promised to make some urgent enquiries and get back to him - but for now it was time to meet the "wife".

Clooney and his new family enjoyed, if that was the right word, an Indian takeaway that night. Mandy seemed more like her normal self, Paula was a real star, hiding her sorrow while being the perfect host, and Jess, she was just herself: sad, needy, yet supportive to her mum, loyal to her sister, loving to her *fiancé* and caring for the rest of the world. He longed to get her on her own and embrace her.

Paula had made some decisions. She would sell the house and buy something in Kettering. It held few pleasant memories and it was high maintenance. For a while she was going to stay with Mandy, away from the goldfish bowl she felt she was inhabiting at present. Clooney's aunt and uncle in Canada, Ross and Cynth, had invited her to stay with them. Though they had never met they had spoken on the phone, got on well and she thought she might take them up on that kindness. The two families continued to develop even closer ties George felt, and he was both pleased and proud.

Being selfish, he hoped this would mean that he and Jess could get some time together at last, maybe even plan a wedding? Have a bit of fun and get back to normal whatever normal was. The girls, despite some reservations, were in agreement with their mum's wishes and the mood was lifted by the conversation. They even felt able to relax in front of the box and watch a rerun of *Who Wants to be a Millionaire*. Shouting out the answers and even laughing as the evening drew to a close.

Finally alone, Jess and Clooney whispered together while clutching each other beneath the quilt of their bed. George brought her up to date on matters at the football club, she gave him her thoughts and ideas about the future, their wedding and a whole lot else. Later their lovemaking was slow and passionate, deeply rewarding for both, as they ended this particularly stressful week with a relief of tension both needed. Afterwards, comfortable, satisfied, safe and happy, they fell asleep in each other's arms.

After breakfast they drove over to the flat, checked mail and messages, changed clothes then headed north arriving at his parent's home around noon. They lunched on salad and pizza. He wondered if he'd upset his mum. Then she reminded him that as they were dining out that night something simple seemed appropriate midday. While the girls cleared up, Clooney and his father whispered in the garden. His dad believed he should meet up with Blister sooner rather than later or it might never happen given the old man's illness.

Tony Miller's arrival interrupted everything and after brief introductions and pleasantries the player and George retreated to his father's study for some serious discussions. Clooney took an instant liking to the Scotsman and though he didn't know it the feeling was reciprocated. Millar had been stunned when his contract had not been renewed. He knew the club was struggling financially, it was there for all to see, peeling paintwork at the stadium, minimum staff, great discussion about the most minor of purchases, but it was still a shock to be let go. At least in his case there was tons of interest, almost too much for him to choose. Clooney, demonstrating a natural instinct for management rather than a style he had been taught, turned the conversation on its head. He didn't attempt to sell

Kettering at this point, but rather congratulated the player on being popular and asked him what he wanted out of life and what if anything he could bring to Clooney's club.

Miller launched into his financial requirement, paid house move, travel and accommodation paid until he moved, signing-on bonus, new car, wages, three year contract, loyalty bonuses, image rights payments, the usual catalogue of demands that most players trotted out. Then he reminded George of his career to date, his forty-two caps and his Player of the Year awards. Clooney let him finish, paused, then reminded him he'd missed the point, what did he really want out of life and what could he bring to the club? The player was stunned, not really understanding what he was being asked, baffled as to how he should reply. George was in control now. He remembered the old *Huckleberry Finn* story about someone being stuck painting a fence instead of playing with his friends, and how the novel's hero had made the chore appear such a great time others had begged to join in.

Borrowing from that and the vision and the passion of Dave Evans he explained how different to any other club Kettering was. He told him about the Chairman and his dream of returning football to the people, of the commitment to charity. How the profile of the club now was such that the world's media was camped on their doorstep, more Real Madrid than Football League two. How players from all over the world were clamouring to join, how the sky was the limit for all involved. He told him about International Organics, about Jess, about the mood and the optimism, then he asked him again, what could he bring to the club to make them want him?

Clooney stayed silent, the pressure was now on Miller. Previously all those other clubs who had come calling had done the hard sell, how much they would pay, how much they wanted him, but George hoped he'd turned the tables by demanding the player sell himself rather than the approach he believed the rivals for his signature had taken. Tony proved his mettle, that he was indeed the man for the job with his reply. He told Clooney how at thirty-one he'd become a father for the first time, the boy Duncan was now two years old, they had resorted in the end to IVF treatment and been lucky. To him it was the most important happening in his life, his son, and for the first time probably had made him think about the future. He knew he only had a few years left as a player. He was already taking his coaching badges, studying management and trying to read up all he could on business, how it worked and whatever. In three years' time, at thirty-six, no one might want him as a player; he was planning for that day. He owed it to his son and his long suffering wife Lucy. They lived in Grindleford in the Peak District of Derbyshire, in a beautiful stone cottage in one of the most scenic parts of the world. He would keep the house, rent it as an investment and buy something near the club he moved to, but everything had to be right for all his family or he wasn't interested. Lucy googled the prospective area he might move to and had spotted a property in Bedfordshire that might suit them, only thirty minutes from the ground. So nothing was a problem. As to what he could bring to the club he was sure with his experience and his attitude to life now anyone signing him would get the model pro. Good trainer, experienced useful player, committed to the cause and thinking seriously about the future; not a gambler, womaniser, drinker or drug user. So yes Kettering did seem like the right place to him but equally he was the right man for the club.

"I've got him," thought Clooney when the man

finished. "Shit, I've bloody done it." There was a long silence, and then Clooney offered a handshake. He told Tony he would fit in at Kettering and why didn't he and his family travel down and meet Dave Evans, see the ground, view that house and the area and, if he then still believed it was right for all concerned, have a medical, agree terms, job done. Miller agreed.

They talked about matters then over a tea George's dad deliberately made so he could meet and chat with the player. Inevitably they both knew many of the same footballers, had enjoyed similar experiences in the game and because of their respective ages shared similar views of the world and had even enjoyed an upbringing not dissimilar to one another. Tony's dad was manager of an insurance brokerage in Aberdeen, he was an only child and like Clooney had briefly lived and played abroad when he had a spell with German side Bayern Munich early in his career. Both men instantly had got on and the more they talked the better it got.

Leaving his dad to keep up the hospitality Clooney phoned his Chairman from the garden. In football parlance Dave was 'over the moon' at the thought of capturing such a signing. He promised to book Miller and his family into a nice hotel for Sunday and Monday night if they travelled down tomorrow. They could look at houses, he would lay on a driver, guide, to show them the best spots then meet at the club after breakfast Monday, wow him, medical, sort out the deal and he would be one of their players by lunch time. Press conference Tuesday to let the rest of the world know. Job done.

Clooney re-joined his dad and Tony, smiling to himself as yet again Dave Evans's enthusiasm and praise had made him feel good. Tony was agreeable to the

Chairman's plans, thanked George and, after briefly meeting the Clooney ladies, said his goodbyes and left.

The ladies approved of Tony Miller, as did his father. For being the one who alerted them to his availability, dinner tonight was on Dave Evans. He had insisted when Clooney called him. As they passed the afternoon in pleasant banter George realised just how content with life he was. He didn't even protest when Jess told him she had decided on a May wedding. So, at the end of next season, football finished, Jess and he would tie the knot. Very sensibly he left all the arrangements to the girls.

His folk's favourite eatery was the Dore Grill, an inexpensive, old fashioned, Spanish owned restaurant in one of the poshest parts of the city. The owner and his family had been friends for years and he always enjoyed his visits there. Such was the mood of the moment that Clooney persuaded Jess to make love before they went out to eat. The first time they ever had been so intimate in his parents' house. For both of them it was something special, another new beginning they felt, after a rather bizarre courtship to date.

The taxi collected them on time and, while on the way, more good news was received. Dave Evans phoned to tell them to enjoy themselves and go heavy on the champagne if they liked, for he had just heard from South Wales; Bryn Jones was also arriving at the club on Monday for possible signing talks. Though he wouldn't of course be driving given his past. George was thrilled and told his boss, "Well done and have a drink on me!" which promoted a funny if somewhat rude answer in return.

Chapter Twenty Three

As they drank and were merry, George truly believed this heralded the start of better times. If Miller and Jones did both sign, coupled with the other acquisitions he'd made, he could see them challenging for promotion rather than fighting against relegation as everyone would expect. The evening was memorable and hopefully was the first of many to be enjoyed with the owners Joe and Delores.

Later, when Jess and his mum had gone to bed, George and his dad enjoyed a nightcap and finally discussions regarding Thresham's death. Neither knew quite what to do for the best. Clooney senior advised his son still to refrain from telling Jess. "Why spoil her obvious happiness for no reason?" he argued. George was determined to speak to Mandy and see what she thought and then he would have to speak to his *fiancée* - she couldn't be the only family member not to know. Anyway it was late and time for sleep, so without further ado they bid each other goodnight.

The next day after a mid-morning brunch, Jess and Clooney set off for Kettering. Both comfortable with the silence in the car, as their minds considered future plans. His the week ahead and football, hers the wedding. At Loddington they checked the house was okay. Jess's mum had gone to stay with Mandy. Then, home at last, the two of them could relax. Electronic mail read, messages listened to, they switched on the music, turned down the lights and enjoyed the moment.

Tomorrow Jess was being interviewed by local radio. They wanted to come to the ground to ask her about her role with the club, but George had persuaded her to go to them, he didn't want them knowing what was going on that day: breakfast meeting with the Chairman, then hopefully some players to sign. Tony Miller was due in at 11, Bryn Jones at 2.

Dave Evans was in fine spirits. He told Clooney all season tickets were now sold, as was all sponsorship and perimeter advertising and there was now a waiting list for the vice president's club. Despite the precarious times the club really was bucking the trend. International Organics had booked the ground for their sales conference, press launch and staff open day. Mandy, who else, was organising it for next week and would be detailing George at the special meeting at 5 that day. They agreed the monies they were prepared to offer Miller and Jones; then the Chairman swept off to his next meeting, giving Clooney the chance for a quick training session and a chat with Mark Norman before Tony Miller arrived.

The Scotsman was on time and had been impressed by the hotel and the general area. Yesterday they had looked at properties in the villages and towns around Rutland Water. His wife had taken a fancy to Oakham and Stamford and he had left her in their room, trawling the net for properties in that area. They got straight down to business. Tony had been impressed by Clooney's different approach and it appealed to him being at the start of something new and exciting, but equally he wasn't daft either and had a list of demands to be met in return for his signature.

Clooney studied the list in front of him. It was so

similar to what he and the Chairman had agreed it wasn't worth arguing over the difference. Bingo, it was done, they shook hands and while George set up the player's medical Mark Norman took the latest signing on a tour of the ground. Clooney phoned Dave Evans with the news. He was in a meeting, but would do doubt pick up the voicemail at the earliest opportunity. Mandy called, putting back their meeting by twenty-four hours. It suited him. He heard from Lindsay: Thursday was looking pretty full with interviews, photo shoots, personal appearances and more meetings. MotorGiant were offering Jess a Peugeot 207 Cabriolet in silver with red and black leather interior, only six thousand miles on the clock and a two year warranty. He agreed on the spot. It would be fun meeting them again after all that had happened. Mandy asked him to call, as did Blister, his folks, several players' agents and numerous newspapers. He would get round to them all eventually but first he called Jess. Her interview had gone well, she thought and was being broadcast at 1.30 p.m. He promised to listen before Jones arrived. Then it was paperwork and phone calls until he and Mark Norman met up for lunch.

"His assistant was flying," thought Tony Miller, "the best signing the club had ever made, apart from the boss!" He was looking forward now to meeting Bryn Jones. Dave Evans appeared, Mark got up to leave but the Chairman signalled him to stay. All were elated at the Wednesday captain's joining them, but for now discussion revolved around their next target, the young Welshman. All the Chairman's research in his home country had determined the lad was a great prospect who had made one silly mistake and, provided he didn't repeat it, could go on to be a fantastic acquisition.

The three of them then listened to the future Mrs

Clooney on the radio and all had to agree the girl done good. The club was now generating as much media coverage as any of the top sides in the country, with stories about them popping up all over the place. It was a far cry from a few years ago when they had almost gone out of business. Their daydreaming came to an abrupt end when reception buzzed to announce the arrival of the young Welshman.

Bryn Jones was nineteen years old, fresh from prison, very embarrassed and carefully considering his future. His contract had been cancelled by Swansea, so he was a free agent and much in demand. Knowing other clubs would be trying to sign him and sell him their advantages Clooney took the tack that his club offered the boy the perfect place and the perfect environment for him to demonstrate he had learned from his experiences. He could get involved with charity efforts, be seen to be doing his bit, and as the club grew he would grow with it. Everything George said seemed to strike the right chord, as the lad nodded yes to every point that was made. But the icing on the cake that probably swung the deal was Dave Evans. As a young man Bryn's father had played briefly alongside the Kettering Chairman. He had told his son that whatever else could be said about George's boss he was a true Welshman, a man of his word, and, for that reason as much as anything, Clooney got his man.

Jess cooked a meal for them that evening and both had much to say about their respective day. All of it good. As they settled in front of the television all jobs done for once, they were able to think about other things than the club.

Wedding plans and house moves were the order of the day and both enjoyed the process of planning things together, rather than alone. Blister's daughter phoned to say her dad had asked Clooney to visit him if he could. The old man's health was declining fast but she apologised for bothering him; George was there within the hour. Blister's pallour was grey; he didn't even get out of his chair to greet his visitor. Babs, as he referred to his offspring, produced tea and biscuits before leaving them to talk.

Clooney was able to tell him about the new signings, not to be announced publicly until tomorrow and all the other happenings. The old man was genuinely pleased for him. But he wanted to impart news of his own before it was too late. Since his wife's death he had just been marking time, he said. Then, when he had the chance to help George and at the same time have a go at Thresham, he'd jumped at it. For a while it had felt good, but in reality nothing had changed, except Thresham was dead and he would be soon. He had grown fond of George and Jess and was sure they would do well together, of that he had no doubt, but he felt bad that he hadn't put them completely in the picture about that man's demise.

Blister would always hold Thresham responsible for his wife's death. He had cost him a best friend, his daughter her mum, and his grandkids a grandmother. Life had changed for ever the day she passed away, everyone who loved her moved through each day because they had to, but it was only existing, not living. When Mandy had been to see him they had shared a hatred for one man, a wish to see him punished and a fear he would escape justice again, as he had so many times before. Blister admitted he had spoken to some of the lads he knew, serving soldiers and recently retired ones. The word was out that there was a score to be settled, a job to be done.

Two days later a caller had explained it was completed, no names, no pack drill, no reward sought. But a signed confession had been posted through the old man's letterbox and he gave it to Clooney to read. After all the shocks of the last couple of months this one shouldn't have surprised George, but it did.

Thresham confessed that he had killed Jess and Mandy's father, to prevent him blowing the whistle on the crook's activities. He went on to admit to many and various other misdemeanours before ending with no regrets, not one cry for forgiveness. Clooney tried to hand the note back but was told it was his to keep. Now, yet again, it was up to him what he did with the information. As he sat and pondered his actions he realised Blister had fallen asleep, so, quietly as he could, he left the room, said his goodbyes to Babs, and drove home.

He sat in the lane behind the flat, switched off the car's engine and thought long and hard about his next move. Did he tell her about her father's murder by the step-father she grew up with, or did he keep quiet? He phoned his dad for advice. The last few months had brought him and his parents closer than they had been for years. Clooney senior advised him to sleep on it, then they could talk again tomorrow, a sentiment George shared. Then after a few words with his mum he returned home to Jess.

She was waiting for him in her dressing gown and nothing else. For the first time in their relationship he lied to her. Assuring her that Blister just wanted to chat about football, he succeeded in putting her concern to rest to such an extent that off came the gown and they made love on the floor. In the remaining time before going to bed to sleep they discussed wedding plans. There was a hotel by Rutland Water Jess would like to marry at and Dave Evans had promised to sail with her over the reservoir from his lakeside home. Quite an entrance for the bride on what was otherwise to be a simple affair. Clooney agreed to visit the hotel with her the following weekend and check it out.

A last check of the electronic mail turned up few surprises and Mandy had confirmed tomorrow's meeting agenda, which he scanned with little enthusiasm. Sir Alex Ferguson had followed up his call with confirmation of an open invite to visit him in Manchester. "What an amazing guy he is," was Clooney's last thought of the day.

The new car was delivered to the club and Jess was thrilled, surprised and even happier, if that was possible, than she ever had been. The media turned out in force to meet the new signings, and Clooney finished work with Mandy discussing the International Organics' day at the ground.

Basically he had to be there and pose for photos. Mandy also wanted as many players on show as possible and there would be a fun game between the stadium sponsors' side and a Kettering select team. Clooney was expected to play for at least part of that game and be available for a question and answer followed by prize giving. "All in a day's work for an up and coming new boss," he thought.

Jess travelled to London. She had gone by train rather than her new car. So Clooney and Mandy sat with a coffee in the club restaurant, neither hurrying to end the meeting or seemingly conversing much either. George broke the silence by talking about Thresham's death. He also told her he had made his mind up to talk to Jess but as far as he was concerned he would not be taking the matter of Thresham's death any further. What Jess did of course was up to her. Mandy offered no comment other than to thank him for just being him. She kissed him on the cheek and left without further ado.

Dave Evans popped in for a news update and they

finished with a whiskey in the Chairman's office. Well a whiskey for Clooney, several for the boss. Then it was time to head home and a heart to heart with Jess upon her return.

He was almost knocked to the floor by the strength of her greeting. The car was a gift beyond imagination for her and she was eager to let him know how grateful she was. She wanted to take him out for dinner, her treat, in the new motor of course and there was no way he could say no - so he didn't.

They drove the half hour or so to the Normanton Park Hotel with the roof down, the music playing and Jess as happy as she had ever been. It was not going to make it any easier telling her, he thought. Of course she had an ulterior motive in choosing this particular venue. It was where she hoped they would marry. Clooney had to admit the setting by the lake took some beating. Across the Rutland Water he thought he could make out the lights of the Chairman's house. It certainly would be something for the bride to arrive from there by boat. Their meal was excellent and as darkness fell they could see the water in the moonlight; the whole place had an atmosphere that seemed perfect for anyone's big day.

Clooney debated with himself, was he a coward putting off the moment or was he not wanting to spoil her day by telling her? He certainly was quiet on the drive home but Jess talked enough for both of them so there was no problem there. She pulled him into bed the minute they were through the door and their lovemaking was breathtaking. Afterwards George decided now was not the hour and they fell asleep in each other arms

Clooney came awake with a start. It was now just three weeks or so 'til pre- season training started in earnest. He had friendlies to arrange, players still to sign and he still hadn't told Jess. He made her breakfast in bed and then as gently as he could be broke the news to her. Colour left her face and she looked as if she might faint. Then she sobbed in his arms for a good twenty minute before locking herself in the bathroom - and that was it. On the surface at least she was composed, getting ready for another day at work and nothing had changed, though obviously everything had.

Before they could talk about it the phone rang. It was Burns, to say Blister had died in his sleep and he wanted to be the one to let George know. For the second time since waking a short time before both of them were upset and again her tears flowed. Clooney comforted her until they both felt able to face the thought of work and they dressed in silence, each deep in thought and memories.

The day was a blur, he spoke on the phone, had meetings with people, but it was as if he wasn't there. Amanda phoned, she'd heard the news, was as devastated as they were; this certainly was not a day Clooney would have wished or planned for if he had any control of destiny. Dinner that night was a sombre affair, Amanda joined them and George spoke to Blister's daughter to express his condolences. The only good news came when Mark Norman phoned to say Alan de Toure and John Middlesman, two of the players they were chasing, had agreed to sign. On such a day George found it difficult to react positively, even to this good news.

Dave Evans contacted Vic Burns and offered the club's restaurant for Blister's wake. Free of charge. It was typical of the man that he always knew just what was the right thing to do. The funeral would take place next Wednesday and Blister's daughter had asked Clooney if he would say a few words. He was both honoured and scared at the thought, but thanked her and promised to let her have a copy of his speech for her approval as soon as possible.

Then the day to day work at the club overtook him, pre-season friendlies arranged at Stamford, Northampton Town and Peterborough. A quick tour of the South West, playing Yeovil, Exeter, Torquay and Plymouth, before it all began for real with that opening fixture against Evesham Town. With the young players on board the playing squad for the new season now stood at twenty-six, with three players unable to start with injuries. They had just about enough men and boys to work with, but not enough to run a reserve team. Still with the Chairman's support he knew it wouldn't be lack of finances that held him back if he needed reinforcements.

He was invited to sit in on an unofficial board meeting, joined the directors for lunch where he was quizzed on transfer activity, and then spent an afternoon answering mail and doing interviews with local media before he ended the day with a brief catch up with Mark Norman. Who was the one who should be congratulated for work on the playing side, George thought. He was conscious that not only was he nowhere near match fit, he hadn't been involved in any of the other players' training either. He promised himself that would change.

He pushed himself hard on his morning runs, even harder in training, but he knew he was out of shape. On an impulse he booked Jess and himself into a spa hotel for the weekend. She was thrilled but had no intentions of following his proposed exercise. So, with work done, he tried to compose his tribute to Blister. He wanted to say so much about his admiration for the man he had known only a short time but who had done so much for him. It was a hard task for a man more used to football than writing but he believed he'd done his friend justice.

After last minute catch ups with all and sundry he and Jess were able to drive over to Oakham in the early afternoon. Checking in at 4 p.m. they both used the swimming pool, had massages, then walked the extensive grounds before pre-dinner lovemaking. Clooney ate sparsely and drank only water, his pattern for the weekend. He practiced his speech on Jess and she burst into tears, was very proud of him, and when they retired that evening demonstrated just how much she loved him.

Saturday he woke at 6 a.m., ran for an hour or rather walked, ran, and limped his way around the estate. After a light breakfast it was a day of swimming, treatments, tennis, walking, eating, sleeping and love making. Not only did he feel better he was enjoying it very, very much. They watched a movie in their room, talked about the wedding, then Jess told him her news. He was going to be a dad! It seemed after all the stress of Canada, him, their step-father, and everything else she had forgotten to take the pill but dared not tell him in case he was mad. They fell asleep with him still reassuring her she'd made him happier than ever.

When he woke he wondered had it been a dream? Was he really going to be a father? They would have to bring forward the marriage plans, buy a house. Should he tell his folks; did any of Jess's family know? He was tempted to wake the beautiful woman lying beside him but instead just watched her sleeping peacefully. He felt great pride and pleasure that this lady was to be his wife, the mother of his child. The excitement was such he had to do something, so, quietly as he could, he went for the hardest, longest run he had done for a long while. On his return his gorgeous *fiancée* was waiting for him and they embraced with passion before he hit her with a hundred questions about the future. Jess was relieved and excited that rather than be angry he was so obviously delighted at the news. She had been so scared to tell him she had not dared to make plans, fearing he would blame her for allowing it to happen.

She was sure the child had been conceived when they were in Canada. "Did that mean it would have dual citizenship?" she considered jokingly. Now George was in the picture they could talk, make plans and look forward. Perhaps this was fate's reward for some of the cruelty previously dished out. Over breakfast, a vocal, excited affair that caused other restaurant users to stare, they made their plans. The wedding would be brought forward to August 1st if they could, the Saturday before the season began. They would look for a new home around the Stamford, Oakham area and get the flat on the market. No one else did know she told him, stupid. So parents and Mandy, Dave Evans and relatives and friends would need to know; they were having a baby.

They swam and had some treatments again that morning, but now they couldn't wait to get going. They checked out, then drove first to Oakham and then to Stamford. Gazing in the estate agents' windows noting properties they might want to follow up on, they took afternoon tea at the Falcon in Uppingham, perused more estate agents' wares before heading for home; a mixture of tired, excited, happy, worried, but very much in love.

Ignoring answering machine and electronic mail when they got home, Jess called her mum, Clooney his folks. They told Mandy and Dave Evans. Everyone was excited, pleased, happy for them and full of ideas. They looked up baby names on the internet, checked out more houses, other possible wedding venues if their first choice Normanton Park couldn't take them. Then they took the plunge and found to their absolute delight that, due to a cancellation, they could do it. They booked it on the spot, then rang everyone again to tell them it was on. The Chairman insisted Jess stay the night before the wedding at his place, then he and his wife would bring the bride over by boat for the ceremony. As George and Jess had previously discussed, they then asked him if he would do the honour of giving the bride away. This was too much for him and he broke down in tears while accepting with delight.

Finally, after a bottle of champagne to celebrate, or rather two glasses for Clooney cutting down on the booze to get fit and Jess also so as not to harm the baby, they headed for bed; after another whirlwind of a day in the life of the happy couple.

When he told the staff and his mates everyone seemed genuinely pleased. He trained hard that morning with the players and felt a little bit more like his old self, even scoring one thumping header in the daily knock about after training. On July 1st, just twenty days away, everyone would be back for pre-season. The weigh-ins, get-togethers with new recruits, team photos and the beginning of a new journey; their first ever taste of League football.

He had a long but enjoyable meeting with the Chairman. Dave Evans was pleased about the baby, delighted about the wedding and generally happy with life. His own health was improving and he felt years younger. Both men still felt they were about four players short of the squad they would need if they were more than to hold their own in the League. They studied the PFA list of available players, read the available for transfer information from other clubs and reviewed the applications for a trial posted on line or received in the post. One name jumped out at Clooney, a player he had played with albeit briefly at Forest. Eamon O'Keefe, twenty-nine, midfield general and alcoholic! The midfielder on his day was world class. His vision, passing, shot and speed put him in the superstar class. But his drinking had turned most of his performance into comedy. O'Keefe had just been released by Brentford, after only two months. Before that he had racked up appearances at Linfield, Rangers, Hearts, Preston, Huddersfield, Notts Forest, Luton, Plymouth, Torquay and Northampton. Ten clubs in twelve years was hardly a recommendation, more a suicide note, but then George noticed a brief covering letter penned by the Irishman's long suffering wife Cara. Her man had not had a drink in a month, a first for him since the age of seventeen. She was pregnant for the first time and he wanted to turn over a new leaf. With the Chairman's blessing he contacted O'Keefe, who lived just down the road in Milton Keynes. They chatted about old times and old friends and Eamon agreed to drive up for a meeting that afternoon providing he could bring Cara with him, to which George readily agreed. Clooney devoted the rest of the morning to training, paperwork and meetings, before a light lunch with Jess where he surprised her by asking her to sit in on the meeting with the Irishman and his wife.

O'Keefe was heavier yes, but his skin tone was better and he carried with him the air of a contented man. Cara and Jess hit it off straight away and got down to the serious business of baby talk. Eamon was honesty personified. Admitting his sins, talking freely of his past drink problems and swearing he was a changed man. George invited him on a stadium tour and they joined some of the staff in an impromptu kick about. O'Keefe had not lost his touch and Clooney knew he wanted him on board. Over a much needed rest and drink of water(!) they discussed a one year deal with a monthly get out for the club if Eamon strayed from the straight and narrow. Though both men shook on it, the Chairman still had the final say and they met him in the boardroom.

Dave was brilliant, no ranting and no raving, no talk of this being the last chance saloon. Just an appreciation of his talent and the hope that this would prove to be the place he settled down. Eamon had had so many people read the riot act to him he was taken aback by the Chairman's approach and instantly committed himself to the cause. When they re-joined the girls Cara thanked George from the bottom of her heart and Jess threw her arms around him, so proud was she of her man.

Clooney worked on his speech about Blister. He was more nervous than he could remember, only the list of commercial assignments Lindsay had organised for Thursday took his mind off it, though they were scary for different reasons. He was to record an in depth interview for Sky, looking forward to the new season. He would be appearing in a commercial for a new football magazine and was lunch guest at a Red Cross fund raising do. In the evening he had to do a phone in for Talk Sport and would round off the day by meeting the sales force of some software company who were paying him to meet and greet their winning team of go getters. Lindsay he knew would be there to fill him on the details, thank God.

Jess had really taken to Cara and they were due to meet again while he was enjoying his day in London. On Friday there was a press conference planned by Mandy to announce O'Keefe's signing, but it was the thought of that eulogy that was taxing him now. A workout with the team helped put things in perspective. Though he had let his fitness drop he felt each day he was getting nearer to his playing level. There were photo sessions in advance of Friday's press launch with all the new personnel who were getting used to the club and the area. O'Keefe and Bryn Jones hit if off right away, both being Celts and having had their respective personal problems. Tony Miller as well as being a fellow Celt immediately assumed the skipper's role that George had planned for him. Clooney felt he really had the makings of a team here; when Brendan O'Grady joined them it dawned on George for the first time, the common ancestry the four shared, which would perhaps bode well for the future - or would it?

The sun shone and the crematorium was packed. Family, friends, servicemen, football people and sightseers were all there. Vic Burns made an eloquent speech about his father-in-law and read a poem from Blister's grandchildren. There wasn't a dry eye in the house when George made his way to the lectern to pay his own tribute.

Clooney told the assembled mourners how he had only known the deceased a short time, but how he admired him as a true gentleman, a man of honour, a friend and someone he was very proud to have known. His speech was from the heart and his respect was plain to see. George again impressed a lot of people that day and it was a wonderful send off for a remarkable old man.

The club restaurant was heaving and George found himself engaged in conversation with many who wanted to congratulate him on his words. The hug and kiss from Blister's daughter moved him to tears and seeing the old soldiers he'd met that fateful night when they had attacked Thresham's empire made him feel proud to be among them again. He even had the chance to exchange words with old team mates, now his players, like Pernod and Wethers. It made him realise how much had happened since Jess came into his life and how much he'd neglected good friends, for which he was ashamed. His parents rescued him from his melancholy. They had never met Blister, only spoken to him on the phone, but they too had wanted to show their respects. Eventually proceedings drifted to an inevitable conclusion and Clooney, Jess, Mandy and his parents retired to the flat to enjoy a cup of tea or something stronger and to wind down from the emotion of the day.

The next day, standing at Kettering station waiting for the London train, Clooney was aware of the attention he was receiving. He and Mandy were so close in every way people assumed they were an item. But the truth was they were more sister and brother than lovers.

From the moment they took their seats in first class to their arrival in London the pair of them were engaged in non-stop conversation. Yesterday's events, Mandy's late step-father, Blister, the club, George's new house and finally, as St. Pancras was announced, Mandy told him she was seeing one of his players. He just hoped it wasn't one of the married ones!

It wasn't, but it still was a surprise. She was dating Pernod, once one of Clooney's best mates. Perhaps part of the uncomfortableness yesterday then was this, not just the fact that he was now the boss and had seen little of his mates outside of the ground this last few months. What could he say, except he was pleased for her and thanks for letting him know. But it gave him something else to think about as he left the train. He got a taxi for Mandy, who was heading for a meeting with some International Organics' big wigs, while he searched for the car Sky had sent to collect him. He didn't spot the car but he did find the lovely Lindsay, who beckoned him to a waiting Volvo.

After kisses and pleasantries Lindsay briefed him more fully on the day. Former England manager Trevor Everable, who had worked full time in television since leaving the national side ten years ago, would be doing the interview. It would not be vicious, more an insight to how Clooney was preparing his team for League football, new players, tactics and expectations. George had always admired Everables and was almost looking forward to the meeting.

Just after 9, while the make-up girl prepared him for his ordeal by cameras, Everables came over and introduced himself. He might now be sixty-five but he was still a handsome man who had kept himself fit and he oozed a natural charm. They immediately bonded and Clooney found himself talking freely, as his butterflies flew away.

For the interview they were in a tiny studio with two armchairs, a coffee table and a fake gas fire. He was surprised how small the room was, though on camera it would appear as if they were in someone's lounge. After some banter, chatter to get sound levels, lighting checked, they started to record the process.

In a very gentle way Everables persuaded Clooney to talk about football in Australia and England. He asked about Kettering the place, and for his views on non-League football. He congratulated him on his engagement and the remarkable story of his involvement with Jess. Clooney was concerned about what next season would bring but confident that they would not disgrace themselves or the town. When the cameras stopped rolling George was amazed to discover they had chatted for over an hour. The edited interview would go out the following weekend, lunchtime Saturday and a repeat on Sunday morning, and would be a fifteen minute slot. The two men wished each other well, Everables promising to come up to Kettering to see a game, and with that George was in a taxi with Lindsay off to his next appointment. She was full of praise for his television appearance, describing him as a natural, and was sure the finished interview would win him more admirers and more commercial contracts.

The filming of the sports magazine commercial consisted of him and several other football players and managers being photographed in different situations, all of them achieved by the use of blue screens and props. So although he was actually standing in a studio at London Docks it would appear on screen as if he was on a beach in Australia giving the thumbs up, as all the others did, to *International Soccer Monthly* the new football magazine. He recognised Arsenal's manager, Arsène Wenger and Wayne Rooney from Manchester United; there was Ally McCoist from Glasgow Rangers and Martin O'Neil, Harry Rednap, Tony Adams, Stephen Gerrard, and a host of others with their commercial minders. Out of the chaos Lindsay appeared with mugs of tea. They watched the proceedings for a while then, after they were told it was a wrap for them and they were free to go, they made their way to the Park Lane Hilton for the Red Cross lunch.

Top business names and wealthy potential charity donors had been invited to lunch and an opportunity to rub shoulders with invited celebrities, in the hope that after listening to the great work the Red Cross does they would be moved to donate. Clooney wasn't earning from this, which was fine by him, but Lindsay thought it would provide a good positive photo opportunity and, squeezed between a day of earning, they could afford to do it. Lunch was good, you would have had to have a heart of stone not to give the charity some cash after listening to what they did for humanity, and as a bonus for George he bumped into fellow guest Nathan Jones outside the gents' toilet. He remembered the former Welsh International from when he'd watched him on TV, in his heyday playing for Man U; though he was both older and heavier he was still the imposing figure he had been at his top as a player. They talked briefly, then Jones gave him a tip; Reece Morgan the Leicester defender and former Welsh skipper was unhappy at Leicester City, now thirty-five years old the club had only offered the player a twelve month deal. According to Nathan if someone decent in the East Midlands area offered him a two or even three year deal he would be interested. Clooney couldn't stop himself asking, how did Jones know? The Welshman explained that he had met Morgan at a motorway café a week ago and the player had told him.

George couldn't believe his luck. Had he not bumped into Nathan, literally, this opportunity would have been missed. He knew the player of old, they had faced each other on a few occasions and Clooney had nothing but respect for the hard but fair Welshman. Before returning to the table he asked Jones if by any chance he knew the player's agent. Which he did, and he even gave Clooney a card with the man's name on. It was Nathan Jones! No wonder he'd smiled.

Clooney texted Mark Norman. He replied in minutes to say he was on the case. Then it was photos, goodbyes and off to the next assignment. With two hours to go before he had to be at Talk Sport he and Lindsay found a quiet corner of the hotel and over endless teas played catch up. Next Thursday he had to revisit his old employers MotorGiant for a photo shoot and meet and greet. Payback time for the car. That would be fun! But Lindsay had more news for him, though until he spoke to Jess he wasn't sure if it was good or not.

As an extra wedding present for him and his lady, Lindsay and Mandy had been speaking to the celebrity mags and *Today* had agreed to foot the bill for the big day in exchange for exclusive pictures and an interview. George couldn't believe that someone wanted to pay for his nuptials and wasn't convinced he wanted it anyway. But, if Jess agreed, it would give them thousands more for the house and baby he thought. If he agreed it meant no one at the event could take any photos. The publication would take them all, freely making copies available after the magazine came out. A quick answer was needed, so he contacted Jess. Like him she was apprehensive, it didn't seem right, but the money would be useful; so it was a yes.

They made their way to the Talk Sport studio. Clooney would be alongside regular broadcaster Tony Fitzwaren, the former Spurs and England midfielder. As a player his wit and repartee had been legendary and now he was putting it to good use on radio. They got on instantly and the banter was brilliant as they hosted calls from Kettering fans and others jealous of the club. The hour flew by and afterwards an official of the station spoke to Lindsay about dates for him to return. After a freshen-up it was time to be top table guest at the Rapide Softwear dinner. He met the winning sales team, posed for photos and presented them each with a cheque before answering questions, signing autographs, avoiding chat ups from a couple of the very attractive girls there.

He adjourned with Lindsay to the first class lounge at the station. She congratulated him again on the way he had handled the day. Talk turned to some of the other business opportunities there were for him, but a conflict arose when they discussed boot deals.

In his career to date, Clooney had always bought his own footwear, at bargain prices of course. Now it seemed every manufacturer wanted him to be in their boots and were prepared to pay handsomely for the privilege.

He had always favoured Puma, but Lindsay showed him some eye catching offers from rivals, if he would change his allegiance.

Now she too would discover how Jason 'George' Clooney was so different from most players. He was adamant he would stick with the brand he was comfortable with, and if Puma provided free boots and a bit of cash, which would be a bonus, then that was good enough for him.

Lindsay never ceased to be amazed at her client's integrity. So many of her portfolio would say anything for more money. He truly was an exception to the rule.

Business done, after she promised to organise a deal with Puma, conversation turned to more personal issues. She told him of her background growing up in Auchterarder Scotland, and he shared his experiences of his childhood in Sheffield. By the time he left her to catch the last train from St. Pancras to Kettering he was knackered.

Chapter Twenty Four

He didn't want to get out of bed. Unusual for him. But Jess had insisted on knowing everything that happened when he got home and they hadn't left the lounge 'til 1. Then, after a bout of the most wonderful love making, here he was awake again after what seemed like only minutes of sleep. Jess was seeing the doctor that day, it was now forty-eight days since they believed the baby had been conceived at Niagara Falls. Not a name they would be calling it!! The pregnancy test had confirmed Jess's suspicions, but now for the first time she would be having it recognised.

Mark Norman broke the spell, when he called to say he had spoken to Reece Morgan and his agent and they would be coming in on Monday for a meeting. That was the good news; the bad was that Colin Smith, the club's right back, was in Kettering nick picked up last night fighting in the town. Within minutes George was on his way. In the car he phoned the club's solicitor Gary Wicks, who agreed to meet there, and in no time he found himself - not for the first time - at the town's police station.

Gary arrived shortly after and was able to fill him in on what had happened. It appeared Smith's lady had been outside the nightclub giving some local a hand job. Colin had caught her, punched her, and then given the bloke the thrashing of his life. Others had joined in and when the police arrived Smithie was about to take on half the nightclub. He had spent the night in the cells and would probably be charged with disturbing the peace, causing actual bodily harm, aggressive behaviour, being drunk and disorderly plus who knows what else. Or, rather, he would have been, if Vic Burns hadn't stepped in.

It was Vic's first day back at work since the funeral. Once he knew the circumstances he had swung into action. Mrs Smith, if indeed they were married, was full of remorse for her drunken stupidity. She wanted her man back and would not be pressing charges. The local man, now hospitalised, had been persuaded, after the police found a substantial amount of drugs on his person, that it would be better to forget last night. Both parties had confirmed in writing they had no intention of taking matters further and Vic had persuaded his colleagues who made the arrest to let this one go. George couldn't thank him enough, but Burns reminded him this was one last favour on behalf of his late father-in-law. Clooney thought he knew what he meant. Debts honoured, past buried, say no more. But don't expect such favours ever again were the Inspector's thoughts.

George drove the very sheepish player straight to the ground and told him to start training. Then he and Gary Wicks had breakfast in his office. Catching up on the news and briefing Gary on the flat sale and possible house purchase, the solicitor promised to help through his network of contacts, to try for a quick sale and a speedy purchase. Certainly if anyone knew how to do it he was the man. On the personal business front Wicks reminded him that neither he nor Jess had signed their Wills yet, an oversight Clooney promised to deal with. Sir Alex Ferguson's secretary rang, if George was interested he could have Tyson Fletcher on a three month loan. The player, born of a Lancashire mother and a St. Lucian father was a no-nonsense centre forward, now aged eighteen, who had everything in his locker but experience. George didn't hesitate in saying yes.

It was now just weeks 'til the squad reported back, a couple of weeks 'til he tied the knot; and still so much to do. After a gruelling training session, particularly for Colin Smith who had thrown up more than once, George told Mark Norman about Tyson Fletcher joining on loan and he could tell his assistant was delighted. They were beginning to assemble a squad that could be a real force in their division - not a side scrapping to avoid relegation.

Since Clooney had taken over a whole raft of new players had joined. Midfielders Paul Wilson and John Henderson, keeper Brendan O'Grady, defender Tony Miller, winger Bryn Jones, midfielder Eamon O'Keefe, defender Reece Morgan if he signed, forwards Alan le Toven and John Middlemask with young players on loan like Tyson Fletcher at centre forward. He would expect every one of them to be pushing for a start next term. Which meant perhaps only three of last season's promotion winning side might make it into League football with the club. Clooney knew that was bound to cause some resentment with both players and fans. It promised to be interesting, he thought.

Jess had reminded him he hadn't yet picked his best man and he was torn between people like Dave Evans, Pernod, and Gary Wicks and, had he still been alive, he thought he would probably have asked Blister; but in the end he opted for Gary Wicks. It was a decision based partly on his friendship with the solicitor and partly that unlike the others Gary was neither his boss nor his employee; "Less potential for misunderstandings that way," he thought. He phoned Jess, who agreed, then he rang Gary who was suitably surprised, delighted and willing. So that was taken care of.

Clooney had his own pre-season check up with the medical team. Apart from being 5 lbs. overweight he passed with flying colours. The club doctor gave him a diet sheet and he then put himself through the most strenuous training session he could, leaving several of the younger players unable to keep up. He felt satisfied with himself and life in general.

Mandy joined him and Jess in the club restaurant for lunch, there was lots of catching up, wedding and baby plans discussed, before George left them to it and popped along for a meeting with the Chairman. Dave Evans was ecstatic when he heard the news about Fletcher and possibly Morgan also joining them, he was convinced they would be chasing promotion rather than fighting relegation and the two men enjoyed themselves, speculating just how far the club might go. August 4th was that big day when they would open their first ever Football League campaign. But he had his own big day to think about before that and he knew he needed to get his thinking cap on with only weeks to go.

At the management meeting that afternoon they confirmed pre-session activities, medicals, weigh-ins, photo calls, friendly games, open day for the fans, there was so much to do, but his sister-in-law to be was amazing; she had with Mark Norman set most things in motion and George almost felt redundant. That evening he and Jess had confirmed their arrangements for the wedding. The hotel seemed even more amazing in the evening light. They decided to stay over rather than drive back, and the hotel gave them a complimentary room, the perfect ending to a day of mixed fortunes. But a weekend to sort things out lay ahead before it was back to the grind on Monday.

They enjoyed breakfast with its view of the lake and the sunken church. Odd to remember this was a man-made reservoir covering fields, villages and farmland. Gary Wicks phoned with amazing news. The flat was sold. He couldn't or wouldn't give details, only tell them they could and should get moving on their house hunting. They were blown away that it should have happened so quickly, though Clooney wondered if friendly helping hands had been at work. It confirmed their decision to stay over had been a good one and now they could devote the weekend to finding a new base.

Back in their room they used the laptop to go online and search for properties. Soon they had likely viewings in Oakham, Stamford and Uppingham arranged. The rest of the day was spent in inspection visits, lots of driving and no results. They wanted privacy but also to be near a town. A safe garden for the third member of the family when it arrived and a place with space to grow. A house with character that they could move straight into, rather than wait for it to be rebuilt. But nothing they saw quite fitted the bill.

Their spirits were dampened that evening as they sat in the hotel lounge, devouring the local paper and magazines for property details. The hotel barman brought over their drinks and, seeing what they were doing, offered to help with his local knowledge of the area. They told him their budget and what they were looking for and he went away to think about it. After dinner he stopped them on their way to their room with his news. A builder he knew had just completed a barn conversion, in the village of Ashwell by Rutland Water, stunning views, home cinema. It would be going on the market, but he would be working on the house tomorrow and they could stop by and view if they were interested. Bill Sutherland the builder had also emailed some photos and details to Tony the barman which they eagerly grabbed, thanked him and went off to their room to peruse. They sat on the bed and studied the photos Tony had printed off. The place was a dream. Brand new, but constructed in local stone. Full of character, prime position and space to expand. The only thing missing seemed to be a garage. But that could soon be built. Spirits lifted, they undressed for bed, but first made love while looking out across the dark water of the lake. Sleep came easy and they woke refreshed, excited and happy, ready for the new day.

Sunday breakfast shared with the papers was the perfect start to the day. Clooney had to smile at the football stories. Most the product of imaginative sports writers rather than hard facts, he reckoned. But one that caught his eye was the news that Arsenal had decided not to offer a new contract as a player to David Street, but instead had offered him a role on the training staff. The former England skipper, now thirty-eight, had declined as he still wanted to play for another season and would now be looking for another club. As he read it his mobile rang; he knew who and why, it was the Chairman. He wanted Clooney's thoughts on Street, before contacting the Arsenal. George was able to tell him that all he knew about the player was good and, with him as Captain, the sky was the limit for the club. Dave Evans promised to do his best and left the couple to their house hunting.

The barn conversion was stunning, combining the best of local materials with the best of craftsmanship. Bill Sutherland was a local man who had been building in the area for thirty years and he took an obvious pride in his work. The lot was set in about half an acre of fields with breathtaking views. Bill had added a circular entrance to the base which made the whole place look more like an old fashioned manor house or very small castle. The *décor* was light, modern with quality fixtures and fittings.

A fully equipped office on the first floor would make a fifth bedroom should it be needed. The home cinema room really was like a mini movie hall. They both instantly fell in love with the place. Cash flow was more important than anything to Bill, so for a quick sale he was prepared to offer a handsome discount. They verbally agreed a deal there and then, subject to survey, and shook hands on it.

Both of them phoned their folks to tell them the news. The lunch was a late celebratory affair at the George in Stamford before they drove home. Back at the flat Clooney googled all he could on David Street. He had met him once at a dinner and liked the guy, but felt nervous at the possibility of having him in his squad. "How could a journeyman player like himself manage one of the all-time greats?" he pondered. Perhaps it would be better if he didn't join. There were the usual assortments of emails, voice messages, texts to deal with; then after sifting and planning for Monday he called it a day, falling asleep imagining watching football in his home cinema. Happy dreams.

Dave Evans phoned while they were still at breakfast. Phillip De Sousa, Dave Street's agent/manager, had agreed to consider a proposal from the club. The Chairman wanted Clooney to help him draft it, now. With a quick goodbye to Jess, George headed for the ground. On the way he phoned Gary Wicks, who was unavailable, so he left all the details of the new house with his secretary, need for survey and property register search. The Chairman met him in the car park and within minutes they were ensconced in the board room planning their offer letter to De Sousa. Dave was astute enough to pick up on George's nervousness. He also suspected the reason. Quickly but convincingly the Chairman explained that Street would be no threat to him. George was the boss, hopefully for the medium term at least. But Street might be the man to get them promotion, before he hung up his boots and moved on to other things. This made Clooney feel better about the situation and together they emailed an attractive offer letter to the player's agent. He felt better still when, following the meeting with Reece Morgan and his agent, another signing was obtained.

The travel agents' representative came in to see them and presented the details of the club's pre-season tour. Coach arrangements, hotels, meals, travelling facilities. The fixtures had already been agreed. It looked good: a South West of England tour, playing to holiday crowds - a bit of bonding, getting to know his squad and hopefully his opening fixture formation. Further meetings with the club staff followed before an evening appointment with the clubs fans at their H.Q., an office in the stadium donated by the Chairman. The Supporters' Club committee were as positive about the new season as he was, probably more so, and a good time was had by all.

Clooney arrived home about 9.30 p.m. and Jess greeted him with the news that Gary Wicks had been in touch. It was the club, Kettering, that had bought the flat for cash, done deal. Clooney was furious that the Chairman had not told him. He felt manipulated and for the first time wondered if he really could trust Dave Evans.

Throwing caution to the wind he phoned his boss, who was still in the car on his way home. Realising how angry George was he turned around and drove back to meet Clooney and Jess at the ground. George arrived first at the dark empty stadium and switched on sufficient lights for them to make their way to his office. Fifteen minutes later the boss appeared. Jess made them all tea, hoping to calm things down. Dave Evans was as unfazed as ever and quickly took control of the meeting. It seemed the club's directors were worried about the escalating costs of hotel bills the club were facing, with all the new signings requiring temporary accommodation. He had come up with the idea of buying a number of houses and flats they could loan to players, which as an investment should grow in value rather than throwing away cash on hotel rooms; and they had gone out and bought three properties. The board hoped that they had shown some appreciation for the hard work George and Jess did for the club by purchasing their flat, but if the Clooneys objected they would look elsewhere. Jess was embarrassed, for herself and for her partner. They had been fools and she apologised unreservedly to the Chairman for their churlishness. She was pleased when her husband to be swallowed his pride and did the same.

They celebrated with a drink in the Chairman's office. Dave's wife Dianne phoned, Phillip De Sousa had suggested a meeting on Wednesday; his client it seemed was interested in knowing more. That called for a second drink, and when both parties left for the final time that day the mood was much improved. Instead of going straight home they ate at the Italian restaurant in Kettering so favoured by the players. But they were the only representatives of the club in there that night and were soon the centre of attention.

Ignoring the audience, Jess spoke firmly and lovingly to her man. He reluctantly agreed the possible signing of Dave Street did make him vulnerable, but it was perhaps more the straw that broke the camel's back than anything. In the two and a bit months since he'd known Jess his life had changed forever. His job, his marital status, approaching fatherhood, moving house, Thresham's death - so much had happened was happening, he felt he was beginning to cry and despised himself for it. She took his hand in hers and told him how it was this sensitive side to his strength that made her love him. They both opened their hearts and their souls to each other, shared only a half-bottle of wine yet felt intoxicated when they finally left and met the cold night air. Together, she reminded him, they had already achieved so much and together in the future they would achieve even more. Lovemaking that night was as good as it gets and both slept like the proverbial logs.

After his most punishing training session to date George caught up with the paperwork, did some media interviews, met with a party on a tour of the ground and then met Jess, Mandy and Mark Norman for lunch in the club restaurant. Each had their own success stories to bring to the table. Mandy had arranged the International Organics world conference to be held at the stadium, which was to be videoed to every International Organics H.Q. in every country they operated in. Jess had been invited to give a keynote lecture on her role with the club at a UK seminar on football and the community. Mark had assembled a youth side which looked promising and was even more excited to report on the attitude, fitness and ability of the first team squad who had been coming in for training. Clooney briefed them on the proposed meeting with Dave Street's agent and they even found time to talk about non-football matters for a short time.

Following lunch George had a conference call with Lindsay and his management team, regarding commercial opportunities for him and Jess before driving over to Corby, where he gave a well-received talk on the club to members of a British management association. Back in Kettering he did a radio interview before arriving at the ground around 6 p.m. He collected his messages, dealt with all the outstanding matters he could, and was preparing to leave when Gary Wicks phoned. The survey on the new house was good and with a bit of luck the Clooneys could look forward to moving in before the end of August. Gary was disappointed there was to be no stag-do, George daren't risk it with so much to be done pre-season but he was assured that the lawyer would not let him down on the day and they would make up for it at a later date. "Some chance!" Clooney thought.

George checked his diary after the wedding ceremony - he would have to be back at the club for lunchtime Saturday as they faced a pre-season friendly against championship side Leicester City. Nathan Jones, as well as being Reece Morgan's agent, had persuaded his players' old club to bring a strong side to Kettering for this attractive pre-season fixture.

Dave Evans popped in to go over again the plan for the meeting with Dave Street's agent. The Chairman passionately believed this potential signing would clinch the club's success. Clooney remained to be convinced. Depending on the player's attitude he could, if he joined, be a catalyst for disaster as much as the opposite. Mark Norman was taking an evening training session with the juniors and George joined him, intending only to watch for a while as a show of support. In the event he stayed until the end, mesmerised by the performance of one player, seventeen year old Alfie Singh.

Singh was from Wellingborough of Indian parentage. His real name was Alfit but the lads had nicknamed him Alfie. He was short, wiry, fast and talented. Operating on the right wing or in midfield he tackled well and in the kickaround he seemingly dominated the game, confidently scoring and making goals with ease. Here was an exceptional talent and George realised he had been slow to recognise the fact, despite Mark telling him at every opportunity. The lad was on a youth contract but Clooney had seen enough in one hour to convince him they needed to tie the boy to a three year deal, or risk losing him. Fortunately the kid didn't have an agent and his parents were as nice a couple as you could wish to meet. After a brief chat with the lad Mark ran him home, and, taking a contract with him, succeeded in tying the deal up by 11 p.m., much to Clooney's delight when he phoned him. The squad was looking very good for next season, even without Mr Superstar Street, but George would be glad when tomorrow was over.

Wednesday was a beautiful day weather wise, hot but not sticky, blue skies and a glad to be alive, feel good kind of day. Clooney hoped that boded well for the meeting. He had never seen the Chairman look nervous before, but today was obviously getting to him. Phillip De Sousa arrived on time; he was immaculately turned out, tall, expensive suit, no tie, short silver hair and briefcase. He looked every inch the very successful man he was. Dave Street was not in attendance. If the meeting went well he would arrive by helicopter later - quite a contrast to young Alfie having a lift to Wellingborough in Mark Norman's car. De Sousa's big problem with the proposed contract centred around his client's image rights. It seemed that under his current deal the club paid for the use of his photograph. The rights were held by a company in the Bahamas. The Chairman had hinted to Clooney that this was a tax dodge and that the money ultimately found its way back to Mr Street. Dave Evans was not happy that if they became the player's employer, they, like anyone else, would have to pay to use his picture. De Sousa would not be moved on this and he wanted a percentage of merchandise sales for his client, no public appearances without payment and one day a week off for commercial activities. The bargaining got serious. Agreement was reached on merchandising, with Street to get 12½% of all merchandising sales, a buy-out fee for the image rights of £20,000 a year, and a yes to the day off for corporate work.

Previously the Chairman had explained to George how the company's marketing department had calculated Street's worth to them in merchandise sales to be around £5,000 a week - so to pay him £625 plus the £20,000 a year for his image rights was worth it to the club. They would be around £75,000 a year better off. The extra opportunities to earn for the club that he would bring through increased sales and media exposure should cover his wages, and giving him a day off cost them nothing, but helped keep him in the public eye, thereby increasing sales opportunities. It was a definite yes to the deal, the only stumbling block being that Street was to get a £50,000 bonus if the club was promoted and the player himself had to want to play here. The bonus wasn't a problem in itself as Dave had already planned to take out an insurance policy or bet that would provide the club with the necessary funds if - please God - they did it. But what was the man like and would he sign?

De Sousa asked for privacy, which was granted, to phone his client and twenty minutes later they received the news that Street would arrive around 3 that afternoon. All senior staff were informed, the club photographer summoned but a media blackout imposed until there was something positive to report. Dave and De Sousa went for lunch and a nervous Clooney attempted, badly, to concentrate on work while his mind turned over thoughts on the meeting to come. Wicks phoned to update him on property sale and purchase matters, Jess called to wish him luck and find out how things were going. Finally at 2.50

p.m. the noise of a helicopter could be heard overhead and George went out to the car park to meet his V.I.P. arrival. Seemingly from nowhere people had assembled to watch the craft land and there was quite a crowd to see the great man disembark. Instantly recognisable, he was greeted with good wishers, cheers and even handclapping. Clooney felt even more nervous as he walked over to meet and greet him. The player was even more imposing face to face, 6' 1" blond, handsome, tanned and athletic; he looked every inch the star he was. His boyish grin charmed men and women alike and George almost unwillingly found himself smiling in return. They shook hands, exchanged pleasantries, then made their way to the board room, where his Chairman and the player's agent waited.

Street's personality was such that he dominated proceedings - even the Chairman seemed in awe of him, though the player did everything to make them feel comfortable. Clooney knew it was a mixture of fear and envy that made him wary of the man, but he couldn't help respecting him for what he'd achieved and for how he came across. As they made small talk Street reminded George of a meeting they'd had many years ago at a League game when they had been opponents, but both of them had ended up laughing at the antics of a now famous referee who had wanted to be the star that day, made a right ass of himself and then to everyone's delight had slipped, fallen and landed in a piece of wet turf almost swallowing his whistle at the same time. Clooney remembered it well but had forgotten that Street had been there. It certainly hadn't been a game the player had dominated. It made him realise the bloke was like him, only human.

Now whether Street had told the story on purpose or not to relax him George didn't know, but it certainly made him feel better, not nervous anymore. The get-together was going well, and it seemed the player was interested in coming to Kettering, but Clooney was determined to find out why, when there must have been better offers on the table. The Chairman presumably felt the same way, because he dared to ask out loud what George was only thinking. Street answered without hesitation, and it was surprising to say the least.

Dave Street had been born in a London hospital, but the family had moved to Peterborough when he was two, so he considered this area as home. He owned a house by the river in Cambridge and his folks now lived in the home he'd bought them in Huntingdon; all local to Kettering. His main business interests though were in Italy, where he had played for Inter Milan twelve years previously, and he had a home there as well. His wife Nicki had her own fashion house *Street* and he his soccer academies were all based there. They both spoke Italian and intended to base themselves there in a year's time when he retired as a player and their son finished his treatment at Addenbrooke's Hospital, Cambridge. Of course, Clooney remembered, the boy had a heart problem; it had been all over the papers. So Dave Street superstar wanted to wind down his playing career close to his family before relocating to a new life, business, future in another country. It ticked all the boxes for the player, would keep him in the public eye while allowing him time for his family and business with no relocation issues. More than ever this was looking like a deal might be done.

While Chairman and agent discussed terms, George and Dave toured the ground. It was amazing how many people stopped for Street's autograph or photo and it was heart-warming how pleasant the player was with them all, taking time, making them feel special; he really was a most likeable guy. Eventually they talked shop and the player raved about Arsène Wenger, the best manager he'd ever known. He genuinely seemed to want to go out and enjoy one last season before hanging his boots up. But he wanted it to be special, not just ordinary. With it being Kettering's first ever season in League football, the new stadium, the location, everything, he would like to be a part of it, and if he could help them get promotion at the first attempt then it would be the perfect way to bring down the curtain on his career.

Clooney now was sold on the man, could see them becoming friends and was excited at what the team might achieve with the player on board. Now it just remained for a mutually acceptable deal to be agreed. Thirty minutes after returning to the board room it was done. Signed, sealed, complete. It was agreed it should be kept under wraps until a press conference could be arranged for Friday morning. Dave would arrive by helicopter again, hopefully to surprise the media and gain maximum publicity. They would have a day to produce the lettering on the first Kettering shirts home and away with his name on, and Mandy would work overtime on ensuring all went according to plan. Dave Evans threw a further surprise when he told George that he and Mandy had done a side deal with International Organics so that the club's sponsor would pick up the cost of Street's wages in return for him making guest appearances and suchlike for them. They would be picking up the cost of Friday's press conference and the new player would become an International Ambassador for the company, whatever that meant! Clooney never ceased to be amazed at how clever his boss was and his future sister-in-law. But it was a great day for the club and he couldn't stop himself from thinking about promotion rather than survival. It was a nice feeling.

On his way home Dave Street called him, there was a dinner Thursday night in Cambridge, a fund raiser for East Anglia's Children's Hospices. Street was a supporter of the charity, his sister's late child had received tons of help from them and he liked to show his appreciation. He was wondering if Clooney and Jess would like to join him as his guests? After all he wasn't signing 'til Friday so they would just be acquaintances, not player and boss. George thanked him, said he would check with his other half and get back to him that night. They chatted a bit about the international game Street had played, when Eamon O'Keefe, after a brilliant first half, got stuck into the booze at half time and did nothing after the break - except score the bloody winning goal. God if you could harness that talent, they could walk the League! Laughing they ended the call.

At home Jess was waiting desperate to hear all about Dave Street, one of her idols. Over lasagne, salad, garlic bread and Evian water he described his day. When he told her about the invite for the next day she flipped. Of course she wanted to go, to meet both of them, Britain's most famous football couple. Clooney texted his acceptance, then they phoned Mandy, so the three of them were up to date with each other's news. It seemed Friday's press conference was going to be mega. TV, press, radio, the works. The mayor would be there, and after it was over George and Street would travel with the mayor to the Town Hall for tea, more photos and to meet the great and the good of the area. All of whom, she had assured him, had no idea who the super star was that they were going to meet.

Everything was going well, it made George nervous. But checking his emails and post, voicemail and texts there was much that was good to put him at ease. His folks rang, and his day was complete when they told they too had never been happier in their lives and were so pleased that their son and Jess were an item.

Thursday was supposedly his day off for commercial earnings time, but with all there was to do at the club and the big event that evening he had abandoned that, sent his apologies to Lindsay, then trained as hard as he ever had before doing a full five hours in the office.

They left that evening in Jess's car. Cambridge was a pleasant drive away and the car park at the hotel was almost full when they arrived. The guests were immaculately turned out and he recognised the faces of television soap stars, a well-known newscaster, several stage stars, fellow sports people, radio personalities and writers, plus the other supporters of the charity there that night. Dave and Nicki welcomed them warmly and introduced them to representatives of East Anglia's Children's Hospices and other guests. Former Ipswich legend Kevin McCreedy, with whom Clooney had clashed on the pitch many times in the past, greeted him warmly and they began to relax and enjoy the occasion. After mixing, mingling and enjoying pre-dinner cocktails Dave Street officially welcomed everyone and invited them to take their seats for dinner. The table plan showed George that he and Jess would be sharing their table with a lady from the charity and her partner, TV weatherman Doug Lane and his wife, rock singer Elliot Ness and his boyfriend, plus four couples from the local business community; twelve strangers joined together for one evening for the same cause. Grace was said and conversation broke out everywhere. Elliot Ness was a football fanatic and Arsenal fan and wanted to talk about the game to anyone who would listen. Weatherman Doug

Lane, so dour and straight laced on the box, was amazingly funny and told some hilarious risqué jokes. Clooney and Jess really enjoyed themselves. They bought the almost obligatory raffle tickets and were amazed when they won a balloon flight for two in the draw.

Following dinner a super speaker from the hospice thanked them for their support and reminded them of the work that was done for those life limited kids and their families, and there wasn't a dry eye in the house when he sat down. But the real heart breaker was a short video that followed, showing the kids saying thank you, and when the collection boxes came round all gave generously. Dave Street stood, thanked everyone for the evening on behalf of the guests and publicly pledged his continued support.

Driving home afterwards they had much to talk about and yet were asleep within minutes of getting into bed. During the night Clooney woke needing the toilet. When he returned to bed he lay for a while thinking about what was ahead, but felt calm, yet excited about the future. Pre-season started in earnest on Monday the 18th, two weeks later he got married. "Not much happening then," he thought, before falling asleep again with a great big smile on his face.

The next day George had breakfast with the Chairman at the ground. Television crews had started to arrive, though the conference didn't start until 11 a.m. Everything seemed to be in order, supervised and arranged by Mandy, who was in her element. Everyone was still sworn to secrecy, even some of the club's employees were speculating on what was going to happen.

Over in Cambridge, Dave Street was ready to play his part in the day's events. He and his wife had breakfast in their hotel room, Nicki told reception her husband was "under the weather," and would be having a lie in. At 8 on the dot film make-up artist Zena Coroni arrived, disguised as a nurse. Street was made to look ninety with a wig, make-up and other effects. Then Zena wheeled him to her car in a wheelchair for the drive to Kettering. Confident no photographers or other media hounds were on their trail they drove to Clooney's flat, where Jess welcomed them and made teas and coffees while Dave was transformed back from old man to the footballer with everything. Shortly before 11 a.m. a stretch limo with blacked out windows arrived and, with a blanket over his head to conceal his identity, they set off for the ground. Jess was constantly in touch with Clooney by phone, so the powers that be knew everything was in place and on time.

Following light refreshments, the Chairman thanked the media for joining them in the club restaurant, the only room big enough to accommodate them all. Then he invited them to follow him to the pitch, which they all did, as well as the club staff. The stretch limo swung into the stadium and parked on the centre circle. Clooney, microphone in hand, walked over to the car doors; then announced the club's new signing would be with them in a moment. The rear doors of the car opened, there was a long pause, with everyone holding their breath in a perfect silence, before Dave Street appeared. The throng went mad, he needed no introductions. Soon he and George were mobbed by media representatives from around the world and, in minutes thanks to mobile phones, cameras and the internet, the whole world seemed to know the impossible had happened. Former England and Arsenal captain David Street was now a player for Kettering.

The press conference dragged on over lunch, with Clooney doing interview after interview until at last the media departed and the dust began to settle on yet another extraordinary week in the life of the club. Street set off for his Italian home, George, Jess and Mandy were invited as the Chairman's special guests to his place, and a late but great night was had by all. The television news carried pieces about the new signing and Street was interviewed alongside the private jet flying him from East Midlands airport to Milan. His Italian home was in the wonderful city of Pavia, where he was to spend the weekend. He said all the right things and the Chairman beamed when he saw the bookies were now making the club joint favourites for promotion rather than the drop. Changed days indeed.

After a leisurely breakfast Jess and Mandy left to drive the short distance to Stapleford Park, the luxury spa hotel they were spending the hen weekend in. Mandy had arranged it all. Beauty treatments, trips to the theatre, *Back to Broadway* the musical was playing at the Crescent Theatre in Peterborough. Mandy was friends with the show's producer and lead singer Gina Price and they were going to have supper after with the cast. Both girls had seen the show many times before but it was so good they were happy to watch it over and over again. On the Sunday they were having lunch on a steam train. Then Jess should, if she was lucky, get back to Clooney early Sunday evening.

George was going to go home alone to his empty flat when he suddenly decided instead to visit his folks. A quick call confirmed they would love to see him and he was in Dronfield for lunch. The weather was good enough for them to have the meal in the garden, catch up on the news, have a snooze before dining at the Dore Grill. Like most Saturdays the place was fully booked but Jose promised to make room for his famous guests.

After his mum had gone to bed Clooney joined

his father in the lounge, for a final drink, a chat and some parental advice. Before he was even asked, Clooney senior reassured his son about next season, the wedding and even Dave Street's massive, overshadowing presence at the club. He told his son how people in his life and events had made him at times unsure, but George's grandfather always told his son: "Be yourself do your best and those you care about will love you and it doesn't matter about the rest." Sensing his son was suffering some major self-doubts, he reminded him it was his son's goal that got the club into the League. Dave Evans had backed him with his own money. Players who had signed, like O'Keefe, Reece Morgan and Tony Millar, had joined because Clooney had persuaded them, when they no doubt had other offers on the table; last but certainly not least, indeed the reverse, was the lovely Jess. Both of George's parents loved her like a daughter and couldn't see anything but success for the couple as long as they kept their health, looked after each other and stayed true to themselves.

The passion behind his father's words moved George and gave him the tonic he needed to move on positively, knowing his folks were supporting him one hundred per cent of the way.

They said their goodbyes after lunch and George drove home for his meeting with Blister's old mates, with their plans for pre-season training. No sooner had he checked his messages than the doorbell rang and the guys were there. They talked about Blister and the funeral, they were in awe of Dave Street and a little bit self-conscious now with Clooney, his world being so different from theirs. They laid out their plans for the week and Clooney knew a lot of pampered footballers were in for the shock of their lives with what was in store. A coach would collect the squad the next day at 4 p.m., then it was off to the toughening camp which, surprise surprise, was the old base by Grafton Warren they had used as their headquarters for the raid on Thresham. Half a dozen ex-military were helping, and Clooney's team would get the shock of their lives he was promised.

An exhausted Jess arrived home around 10. She had many stories of her fabulous hen weekend but was shattered and the pair took themselves off to bed where she brought Clooney up to date on the happenings, while he enjoyed her company, her body and the pleasure of being together.

All of the players made it on time. They were weighed, fitness assessed, then kitted out. Photographs were taken an hour later and an hour's light training took them up to lunch. As ever Street was the main attraction for the media, staff and players - even a couple of hundred fans turned out to watch the first day back. Naturally lunch was in the club restaurant, where the Chairman joined them. Dave Evans welcomed them to his club and Clooney set out the club rules. This was followed by media interviews and the club's programme editor grilling the guys for stories and profiles for the club's publication and website.

At 3.30 p.m. the troops arrived and equipment was loaded on to the coach, introductions made and, bang on time, the group left for their secret destination. The players were boisterous but also nervous of what was coming, and when they pulled up at the old camp they wondered what indeed was coming next. They soon found out when a squad of ex-soldiers marched them faster than they'd probably moved in their lives to their huts. The spartan accommodation was greeted with disdain and when they were told they could not leave the camp and would be called for breakfast at 6.30

a.m. there was a near mutiny, but soon the card schools and computer game competitions started and they settled down. Dinner was served at 7 p.m., a barbecue; lights out was 9 p.m. Those clever sods who tried to go AWOL were brought back within minutes of their escape attempts and eventually everyone settled down. With the lights off everywhere it really was dark and it didn't take long for all of them to fall asleep.

The ear shattering alarm at 6.30 a.m. was designed to wake even the heaviest of sleepers and it worked. The bleary eyed players were marched to the shower block and toilets before assembling in the breakfast room at 7.15 a.m. By 8.30, warm up exercises complete, they were on their first exercise of the day - a five mile walk where the pace constantly changed. After a water break at 9.30 a.m. it was PE in the gym, then a run of twice round the football pitch, about half a mile. It was now 11, and to players unfit after the summer break and not used to more than three hours compulsory daily training in the season this was a real shock to the system. But they hadn't finished yet. It was time to go swimming in the camp pool before saunas, massages and rub downs, administered not by pretty girls but rough old ex-servicemen. When they sat down for lunch they were knackered. At least they had the chance to recover from the morning before they were taken to the rifle range and given the chance to play soldiers. Typically, as with everything, Dave Street was an excellent shot. But Clooney, who had never used a gun before, proved a natural and beat him to the winner's prize, a silver salver to be inscribed in memory of the day. Another long walk followed before they finally finished the day at the gym with warm down exercises. First day over and no sign of a football. After dinner they were taken to the cinema to see the latest Bond movie and a few of the lads fell asleep on the way back.

Everyone slept well, all that fresh air and exercise cured even the insomniacs. The next day followed the pattern of the first except instead of the rifle range they had a golf tournament. In the evening they watched *Back to Broadway* in Peterborough, every bit as good as Jess had said. While West End musical numbers were not to the taste of everyone you couldn't fault the ability and the energy of the performers.

By now the lads were desperate to see a ball, two days training gone, no football, they looked forward to actually getting on the pitch the next day.

Thursday was all about playing football. Coaches came in to work with the goalkeepers, others the strikers, and a third the defenders. They worked with a ball all morning and finally, after a light lunch, for the first time the squad was to play a game. Names were drawn out of a hat, Clooney made adjustments where necessary, and finally a game happened. O'Keefe, fitter now and sharper because he was off the booze, was outstanding. Dave Street demonstrated his obvious class and George could see there was going to be a real fight for places which was good news. The old soldiers watched their charges go about their work and had to admit they looked good. Then the Chairman arrived for an end of course dinner and prizes were handed to best and worse at events before a happy group called it a day.

Friday they were allowed to sleep in after the party. Breakfast was served at 8 a.m. and by 9 they were on the coach to the ground; training started at 10 a.m. as it would throughout the season. After lunch together to compete the bonding the players drifted off. Tomorrow they would play a closed-doors friendly against Northampton Town. Until then they could do what they liked.

Clooney briefed the Chairman on the week, caught up on mail, messages, events, before touching base with Jess, Mandy, Lindsay and his folks. The world had carried on as normal without him, so he was able to relax that night and enjoy the luxury of a quiet night in with his wife to be.

The closed-doors game would actually have almost five hundred spectators from the club sponsors International Organics and a whole raft of entertainment and food, drink and prizes was being laid on for them. Clooney picked his opening team, then pinned it on the club notice board. Over a light lunch with his players he explained his team, tactics and that keeper Brendan O'Grady was captain. As an ex-Northampton player it seemed only right. Millar, O'Keefe, Street and local lad Alfie Singh would also make their debuts, while the rest of the side would be made up of last season's team, including the boss himself. Mark Norman would manage the side, allowing George to concentrate on the game. With Northampton, the Cobblers as they were called, being a local side everyone knew each other and prior to kick off all was amiable and good natured. Mark's tactics, already agreed with Clooney, were simply don't get hurt, pass the ball to feet and enjoy yourself.

The game was played at walking pace. The sun and the pre-season stupor saw to that. But O'Keefe was bossing midfield, spraying passes about and from one of them Alfie Singh ran at the Cobblers' defence, beating them for pace before slotting the ball home. A Dave Street free kick on the stroke of half time ensured the home side was the happiest in the dressing room during the break. Mark made two changes, bringing Street and Clooney off which was greeted with much merriment by the lads. Paul Wilson and Tyson Fletcher took their places, and it was Tyson who netted the club's third goal before O'Keefe netted the fourth and final one of the afternoon, a fitting reward for his magnificent performance. As the players left the pitch the applause rang out deservedly for a job well done. Best of all, no new injuries, only minor knocks. It had been a great start for a team of whom so much was expected. Tomorrow they would leave for their West Country tour with games at Yeovil on Monday, Torquay Tuesday and Exeter Wednesday. Clooney intended using the whole squad before the weekend's game against Leicester, the day before his nuptials.

The coach was given quite a send-off when they left that Monday morning, arriving at their team hotel for 4 p.m. after a light meal en route. An hour's sleep, then the team meeting, lots of changes, lots of opportunities for players. After a brief walk to waken tired limbs it was off to the ground for final preparations, pre-match massages, high energy drinks and snacks; then a warm up on the pitch before getting down to the action.

The game gave them quite a workout, with Yeovil at near full strength compared with Kettering's makeshift side. The home team were a goal to the good at half time but second half strikes from John Henderson and Clooney, both on as substitutes, turned the game in their favour and the players were allowed a minor celebration back at the hotel.

The next day they travelled for a morning at Lyme Regis. Bracing sea air, a walk on the sands and a swim in the sea for those brave enough, before they left for Torquay arriving at 4 p.m. for the usual routine of sleep, team talk, massages and high energy sustenance before travelling to the ground. It was another great result, three on the bounce now as they won 4 – 2 with goals from Street, Singh,

Wilson and Fletcher. Paul Wilson again caught the eye and he O'Keefe and Street were a more than useful midfield combination, while Fletcher up front allied with Singh's pace would cause problems for any side. At the back Miller was truly outstanding and O'Grady was looking as reliable a keeper as you could ever wish for. There was a really solid side developing already, with strength, flair, pace and goals in it, and George was getting excited even though he was struggling to make the team. There were more moderate celebrations at the Torquay hotel before they turned in but Pernod asked the boss for a private word and for a moment Clooney feared the worst. But he needn't have, it was good news, the player had proposed to Mandy, been accepted and wanted George to be the first to know. They celebrated over a glass of champagne, then Jess phoned to express her delight as Mandy had just broken the news to her. It was another good day and night for the Clooneys-to-be and the club.

For the Exeter game Clooney again rang the changes. Reece Morgan was, at last, match fit and desperate for a run out before Saturday's game against his old club. He decided to start with Bryn Jones, giving Alfie Singh his spot on the bench. Alan de Toure and John Middleman would start and by the end of the game all of his squad would have played some part in the opening four games.

Exeter were a division higher than Kettering but you wouldn't have known it that first half hour. Bryn Jones was tearing them apart on the flanks, the tricky Welsh winger was fast as well as skilful and Exeter knew only one way to stop him. From one of the many free kicks Bryn earned the team Street smashed home a stunner, and at half time they were well on top. Clooney joined the fray for the second half with O'Keefe, Miller, Henderson and youth player

Jermains Oghala who was making his first team debut. The home side made several changes themselves and dominated the opening exchanges, equalising after fifty minutes and taking the lead on seventy. Clooney was determined they were not going to suffer their first defeat under his leadership and he rallied his troops for an equaliser. With only minutes remaining Bryn Jones salvaged a draw with a superb solo effort. They could look forward with confidence now to Saturday's visit from Championship side Leicester. The only sour note was news that Paul Wilson had an injury and could miss the next game. Otherwise everyone was fit, happy and looking forward to what lay ahead.

Jess phoned with last minute reminders for Sunday's ceremony and George promised himself a day off on Friday to sort a few things out.

The coach had them back in Kettering for 4 p.m. and Clooney checked in at the office and spoke to Lindsay and Mandy by phone before heading home. His bride to be had a million jobs for him before bed but when you were as happy with life as Clooney was, he was able to do them with a smile.

The next day they visited the Normanton Park to check final arrangements. Unbeknown to Jess her husband-to-be had arranged for them to be whisked from the hotel by helicopter, then a private plane to Paris, where they would honeymoon for two days before he prepared for the season's opening. Mandy joined them after lunch with Lindsay and a representative from *Today* magazine who had paid for the exclusive media rights to the big day. The afternoon talk was all about deals, offers, freebies and a load of stuff Clooney felt almost embarrassed about. His big day which he should have organised and paid for had been taken over as a money spinner and it left him feeling somehow dirty and embarrassed about the whole thing. But nothing could spoil the day, particularly when they heard from Barry Wicks that the exchange of contracts on their flat and the new house had gone through, completion to take place on the 15th August, when they would move into their new home. Now the girls started planning the commercial opportunities there, free carpets, furniture, and electrical equipment. Clooney felt he wasn't part of this crazy world and wandered off to view the old sunken church created when the reservoir was formed. Dave Evans sailed over to join them. "Practice run for the big day," he said, and they all enjoyed a trip to his home for drinks, then back for a light meal on the house, of course! Then home.

Clooney arrived at the ground by 8 a.m. Too nervous to lie in, friendly or not it was an important test for his team. He had wrestled with his team selection half the night it seemed, but in the end had plumped for a very attacking line up, minus Paul Wilson who missed the game through injury, with both his wingers Jones and Singh on from the start. Tyson should certainly see plenty of the ball and with creative players like O'Keefe and Street they should be very good going forward. He would ask Henderson to play the holding midfield role, he was sure he was more than capable for the day. Reece Morgan was as good as you could wish for and if O'Keefe maintained his form to date they would give their visitors a game to remember. George settled for a place on the bench, though he would have loved to have been playing. Then he did a radio interview, a piece for the local paper and appeared briefly in a filmed piece for the local TV station, all before 10 a.m.

Numerous celebrity visitors were due to attend the game, mostly managers and referees of other clubs wanting to check them out. Dave Evans came by, as nervous as

George was, and the team notice went up on the board. It was a quick meeting with various of the club management, a chat with the sponsors before a light lunch at noon with his players. Everyone was looking forward to their biggest test to date, none more than skipper for the day Reece Morgan, who warned the lads what to look out for from his old team mates. Scarves, programmes, balls, you name it, had to be signed for charities, fans, the sick and friends. Then it was team talk, massage and relaxation before pre-match warm ups in the dressing room and on the pitch.

Clooney met his Leicester counterpart when their coach arrived. Bob McGuiness was a genial forty-five year old Scot, now in his third season as manager of the club. They chatted, agreed to meet for drinks after the game, then George let them settle in while he made his final preparations. Despite the short time they had worked together he and Mark Norman his assistant really were developing a close partnership, each seeming to know exactly what the other was thinking, and Clooney was glad of his colleague's assistance on a day when there seemed so much to do and so little time to do it.

The dressing room was a hive of activity: at 2.30 p.m. the players had been on the pitch, decided which studs or indeed which boots to wear. Now it was almost time. Some were silent, others couldn't shut up, the staff were constantly busy. Then finally it was time. Clooney wished them all the best, reminded them of the team's success so far, though today was their biggest challenge yet, then urged them to play with passion, run like the wind, tackle like men, use the ball to do the work on the ground if they could, and enjoy the day. Then they had a minute's pause for reflection before they burst out of the changing rooms into the team tunnel.

The Leicester players were already lined up to play and were surprised how pumped up their opponents were for what was to them just another pre-season friendly. The Leicester lads joked with ex-colleague Reece Morgan. Then the referee spoke to the two captains before leading the teams out onto the pitch. They're arrival was announced by the playing of the home club's anthem *Star Wars*. When they ran out into the sunlight a capacity crowd greeted them with a roar and thousands of balloons supplied by International Organics were released. It was a real party atmosphere that George was determined not to let the visitors spoil.

It was Leicester who kicked off and began to knock the ball about confidently. But, as to be expected, Morgan soon had enough of that; he won the ball with a crunch tackle and fed O'Keefe. The Irishman was away, after avoiding tackles as if they weren't there he ran twenty yards before slipping an inch perfect pass through to Singh. The youngster tore down the touchline and managed to cross a perfect ball before he was knocked to the ground by a desperate defender. Tyson met the cross with a thundering header which rattled the cross bar before it was hoofed to safety by a relieved opponent. Throughout a well fought first half, more cup tie than pre-season work out, Kettering were on top and were rewarded for their efforts when dead ball specialist Dave Street lashed home a free kick. Both sets of players were rightly applauded off at half time.

There was no time for celebrations, the job was only half done. Alfie had received such a kicking in the first half Clooney was tempted to remove him from the fray, but the player pleaded to be allowed to continue and a reluctant George acceded, but made him and Bryn Jones switch flanks. The gamble of playing with two men who were really out and out wingers seemed to be paying off and they were stretching their opponents' defence, allowing space for Street and O'Keefe to weave their magic. When the buzzer sounded for the next instalment the home dressing room contained the more confident and happy set of players.

It was a confidence that seemed well placed when just ten minutes after the restart Tyson volleyed home a Singh cross. Clooney was relieved he'd been talked into leaving the lad on. But now was the crucial time. Leicester would throw everything at them to get back into the game, they needed to stand firm before the onslaught. But first George made a change. Henderson was carrying a knock and they would need a fully fit, holding midfielder more than ever now, so veteran Kenny McGleish took his place. The tough Scotsman might not now have the legs for a full ninety minutes but over the remaining half hour or so he could be just the man you wanted on the battlefield.

The manager had judged it right. Leicester made three substitutions, then threw everything but the kitchen sink at the home side who never buckled under the pressure until five minutes from the end, when the away team finally pulled one back through current Scotland International forward Jordon Stewart. But to Clooney's delight his players held on to gain an impressive victory over their illustrious rivals.

Everyone at the club behaved as if they'd won the cup rather than a friendly game, but Clooney left as soon as he could, following the promised drink with his Leicester counterpart. Tomorrow was another big day.

Danny joined him for breakfast. Jess had stayed the night with her mum and Mandy at the Chairman's house. Clooney's folks would be en route to the hotel. He signed some papers for the property sale and the purchase of his new home. Then, suitably turned out, the pair set off for the hotel. They had exclusive use of its facilities and security men working for the *Today* magazine ensured their privacy. George greeted his parents, relatives and friends in the lounge bar where champagne was served, but they soon spilled out on to the terrace. The Chairman's boat was spotted, so they made their way into the library where the ceremony would take place. At the last moment Clooney stepped out to meet his bride, who looked stunning in a cream outfit that Mandy, who else, had organised. Together they entered the room to a burst of applause from the guests.

After the simple ceremony was over it was photos on the lawn, all orchestrated by the magazine. Guests would receive free copies, but no one was allowed to take pictures, except the official *Today* camera crew. The wedding lunch was magnificent. Dannie's speech was as eloquent and as funny as you would expect and when the happy couple departed early evening there was real emotion in the air.

Jess still had no idea where their brief honeymoon was to take place and was surprised when they boarded the private plane at East Midlands Airport. On this flight they were the only passengers, with acres of space and privacy. Jess snuggled close to him and they both watched the dark sky pass by, lost in thoughts and memories of the day and their history. Ninety-three days ago, Jess reminded him, they had never met. Now they were married, moving house and having a baby. It had been a three months to remember for sure and now, here they were on their honeymoon. It was truly amazing.

Upon landing a waiting limousine rushed them through the suburbs to their base. The Hotel Banke, a new hotel with ninety-four rooms in a quieter area of the city, it really had been an old bank until a Spanish company had recently converted it into the stunning hotel it now was.

The magnificent lobby, glass domed, light and airy was a welcoming sight. Their room looked out across the city and champagne and chocolates were waiting for them, which they both demolished with relish. They celebrated in the appropriate way, the new Mr and Mrs Clooney making love for the first time as a married couple.

The next morning they did the tourist bits, Eiffel tower, Louvre, open top bus tour, Follies Bergère at night. Mark Norman phoned, no injury problems and he was taking scratch sides to Peterborough and Corby prior to Saturday's big kick-off. Tuesday they travelled to Versailles and in the evening ate as they sailed on a *Baton Rouge*. An accordion player came to their table and serenaded them with *"No Regrets"* before they brought the evening to a perfect end by making love in their honeymoon suite to the accompaniment of the sounds of night time Paris. During the night Mandy emailed them some sample photos of the wedding day and at breakfast they were able to relive the moment again.

Shopping on the Champs-Élysées was followed by lunch at an open air café, before reluctantly they returned to the hotel, packed the newly acquired shopping with their stuff and waited for the taxi. By 7 p.m. they were in the air, looking down on the magical city they had spent the last few days in. Clooney was pleased to hear his scratch team had forced a Nil-Nil draw at Peterborough and hoped tonight's game at Corby would also prove successful.

There was a real surprise for them when they landed. Mandy had arranged for a vintage Rolls Royce to meet them on the tarmac and as a result they were home before midnight, to be greeted by hundreds of cards from well wishes. Mark had phoned to confirm a 2 - 0 victory for the lads; Bryn Jones and Millar the new team captain in place of Street getting the goals. But Alfie Singh had received another good kicking and was doubtful for the start of the season. Clooney arranged to be in early for a breakfast meeting, then caught up with messages and emails before he and a very tired Mrs Clooney hit dreamland.

Honeymoon over, it was back to work for George and he was at the ground for an 8 a.m. breakfast with Mark, a meeting with the Chairman, then a morning's training with the lads. The club's phsyio Fred Mee reported on Alfie Singh's bruising. He felt at best the guy should be on the bench for Saturday, but preferably rested; he had severe bruising of both legs and Fred had decided a treatment regime for the player that didn't include playing football was the order of the day. That night they played their final fixture of the pre-season, probables against the possibles, though the players didn't know that for sure, and that was it. No scares, serious injuries, or personality problems - they were ready!

After a light morning's training for the lads, a very heavy session for the boss, the players drifted off. They were to report back the next day at noon, but for George there was a frantic afternoon ahead. He had told the players tomorrow's line up. Goal Keeper O'Grady, defenders Miller, Pernod, Morgan, Smith, midfield O'Keefe, Street, Wetherall, Wilson, forward Jones and Tyson. Now he briefed the media, caught up on paperwork and spent as much time as he could with the non-playing staff at the club, showing all the interest he could muster in their plans for the season's opener.

It was after 6 when he got home, collected Jess and they dined at her mum's house with Mandy in attendance, where they were able to view all the film and still footage of their big day. It had happened less than a week ago but already was becoming a faded memory. The pics brought the day back to life and they expressed their preference for the ones to appear in next week's magazine. A whole host of family and friends were coming to tomorrow's game, including parents, Vic Burns with his wife Blister's daughter, Danny Browne, Gary Wicks, his manager Fraser Wiltshire and the lovely Lindsay. Karrina was coming down from Scotland, his Aunt Cynthia and husband Ross had stayed after the wedding for this day, Scowcroft, Davison and some of the other ex-troops. It was some size of party that was coming and Clooney was moved that they all cared enough to want to be there.

Finally it was time to leave. Butterflies had begun fluttering and George wasn't sure he could sleep, but with some gentle manipulation from Jess he actually did, like the proverbial baby. It was his wife who lay awake for hours after soothing her husband to sleep, thinking how much the game meant to him and praying he wouldn't be disappointed. So much had gone right for her since she met him, she hoped there wasn't a major disaster ahead.

Before breakfast he took himself out for a run. He was at the ground for 9 where he was joined by an equally nervous Chairman. Dave Evans told him the game was definitely a sell-out, television would be there and the weather promised to be kind; all they needed was the right result. He recorded a piece for the BBC's lunch time football show, he spoke on the phone to Jess and his folks, then it was down to business with Mark Norman. Final tactics agreed, he had half an hour before his players arrived and he spent it walking the length and breadth of the stadium, soaking up the atmosphere.

The club shop was open and he popped in to sign souvenirs, greet the staff and say hello to the fans. All over the place people were at work, food outlets preparing for custom, cleaning staff finishing their duties, security personnel beginning their day. The atmosphere was electric and Clooney felt his own tension rise. But he kept smiling and he kept moving and before he knew it the lads were arriving for lunch and he was hurrying to join them in their private dining room. You could cut the mood with a knife, everyone was nervous, but it was now Dave Street came into his own. When you had been everywhere and done it all like him that experience stood you in good stead on a day like this. To his credit he put everyone at ease with his humorous stories of celebrities he'd met and places he'd been.

It meant most of them managed some lunch before the familiar rituals of massage, rest, signings, dressing room warm up, final words and then the line up in the corridor alongside your opponents ready for the off. Evesham had not had a bad pre-season themselves, they had signed two former Scottish Internationals in Douglas McKenzie and Kyle Johnsone, and they had only lost one game and that by a single goal, so they weren't here to roll over.

At last, to rapturous applause, George took his place in the dugout just as he had done ninety-nine days ago. But this time as the manager.

Kettering attacked from the start, Bryn Jones delighted to have got the nod, in part due to Alfie's injuries, played like a man possessed. They couldn't stop him by fair means and it resulted in a string of free kicks for the home side, but a combination of nerves and bad luck kept the game scoreless at half time. Within one minute of the restart all of that changed when, totally against the run of play, the home team's defence was breached by a through ball from McKenzie and Kyle Rafferty was able to score a debut goal.

There was almost total silence in the ground, only the few hundred Evesham supporters behind the goal celebrated. Clooney wished the earth would swallow him. After all the hype and all the hopes and dreams, the reality was they were losing their opening game at home. The worst possible start they could have made to their inaugural season in the Football League. George vowed to give them twenty minutes to compose themselves before he made changes, and to their credit the boys responded. Young Tyson was being well held by his experienced veteran marker and O'Keefe and Street were restricted to long range efforts but they kept pressing forward - only to pay the price again when they conceded a second goal. Poor Wethers caught napping at a corner.

Now there was only half an hour to salvage something, Clooney had to change things. He pulled off Tyson and the exhausted Bryn Jones who had run himself into the ground. He decided to risk Alfie Singh and also to lead by example and take to the field himself. His arrival was greeted by muted cheers. The fans had not expected to see their favourites trailing by two goals to nil and George realised he had to do something to raise the team and the crowd. He told Singh just to get the ball to him whenever he could; he would try and make something of it and hoped he could get them back into the game. Within five minutes he did just that. Alfie crossed, Clooney headed against the bar, O'Keefe followed up and they had pulled one back. Now the mood changed, the crowd were urging them forward, the whole team believed they could do it and their adversaries were desperately defending in depth.

Something had to give, and it did after seventy minutes when Wilson raced in from the flank to rifle an equaliser. Now the proverbial flood gates opened, a Street free kick to Alfie, Singh tapped it in and they had gone from two down to three goals to two up and the crowd wanted more. The closing minutes were amazing as shots and headers were cleared off the line, the ball cannoned of the post and crossbar and then, with almost the last piece of action in the game, a cross from Pernod was met by the boss; and just as he had done in that final game of last season, he buried it. They had won, 4 - 2 and he had done it again. As they left the pitch they were mobbed, everyone except the away team and its supporters were going crazy. In their very first League game they had defied the odds, turned the score round and were worthy winners. Evesham Town's 'scalp' would hopefully be the first of many.

Dave Evans was unashamedly crying when he embraced his team manager and he was not alone. This was the result they needed to kick start the campaign and George knew he had done his bit. After showering, changing, beating off well-wishers and the media he sought out his wife, family and friends. They were all overjoyed, most in tears, and his dad through sobs told him he had never been more proud of his son. He was too overcome to speak but he avoided all the well-wishers to grab Jess, sitting pale and tearful by the viewing window.

They held each other close, the moment needed no words. Since meeting just over three months ago they had experienced so much and who knew what the future might hold for them. But for this one moment in time nothing mattered. Everything, but everything, was more than all right.